The Christmas Quilt

The Christmas Quilt

→ A NOVEL ←

Blessings!

Thomas J. Davis

RUTLEDGE HILL PRESS™
NASHVILLE, TENNESSEE

A Division of Thomas Nelson, Inc.
www.ThomasNelson.com

Published by Rutledge Hill Press, a division of Thomas Nelson, Inc., P.O. Box 141000, Nashville, Tennessee 37214.

Library of Congress Cataloging-in-Publication Data

Davis, Thomas J. (Thomas Jeffery), 1958–
    The Christmas quilt / by Thomas J. Davis.
        p. cm.
    ISBN 1-4016-0031-X (paperback)
    1. Mountain life—Fiction. 2. Gilmer County (Ga.)—Fiction. I. Title.

PS3554.A937776 C47 2000
813'.54—dc 21

                                                                00-35290

Printed in the United States of America
02 03 04 05 — 7 6 5 4 3

To my dad and mom,
Paul and Christine Davis,
who embody the essence of all that's
good about Smoky Hollow

Preface

SUPPERTIME WAS NEVER quiet when I was growing up, and I've always been glad of that. After all, it's during table talk that a family finds out who it is—a communal reflection, if you will, of the sentiment, "I never know what I think until I say it." Our table talk consisted of a review of events of the day, excerpts from important conversations the family needed to know about, jokes, quizzing about who was going where, when, and why—a veritable feast of words.

It's the stories I remember most. My dad loved telling stories about when he was younger, and we loved hearing them—at least as long as we held on to the wisdom of childhood. There was the occasional new revelation, but often the yarns were brought out and polished up like an old pocket watch—steady, reliable, something you could count on to tell you the time. That's what the stories were—ways my dad had of telling us the time. Of course, instead of minutes and hours, what he counted out were the narratives that marked the movement of a different kind of time—a growing-up time, a time made special by fond recollection, a time rendered precious by the passing of time itself.

Once I left childhood, it took me a number of years (more than I like to think) to wise up to the importance of what my dad had been saying all that time. In fact, I suppose it was only after I had children myself, and felt a need to start passing to them some of the stories that make me who I am, that I began to listen again with ready ears to my dad when he said, "When I was little . . ." One day I had a startling revelation—I realized my dad was a master story-teller. His stories engendered in me as a child—and later as an adult when I was finally smart enough to pay attention—a wistfulness, a desire, a longing, if just for a second, to be in the story itself. If you find yourself walking along a dirt road with a little boy who likes to kick tin cans just because it's the best thing to do at the time, you're listening to someone who can really tell a story. And it's an important story, because at that moment you and he share something special—the memories that make him who he is, which is part of what makes you who you are. Drawing on some of my dad's stories, I have created something that I hope conveys the feeling I get when I listen to him—a heartfelt appreciation for home, family, and land.

"Smoky Hollow" is the made-up community that serves as the

setting for this book, but in the story it lies near a real town called Ellijay in a real county named Gilmer, snuggled in the North Georgia mountains. The plot and main characters are fictional, but many of the things that provide atmosphere are not. My dad will recognize many of the anecdotes that he has told over the years as they are used to provide an authentic backdrop for this novel. I am grateful to be able to use them.

If I learned something about storytelling around the table, I picked up other things as well. I learned, for example, the difference between a table set with food and a table appointed with love. Besides providing the essential good meal, my mom personified hospitality, something that has always made even the simplest meal seem like much more.

And she listened. I remember talking her ear off when I was a child, and she always had time to hear what I had to say. That has stayed with me in a couple of different ways. An important one is that she is still someone I can talk to because she is someone who will really listen. As I grow older, I find that's a gift rarely given. And she has helped me to be a better listener. To be able to sit and listen to life's rhythms is essential for writing, and it is a skill that requires a teacher. I had a good one.

One other thing needs to be said in relation to my mom. I didn't realize until well after I had finished this book that I had given my mom's traits to one of the main characters of these pages—Granny. Again, I experienced a table-talk revelation. As my children and I talked about "Mama Tine," I understood a bit more about Granny's appeal—common sense, yes, but firmly placed within the framework of compassion; hard work because working hard is the right thing to do; and a bone-deep capacity for love, especially where children and grandchildren are concerned. Without my mom, I would not have been able to write about "Granny"—ample proof that some debts require thanks, pure and simple, because there's no question of being able ever to repay them.

I welcome the opportunity to thank other people as well for their contributions to this work. Larry Stone and Rutledge Hill Press have my gratitude for believing in this book. Without them, you wouldn't have it now. There are no words to communicate the thrill of having a publisher call with the words, "We'd like to publish your book." My work has greatly benefited from the expert editorial eye of Anne Christian Buchanan, and I'm glad to be able to say "thanks" to her here. Jennifer Greenstein, managing editor, has been a delight to work with.

My children, Mave and Gwynne, have been patient with an at-times obsessive author. With good humor they have listened to my ramblings about "the book," and this, along with so many other things, makes them a joy to me; indeed, they make life a joy. I love them dearly.

My wife and best friend, Terry, has given me what an author needs, I think, from at least one person—unqualified support. When you don't think you can write another word, it's always nice to have someone who believes you can. She is a blessing, and my life would be much poorer without her. I know a poem about soulmates that says, "I see the world through your eyes, and you gaze on stars by mine; what wondrous gift of grace divine, two souls to live entwined." Some gifts call forth silent wonder because you're in the presence of something too big to be bound by language.

I cannot write about family without recalling the one in which I was raised. Denise Moore, Suzanne Korpeck (1956–2000), and Tim Davis have made it easy to write a book that celebrates family, as this one does; I am thankful for them. The memory of the four of us hanging out the windows of a 1965 Ford Galaxie 500 and yelling good-naturedly across the town square to friends who hollered back with enthusiasm reminds me that it was a good thing to be counted as one of the Davis kids; it still is.

The Christmas Quilt

I

CHRISTMAS 1942 STANDS out in my mind for a lot of reasons. More happened that day than happens most years. For one thing, it snowed. We get snow in the North Georgia mountains, but rarely on Christmas Day. I still remember running around outside the house, chasing fat flakes that fell slow like fluffy seeds off a cottonwood tree. I love snow, just like Granny did.

Another thing that happened that day was that Uncle Joe came home. He'd been gone a long time. When he was young, he'd always tell anybody that'd listen, "I'm gittin' outa here. Gonna be rich and ain't gonna wear overalls or git red dirt under my fingernails. I'm leavin' and leavin' fer good." He left Smoky Hollow when he grew to a lanky seventeen, the way Granny told it. Granny loved Uncle Joe, and she missed him a lot. "Ran off to Dee-troit," she'd say, "hoping to be a big shot. Well, he may be a big shot, but he's still my Joey, pure and plain." Most things Granny liked best were pure and plain.

It's too bad I love Christmas so, and I love snow, because I don't think I'd ever want to see another white Christmas. That's because of the other thing that happened on Christmas of '42. Granny looked out her bedroom window, and the snow made her happy. Christmas joy at its purest, she always said, talking about the couple of white Christmases she'd seen when she was little. But on the white Christmas in 1942, Granny died.

I love Christmas, and I love snow, but there's no joy for me now in remembering a white Christmas.

It all started back that June with big news. Uncle Joe was good about writing Granny letters. How she loved those letters. She kept them in a box with a special lid. It had an Oriental kind of picture on it, with the women decked out in red robes with black belts, green mountains sparkling in the background. I think they were pushing one another on swings.

Ralph, our letter carrier, would always knock on the door when Uncle Joe's letters came. "Important-lookin' mail here, Miz Smith," he'd say. And Granny's eyes would gleam like two possum eyes staring into a lantern at night—she was that proud. But all she'd say was, "Oh, it's from Joey."

The envelope's return address boasted a dignified lettering. "Office of the Vice President," said the first line. The second line read, "The Ford Motor Company." "Lordy, all the way from Dee-troit," Granny would say. Then Ralph would say, "Reckon people's all the same no matter where they mail their letters from." And then Granny'd allow, "Reckon yore right."

The way I'd heard it growing up, Uncle Joe had gone off to Detroit, and he'd worked his way up to vice president at Ford. That's why we always drove Fords in our family. Granny wouldn't hear of us even talking about any other kind. I'd sit and whittle sometimes with my friend Bobby, and we'd argue cars. "Yore a buncha danged idjits," I'd tell him. Believe it or not, his folks drove a Chevrolet.

The June letter carried good news. Uncle Joe was courting some relation or another of old man Ford, the letter said. A grand-something or another, but not daughter or anything like that. He offered to send Granny some money, just like in every letter, but Granny wouldn't ever let him. "Save it fer the grand-childern," she'd always say out loud after reading that part to all of us. But anyone could tell she was proud that he had the money to offer. She'd better hope this courting went better than the others, I thought. Uncle Joe seemed to go out with a lot of girls, but he never married any of them.

The big news came at the end. "PS," Granny read, "Might be able to git away this Christmas fer a visit." Uncle Joe, the way I understood it, used to promise a Christmas visit every now and again in his letters. Seemed Ford was always in some sort of crisis though, especially at Christmastime. So Uncle Joe'd have to stay and sort things through. "I'm sorry, Mamma," he'd write, "but it's my job to fix broke things." Summer was always out of the question. Any danged fool knows that's peak production time. There was never any notion that Uncle Joe could come in the summer. But it'd been a long time since he mentioned Christmas, so maybe it'd be so, Granny said. My daddy didn't agree. "He ain't comin' here," he said. "Got no reason."

"Maybe he's gonna show off his new bride," Granny offered. "Maybe that's why he mentioned the courtin' and the visit in the same letter. He's a-comin' to innerduce his bride. It'd be the right thing to do." Then Granny gave Daddy a look that meant, "Don't go 'gainst what I say." I saw the look a lot, and Daddy got the look a lot, and he never did go against her.

"Yep, yore right," Daddy said. "It'd be the right thing."

"You figure Joey could use a new quilt?" Granny asked Daddy.

"Reckon so."

"Then reach over yonder and git my stuff," Granny said.

Daddy went over to a little cedar chest that sat at the end of the couch and took it over to Granny in her rocker. She reached down, lifted the lid, and started to rifle through its contents.

"Lots of blues and grays and whites. Them's good Christmas colors, if'n you think 'bout the night sky and the star of Bethlehem and all. Since he's a-comin' fer Christmas, I reckon a Christmas quilt would do good."

"Reckon so," Daddy said.

"I could do this 'un up real nice, make a good quilt, and it'd keep Joey and his bride warm up yonder in Dee-troit."

"Ain't no 'mount of money can buy a quilt like'n Granny makes, can it Daddy?" I said, wondering if Uncle Joe would really marry old man Ford's relation.

"Nope, not any more," he said. "Makes a fine present, if'n fer a wedding or fer Christmas."

All of a sudden, Granny had a hacking fit. Daddy went over and patted her back. "Go fetch a little water, son," he said.

I ran to the kitchen, grabbed a glass, and went out to the water pump. I pumped up and down once, then twice; then I stuck the glass under on the third time, wanting to make sure there wasn't any sediment in the water. When I came back with the full glass, Granny's fit was over. Red-eyed and teary from the coughing, she took a sip of water. "Lordy, that's good," she said. "Wouldn't walk two feet fer that water in town. Pumped all over creation and who knows where. This here's water from the good earth herself, drunk the way God wanted it drunk."

"Kinda bad hack there, Mamma," Daddy said. "How long's it been? Two, three weeks?"

"Don't rightly know," Granny said.

"Sounds worser than a few days ago."

"Sounds the same to me," Granny said.

"Then you ain't hardly listenin'," Daddy said. "We orta go see Doc Miller."

"We'll see," was all Granny answered. "Now, you two skeedad-dle. Go out to the porch or something. I wanna set a spell and think 'bout this here quilt." So Daddy and I went on out.

"Granny'll be alright," I said as soon as we were out. "She's tougher'n nails. Ever'body says so."

"Reckon so," Daddy admitted. He seemed to think awhile; then he grabbed me by the ear and gave a twist. "Reckon we orta do some work instead of just settin'." Before I could say anything, he patted my back and said, "C'mon. Weeds don't git up and walk off by theirselves. Gotta give 'em a shove."

Daddy knew I hated garden work. "Same as Joey," Granny once told him, me standing behind a tree listening. "Make 'im work at it, Robert, but don't pretend he gotta like it. That's the mistake yore daddy and me made with Joey. Tried to make 'im think that not only he's gotta do it but like it, too. You like it. I like it. I like being down on my knees on God's earth, tending stuff needs tending."

"Yep," Daddy said. "I 'member Daddy saying that a garden was better'n any church most of the time. I 'member 'im saying that that's why people pray on their knees at bedtime, and at the altar, too. Said that long 'fore 'tware beds to kneel by and altars that called us to prayer, 'tware God's temple with the red-dirt floors."

"That's right, he did say that," Granny replied, "though you know he wasn't saying nothin' 'gainst church. I reckon, deep down, he figured a garden fer a prayer. And it is. You know it. I know it. That'n yorn, though, he don't hear the words. Neither'd Joey. Don't make 'im listen fer what he can't hear. Push too hard, and you end up pushing away." So I had to weed, but Daddy never tried to make me like it.

June can be hot in Smoky Hollow, but nothing like August. Danged August is like wearing a wet blanket while the clay bakes hard under your feet. But June's hot is usually nice, bringing out a sweat but then giving a breeze to blow it away. My kneecaps were stained red where I dug them in the ground. It was a whole lot easier scooting along on my knees than having to raise up every couple of feet and move. Summertime garden work made sure my kneecaps and the tips of my toes that dug dirt behind were dirt-red most all summer long, lying along top the sun-burned skin I kept that time of year. So there I was, red head, red knees, red toes, red skin, sweating a good summer sweat with Daddy over in the next row. If I didn't hate working the garden so much, it'd been kind of nice.

"If'n Uncle Joe comes," I said, "reckon he'll drive a great big new Ford?"

"Joe ain't a-coming, son. Got no reason to."

"But, Daddy," I said, "why not? He practically promised Granny. And what 'bout his new girlfriend? They could come together and greet Granny proper-like, like she said."

Daddy stopped hoeing, leaned on the old work-worn handle, and looked at me. What he said surprised the fire out of me.

"If'n you ever left, would you come back?" he asked. There was no accusation in his voice—nothing of the sort. It was a plain question.

"Well, I dunno," I said. "Probably. To visit."

"I look at you, son, and I see Joe all over again. Yore smart, full of energy, but you hate garden work and you hate being where nothin's happening. Not much a feller can do 'round here to make 'nuff of a living to git out of puttin' in a garden. Son, I know you don't much care fer the hoeing and the weeding and all, but it's what we eat. Round 'bout winter we wouldn't eat none if'n we didn't can our garden's harvest. And that's alright by me. Me and yore Granny love to get our hands in the dirt. My daddy loved it, too. Lordy, he could put in a fine garden. Now you, you eat, but you don't care fer the work. Same as Joe."

"Well," I told Daddy, "I try hard. I don't slouch off or nothin'. Least not most times."

"No, son, you don't. And that's good. Not only got smarts, yore a worker, whether you like the work or not. Naw, yore not as bad as Joe. He'd practically spit out the beans Mamma'd cook up. Said he was gonna have steak ever' night when he got out. Well, son, we still don't put on much steak here. He ain't coming."

Daddy started hoeing again, sweat coming down his forehead and running off his nose like a little creek. You could spot the windings the sweat made as it worked itself down to the tip, gathering itself up a second before dropping off. Daddy was redheaded like me, and it didn't take an August sun to make the both of us sweat like we were made of water.

"I'd come and visit, Daddy, really I would," I told him. "And Granny. She wouldn't git just letters from me. I could be in Florida or California, and I'd come visit."

"Yea, reckon you would, son. But don't hold yore breath waiting on Joe. When he left he never looked back. Can't imagine 'im wanting to bring a bride here to show off. He'd be too embarrassed. Don't reckon even old man Ford's dog'd drink water if'n it hadn't a-come from a gold spigot." Daddy chuckled.

"Reckon not," I said.

"Don't git me wrong, son," Daddy said, putting on his explaining voice. "I'd give anything to see ol' Joe again. Lord, I bet he don't fish and hunt like we did 'fore he left. He wasn't no good at gardenin', and no good at being satisfied with what the good Lord provided from the garden. But he was a good'un when it came to knowing the best fishing holes or knowing where to sit and wait fer deer. My daddy was already down by the time I was yore age, so's 'twas Joe showed me best how to hunt and fish. Daddy'd take both of us up 'til he took sick, so I had a good start. But 'twas Joe really learnt me. Most of what I tell you I got from him. He was a smart'un too. Yep. Love to see Joe. But don't git yore hopes up. I used to. Don't no more."

We worked on for a while; then we moved over to an old oak to sit a spell in the shade. I looked over at the porch, and there sat Granny. She was rocking and rereading Uncle Joe's letter. The first day she got a letter from Uncle Joe, if it was nice weather, she'd end up on the porch a-rocking, reading the letter, or sometimes just looking at it, like it was a picture or something.

Daddy caught me looking and said, "Least Joe writes. Lots of fellers wouldn't. They's others that've gone off with nary a word ever. Joe writes."

"Sure is fancy paper and envelope," I said.

"Yep. Course'n Granny'd love it on a paper poke. But it is right nice paper. Joe's got a good hand, too. Right nearly perfect penmanship. Least his teacher always said so. Mine's more like those chickens over yonder." Daddy laughed.

"Naw, yores is good, too," I told Daddy. But he was right. Uncle Joe had fine handwriting. Strong but pretty, like a girl'd write if she was a man.

"Tried to have his secretary write onct," Daddy said. "All nice and neat and typed. Joe signed it in his handsome style, but the letters was all jet-black block letters stamped on with metal. Them's Mamma's words. She wrote 'im back and told 'im to use his own hand to write her. Typewriting might be good 'nuff fer all those fancy folks he worked with, she told 'im, but not fer her. 'Gotta know it comes from yore own hand,' she told 'im. ''Sides, no one needs know what you tell family but family.' Ever since, all the letters have been from his hand."

"Yeah, but must be nice to know you got a secretary there to type fer you if'n you want."

Daddy looked at me a long time. Then he got up and went back to hoeing, saying, "Reckon some folks think so." Then he looked at me for a second or two more, and he turned his eyes to the red dirt. I walked over and plopped down on my knees with a reluctance he probably recognized.

II

THE NEXT DAY was Sunday. Being another fine June day, with a right cheerful sun beaming like a smile, we walked the half mile over to Smoky Hollow Church. Whenever I think of church, that's what I picture. It was a neat little wooden building, rectangular in shape, and it sat with its far end butted up against a gentle slope. Twelve big steps led up to the front door. Underneath the main floor lay the cinder-block basement, mostly above ground except at the end. In the basement you could see the areas set aside for Sunday School classes and a small kitchen with a wood stove and some cabinets.

The top floor was where we held church. A little room for babies sat off to the right as you walked in the front door. That way, when they'd have their hollering fits, their mammas could take them back there and sit and rock—three or four good chairs for rocking lined the narrow room. That way the hollering came close to tolerable—the wall between the meeting place and the crying room took the edge off the shrieks. A plate glass window had been put in so the mammas could see out at the service, though I bet they couldn't have heard anything except babies yelling. Leastways they could watch the goings-on.

Over to the left as you walked into the church was a place for coats and such, and another, smaller room for the adults who came to Sunday School—guess they didn't need as much space as us children. Usually just five or six of the really old men came for Adult Sunday School.

The main meeting room had a center row with pews on either side—about ten or so on each. They were long enough to hold six or seven adults comfortably, where they didn't have to scrunch up to each other. Up front there was what we called an altar, really just a place to kneel and pray. Sometimes Preacher would come down and lay his hands on somebody's head and help that person pray through something important, like a decision to get saved. That didn't happen as much as Preacher would have liked.

A step up from the altar and in the center stood the big pulpit, and off to the left a big throne-like chair where the Preacher'd sit. The choir sat on the right of the pulpit in three short pews that held the four women and three men that sang, plus the song leader.

Behind the pulpit shone a big stained-glass window. It had a picture of Jesus praying in Gethsemane. There wasn't much happy about that picture. Jesus looked sad, and I reckon he should have. Bible says that he sweated great big drops of sweat like blood flowing. Preacher said it was a good picture because it showed how Jesus mostly felt about us sitting out in church—praying over us sad-like because we never got around to doing right. I never liked to make anybody feel bad, especially Jesus.

Preacher once turned to me and asked, "How'd you like to see yore daddy burning in hell? How'd you like to see smoke stuck up his nostrils worse'n ten colds worth of snot as far as trying to breathe?" Granny broke in then and said, "That's 'nuff." But Preacher's eyes burned the question into me, so I answered, "Bad. I'd feel bad." With a glance at Granny, Preacher said, "That's how Jesus feels, knowing that's what's in store if'n we don't change." I reckon bad's how Preacher felt too, the way he always carried on about not enough folks coming to the altar to get saved.

Before church that fine June Sunday we stayed outside until the church bell rang. That was my favorite part about church, standing around outside. Granny'd talk to her friends, and Daddy'd go off to one side and have a smoke with some of his buddies before going in. During the summer of '42 they talked a lot about the new three percent state sales tax that was going to start up, and they wanted to know if their dime can of tobacco would cost them thirteen cents or only eleven cents. They just didn't know how it was all going to work, and it worried them.

All us children would run around in the churchyard, always stopping a foot or two short of the graveyard, so it wouldn't look like we were showing disrespect. We had two graveyards at church. The hill the church snuggled up against held the old graveyard. It started where the back of the church ended. Mostly older graves sat up in there. Some of them had great big old tombstones, taller than me. Quite a few ran back into the seventeen hundreds. Sometimes the tombstone sat like the center of a wheel, with the graves being the spokes. Each side of the square tombstone would have the name of a different family member. Quite a number of the graves had some man who'd buried a wife first; then he'd remarry and bury her, too. I always thought it to be funny, some feller lying in the ground with a wife to either side of him. I figured it'd keep him company.

Smaller tombstones were for the poor folks, I guess, although I always reckoned everybody in Smoky Hollow to be poor. Granny said some folks would save up for a tombstone like they were saving up for a house. "Danged silliness," she'd say. "Ain't gonna care 'bout no tombstone when I'm in heaven." But, for some folks, having a big stone must have been a comfort, because there was a number of them scattered here and there.

But the smaller markers were for regular folks. Then there were the baby ones. Little stones for little bodies. Lots of baby stones lay nestled in the old part of the graveyard. Granny'd tell me that babies had a hard time long ago. Just a danged old cold sometimes would get a hold of them, and they'd up and die. As graveyards go, our old one was pretty, running up along the sloping hill the way it did. It'd have made an agreeable picture if anybody had wanted a graveyard hanging on the wall.

Across the road sat the new graveyard. When the old one filled up, the church bought up a couple of acres for us newer folks. Some nice tombstones rose up over there, but not like the ones in the old yard. There weren't any of the big towering tombstones. The new ones were mostly nice and mostly rectangular, a couple of feet high with a curved top that bounced the rectangle out of shape a bit. Lots of husband and wife tombstones, with each couple lying next to each other in the sleep of death like they did in the sleep of life. Quieter though. No snoring or such.

My mamma's grave sat in the new part. "Sarah Smith" was what the stone said, "1899–1932." She fell sick while I still wore diapers; then she slowly wasted away, to hear Granny tell it. Daddy never talked much about it. He talked about Mamma a lot, but not about when she fell sick and died.

Right under her name and dates, Daddy had them engrave what he felt: "I miss you." And I reckon he kept on missing her. Leastways, he never paid any mind to other women, even though Granny said lots of them that was widowed or had never married thought my daddy a fine man.

I missed my mamma, too, of course, though I don't rightly remember too much about her, just a few things here and there. Daddy remembered a lot more, so I reckon he must have missed her a lot more, and that'd be a lot, because I missed her something sore, even though sometimes I didn't know exactly what it was about her I missed.

Well, we all of us heard the bell. I stopped running and looked around and, in my twelve-year-old way, appreciated the sight of the church and its graveyards. A handsome air to the place, that's how Daddy would talk about our church. And I thought the same. Over in the area where all the old women gathered, I saw Granny folding up her letter from Uncle Joe. She stood ready to share her letters with anybody that'd listen, especially the ones from Uncle Joe.

Daddy and the other men all dropped their cigarettes and ground the butts into the ground with the toes of their good Sunday shoes. Daddy's shoes were always shiny on Sunday. He paid me a dime a month to shine them up good. First, I'd clean them proper; then I'd get out the black shoe polish along with the polishing rag and rub on them something fierce, working the polish into the leather. Then I'd grab the brush. My hand would fly, and by the time I had finished, those shoes would shine like brand new. I always had pride in how my daddy's shoes looked. I told him once I figured he had the shiniest shoes at church. He reckoned as how I was probably right.

We all filed into the church and took our seats. I sat with Granny, and we reached for the hymnbook. Daddy sat up with the choir, like most Sundays. Daddy had a tender-sounding tenor voice, and he could make it all warbly, especially if he was singing a sad song, and that made it sound a whole lot sadder. Daddy's

singing could bring tears to the eyes of the old ladies, and even
some of the men could get all choked up. Daddy would often sing
at funerals, and sometimes those songs meant so much to the men
whose mamma or daddy had passed on that every time they heard
Daddy sing them they'd get all misty eyed, least after the first
little while after the funeral. Daddy had his guitar up there with
him on this particular Sunday, so I knew he was going to sing.

Over in front of where the choir sang, off to the right side of
the altar, sat the beat-up Acrosonic piano. Miss Rogers could
make that thing practically hop off the floor. The sad songs she
could play sad; but on the good old foot-stomping songs, she'd
work that pedal, stomp her other foot, and, I swear, I don't see
how she kept from breaking the piano keys sometimes.

We started out with one of my favorites. We all stood up—the
song leader always said we could sing better standing up, and by
better he meant louder—and away Miss Rogers went, pounding
out the introduction. Then Mr. Charles, a man who could sing
louder than anybody I knew of could holler, brought his arm
down and away we all went:

> I am resolved no longer to linger,
>   Charmed by the world's delight.
> Things that are higher, things that are nobler,
>   These have allured my sight.

Then the chorus would start:

I will hasten to him, hasten so glad and free.
Jesus, greatest, highest, I will come to thee.

I always loved the chorus. Everybody'd sing "hasten so glad and free" and then right afterwards all the men'd sing "hasten so glad and free" as a kind of echo. Always sounded right nice, the women holding out the high note on "free" and the men stepping down the scale with each syllable they echoed. I still think the sound of heaven will be the sound of a country church that knows how to sing.

After the song Preacher would welcome everybody, and he made a special pitch for the visitors, if we had any, though that wouldn't be very often. Then we'd catch up on the week's news from around Smoky Hollow, which came in the form of "announcements" and prayer requests. The social life of the Hollow focused around that church, and it served during the week as a meeting place for folks. We'd hear about every couple that was expecting a baby, whether they lived in Smoky Hollow or no. Everybody figured prayers prayed in Smoky Hollow were good for kinfolk no matter where in life they'd ended up. I used to listen and just soak up all the names of places I'd never been to but was sure I'd make it around to visiting just as soon as I got old enough to hit the road. A rich man and a traveling man— that was what I always figured myself for when I grew up, though at the time I hadn't quite thought through how exactly that would all come about.

That morning in church, we found out who'd been sick in Smoky Hollow same as we found out who'd had visitors. "Thank the Lord," somebody'd say, "I had the nicest visit from my cousins over in Redbud." The way it sounded, the Lord worked a miracle every time somebody made it into Smoky Hollow. I laughed, but none too loud. I always figured the miracle was the getting out, not in.

"Uncle Cecil's been down with fever," somebody else would say. Preacher always listened real good during announcements and prayer requests because he'd always say them over again when he prayed. Course, he added a whole lot of Bible talk so that you'd think a visit from the cousins over in Redbud was like Moses crossing the Red Sea. Maybe it was.

After a spell of catching up on things and folks telling Preacher what the Lord needed knowing, Preacher would call us to prayer.

I once asked Granny why, if the Bible talked about Jesus fussing at people about long-winded prayers in public, why in the world would we want to do exactly what he said not to do. After all, Preacher could pray forever, and that just wasn't any twelve-year-old's idea of a good time. He'd start out low, nice and reverent-like, but then he'd get louder. Sometimes I reckoned even Preacher knew he spoke fierce long-winded, and he figured he'd better get louder if he hoped to keep God's attention.

When Uncle Cecil had the fever, for instance, we'd have to hear every place in the Bible where Jesus healed somebody. "Almighty God, good God, great God to deliver," he'd pray, "we knows you can heal. We knows it 'cause yore dear Word says so. 'Ciples brought the lame man to you, and you cured 'im. Woman a-bleeding fer twelve years touched the hem of yore garment. Healed! The blind were brought 'fore you, and just like the sun breaking over the horizon you put the gift of light to them dark eyes. Jairus's daughter rose up from her death bed 'cause you was asked, sweet Jesus. And when Lazarus lay a-stinking in the tomb fer three days, you just hollered, 'Lazarus, come on out,' and he did."

Preacher paused a minute then. Maybe he needed time for catching his breath. Maybe, after reciting all those stories from the Bible, he had to take a moment to recollect who it was he held forth for in prayer. Finally, he'd declare, "So we know, Jesus, you got the healing touch. Touch Cecil and heal 'im. We can do the believing if'n you'll do the healing."

If somebody fell sick, that'd be the kind of prayer they'd get. If somebody wore out the road traveling, the praying would compare it to the Israelites crossing the desert. Preacher could connect everything to the Bible, even the expecting women. More than once I heard him compare a woman, if she fell a bit past normal childbearing years, to Sarah in the Bible, and he'd say, "If'n you can bring to Sarah, past ninety years of age, a good birth, then we know you can deliver so and so of her child." Finally, when the wind had left him, Preacher would get all quiet again and come to a soft-spoken "Amen."

Preacher always needed time to recover after his prayers—in

the summer, he'd be sweating something awful by the time he finished up, but his jacket would still be on.

Somebody once said, "Preacher, take that thang off 'fore you git started and you won't git so danged hot."

Preacher said, "Can't do that."

"Why not?" he was asked. "You take yore jacket off when preaching."

"That's diff'rent," Preacher said. "When I'm praying, I'm a-talking to God Almighty. When I'm preaching, I'm just a-talking to folks like you and me. It's a matter of respect."

So, on a hot summer's day, Preacher would slump down in his seat after praying over the whole congregation's concerns and goings on and rest a bit. We'd sing to give him a little rest. On this summer day, we sang, "Come, Ye Sinners, Poor and Needy." A pretty melody accompanied some real meaningful words, if you heard them right. "Jesus ready stands to help you," the song said. And I think all of us standing there that Sunday morning believed it, though each of us in his own way.

After the singing, the time for the offering came. The deacons went up to get the plates, and that's when Daddy stood up and took hold of his guitar. I don't know who figured it'd be easier to part with your money if a good song was hanging in the air while you did it, but it made for a fine idea. The collection plates made their way around the congregation as my daddy plucked his chords and sang, "I come to the garden alone, while the dew is still on the roses."

It was a song about the joy of being in the presence of the Lord. Daddy liked that song, and I did too. Granny had a fine set of rosebushes tied up next to the back porch. On early summer mornings, when I went out to pump water, I would see the sun set those roses sparkling. Light would be playing off the dew like the sunshine had nothing else to do but light up Granny's little corner of heaven—which is what it was for her, because she loved her flowers. I always thought of that every time Daddy sang that song, and every time I've ever heard it since his passing I still see the beauty of the roses, and something of the beauty of the hand that put such pretty roses and such pretty words and music together.

But then the offering was done, and Preacher stood up. Daddy's music flew away before Preacher's advance like dry leaves blown away by the winds of autumn. After an hour or so of blustering, and a prayer and a song that brought no one to the altar, we got to go home.

III

"Well, just pick up and leave, Mamma. If'n yore that sore 'bout it all, you orta. Just plain makes sense."

"Don't make sense to me," Granny said with conviction. "Leave the church where yore daddy and me grew up? Yore daddy and me went to church together there from our first squalls in the crying room 'til his burying. Leave? That'd be a fine howdya-do!"

"All I'm a-saying, Mamma," Aunt Lois declared, "is that yore always madder'n an old wet hen when you git out of church, and you spend all Sunday afternoon fretting yoreself 'bout it. If'n what you git outa church is so pore that it takes a whole afternoon to fetch it from yore system, maybe it's time to move on. Plain sense."

Aunt Lois gave Granny one of those looks that Granny hated, a look that said, "If'n you had any sense, you'd see it my way." And there Aunt Lois stood, that look of hers staring out at Granny like she was looking at somebody gone simple.

The fight fell away from Granny. "All I'm a-saying," she sighed, "is that I wish he'd go preach that message of his'n somewhere else. I'll never leave my church, no matter who stands behind the pulpit. It's just so tiresome, though. Don't know why he's like he is now. Didn't used to be."

Granny looked tired, as if Preacher's scalding-hot words 'bout hell and such had gone and burnt off all her energy. Aunt Lois noticed it, too. She looked down her hawk's nose—both her size and her nose came from her daddy, to hear Granny tell it—and with all the best intentions that the rough of manners can muster stated bluntly, "That cough of yores is plumb wearing you out. It'll be the death of you if'n you don't git it taken care of. And where'll that leave me? Having to fetch after that boy of Robert's, I reckon. So you just go git yoreself looked after. I got 'nuff to look after without having to go and look after 'nother brood that ain't mine."

Aunt Lois shot a glance my way. She stood oldest in the family. First Aunt Lois, then Uncle Joe, then Daddy, then Aunt Doris. Aunt Lois was always real bossy. She was also the nearest relative, and so I saw more of her than anybody. I never had seen Uncle Joe—he was off to Detroit making his fortune before I was born. Aunt Doris had married a man that took over an uncle's sawmill down at Canton, a good forty or fifty miles away. About once a month they'd make it up our way. First Sunday usually. But this particular June Sunday was a second Sunday. And second Sundays, like third, fourth, and, when it'd pop up twice a year or so, fifth Sundays, meant just Aunt Lois and her family at Sunday dinner.

Uncle Henry and Aunt Lois lived on the east side of Ellijay, the county seat of Gilmer County. Smoky Hollow lay about seven miles west of Ellijay. Ellijay was a town; Smoky Hollow was just a community with enough folks to have a church and a little school. We went into Ellijay every couple of Saturdays, and we always went to see Henry, Lois, and the girls. There were three of them, and the youngest was about my age. Mildred and I usually had a good time playing outside, climbing trees, and all that, though her mamma always hollered that she should start acting more like a lady and not like some boy without the sense God gave him. I reckoned that meant me, though I didn't know why.

Aunt Lois had a nice house, a lot nicer than ours. It sat on the edge of the east side of town. It had electricity and running water—though Granny wouldn't drink it. It was a strange house, though. Aunt Lois kept the curtains closed most of the time, saying the sunshine would fade the coverings on her new couch or some other thing in the house. She had lots of things I wasn't supposed to touch—or even look at for very long. Once I patted a new china cat—life-sized—that was sitting in her living room.

"Don't you break that," she yelled at me.

"Weren't gonna break it," I said. "I was just petting it."

"Don't give me none of yore sass," Aunt Lois said, "or I'll take a hick'ry to you and tan yore hide." And she would have, so I stopped.

I never could figure how Aunt Lois came out of our family. She didn't seem anything like Daddy or Granny or Doris. As a twelve-year-old, I could never decide if she was the nicest mean person I knew or the meanest nice person. Sometimes I was sure her heart lay stone cold in her breast. More often, I reckoned that beneath that thick hide of hers beat a heart with human feelings, but that she kept them buried under with a disposition I always thought would make for a good reformatory-marm. The kind that'd say, "I'm gonna wear you out with this here strap just 'cause it'll be good fer you."

Anyway, Aunt Lois always did whatever it took to seem to be doing the right thing, even if it meant a lot of trouble for her. I didn't know what exactly she got out of it. Whatever it was, it wasn't joy. I knew if I ever found myself alone in this world, Aunt Lois would take me in because it'd be her duty, and she'd want to do right. But it wouldn't be a joy; it'd be a burden. Maybe the weight of that prospective burden was already heavy on her—she always seemed to look at me with heavy eyes. And with that glance that second Sunday of June, I took my cue and ran off to find Mildred to pass the time with until the adults set out dinner.

After kicking the rocks in the road for a while, we decided we'd play spy and follow after Liz and Becky. They were Mildred's older sisters and the most stuck-up pair of cousins I've ever known. Course, we always let them know we were following them. Made them madder than anything. They'd holler at us to go away, and we'd stand behind a tree laughing.

Mildred told me who their latest boyfriends were, and when the two of them thought they had gotten rid of us, we snuck up behind them and made kissing sounds while calling out the boys' names. Liz picked up a rock and hauled off and threw it—up in the air it went. Liz couldn't throw worth nothing, so I knew she was just trying to scare us. But it gave us the excuse we needed to run back to the house, hollering at the top of our lungs, "Liz's throwing rocks at us."

Aunt Lois met us at the door with a look that I think would've stopped a charging bull. "You git out back and wash yore hands, young lady," she said to Mildred. Then she turned her bull-stopping eyes at me. "And YOU! Go tell Liz and Becky dinner's ready."

I turned around, walked to the front of the porch, cupped my hands, and yelled real loud, "LIZ! BECKY! DINNER'S READY!"

"Young'un, I coulda yelled," Aunt Lois declared. "Now, you stop that and go fetch 'em. No hollering. Go!" And so off I ran up the road, delivered my message to the two, who always looked like they were on the verge of sticking their tongues out at you, and then ran back. I made my way around back, washed my hands, and went in the back door, through the kitchen, and to the dining room. I reached out my hand to grab a chicken leg, but I got a pop from Aunt Lois. "Wait 'til ever'body's here," she said.

"Ain't my fault they gotta walk all prissy," I said. "If'n they'da run like me, they'd be here."

Aunt Lois stood ready to give me one of her lectures about manners and such—the kind my daddy'd let go for a few minutes before cutting in with "Aw, Lois, he's a boy. Boys, they's diff'rent from girls." To which Lois would always say, "Don't know 'bout diff'rent. Worse, that's fer sure." But then she'd hush up because she didn't like Daddy to remind her who the boss of me was. As long as she didn't hear it, she could figure it was her, even though it wasn't.

Granny came in with a bowl of gravy and set it down. Everything was ready then. All of us bowed our heads and waited for Granny to return thanks.

"Fer mercy everlasting, O Lord, we're mighty grateful," she said. "Thank you fer food and family, and look after the young'uns that aren't here. In Jesus' name. Amen."

Nothing ever compared to Sunday dinner at Granny's. I don't know if it was the excitement of being a child or what, but those dinners tasted the best I can remember having. Hunger always seemed to keep me company—in a good way, not bad—and the food satisfied me, and I felt happy after sopping up the last bit of gravy with my biscuit in a way that's hard to capture anymore. All I could figure in that child mind of mine was that, when Preacher read about Jesus and the feast of the kingdom of God, God's chef must be like Granny, and his table hers. Food and love put together fill your heart and stomach to bursting, and I never felt fuller than after those Sunday dinners.

Granny had cut up a chicken and fried it, like on many Sundays. Biscuits and gravy served as the other mealtime regulars. Granny usually made a dark milk gravy with the chicken grease, and I ladled it on thick on top of my biscuits. I'd tear my chicken off the bone and dip it in, licking my fingers as I did. On this particular Sunday, we also had us some new potatoes boiled up, a mess of fried cabbage, and some spring onions and radishes. Another month, and we could expect some big red tomatoes and the beans would start coming in good. Month after that, corn'd be in. As bad as I hated to cut okra, I had to admit how good it tasted all breaded and fried up, crusty on the outside and tender inside. That'd come later, too. Now it was just June, so we ate on the early stuff.

Granny sat there across from me, all of us about finished up. Little bits of conversation had been exchanged between bites of food, but mostly people concentrated on filling their bellies. Our talk time came after everybody had eaten. I lathered up a biscuit with butter and peach preserves—my favorite way to finish up Sunday dinner. Granny had her favorite, too. And, usually, if Granny had any news to share, that's when she'd do it. There she sat, crumbling up the remains of the night before's corn bread into some buttermilk. "Better'n any cake," she'd always declare. Then, after taking that first bite and letting everybody know how good it tasted, she turned to Aunt Lois and said, "Got a letter from Joey yesterday."

"That a fact? Got time to write while running the comp'ny, does he? Ever'time I think he's gone and fergot us, up comes a letter."

"Well, he's mighty busy, you know," Granny said. "Got a couple of good bits of news fer you from it. First off, he's a-courtin' somebody from the family. Shows how far he's made it, reckon."

The "family" was Granny's way of talking about old man Ford and his relations.

"Lord have mercy, you don't say. I never figured Joey fer one of them society types. How in the world will he ever keep up a woman like that?"

Granny dipped her spoon into her dessert. After taking a bite, she said, "Well, you gotta figure somebody in Joey's position is making fine money. And he ain't never had no wife, and no childern either. Probably saved most of what he's made—leastways if'n he's taken my advice. 'Save it fer the childern,' I tell 'im ever time he offers to send something down my way. Lordy, what would I do with more'n I got? I set a good table, house and land's mine, and two good strapping fellers to help me run things. Right, y'all?"

Daddy smiled at Granny. "Reckon as long as I can keep a bit on this here young colt, you'll have two. When he bolts, it may just be me."

"I ain't a-bolting," I said. "Not fer a while, anyways."

"Course you ain't," Granny said. She looked at Daddy when she said it, with more hope than conviction.

"Well, git off them two," Aunt Lois said. "Course they'll be 'round to help. But Joey ain't. You orta let 'im send some money this way. Save yoreself some trouble."

"Ain't got no troubles," Granny replied. "Only vexation I have is that mule-headed preacher that ain't 'parently read nothing but hell in the Bible." We all let Granny mull over that sore spot for a spell before Aunt Lois jumped back in.

"So, Joey's a-courtin'. What else is news?"

"Coming home fer Christmas," Granny declared. She looked up at Daddy and spoke plain with her eyes, "He is." And Daddy never talked back to Granny. They disagreed and fussed some-times, but Daddy never gave Granny any sass.

But Aunt Lois just rolled her eyes. "Mamma, why do you let yoreself in fer heartache?" she asked. "Joey ain't been home since the day his foot hit the dirt out off'n the front porch more'n twenty years ago. And I ain't one to judge a feller, and I know he writes you, Mamma, though not like he used to. I don't hear from 'im, and I figure he don't want to hear from me none." Aunt Lois sounded mad, like when she was fussing over an embroidery that'd gone all wrong, and she had to pull out the thread. Like the thread had gone soft in the head and done something wrong and offended her.

"Reckon Joe does what he has time fer," Daddy offered. "And I reckon he figures he's writing to all of us when he sends Granny a letter."

"Ain't like gittin' yore own, though, is it?" Lois replied. "Lord knows I looked after 'im like a young'un of my own, didn't I, Mamma, when I had to?"

"So you did," Granny responded. "When you was old 'nuff, you always fetched after 'im when I needed you to."

"Yes, I did," Aunt Lois sniffed.

"Course, now Lois, you know why you don't git no letters," Granny started.

"Now listen, Mamma," Lois interrupted. That was something not much done.

"Well," Daddy broke in, stopping a conversation that'd been going longer than the just now of it, "Joe don't need no looking after now, does he? And there ain't no reason to go figuring he's got to git yore howdy doody fer what he does or doesn't do. Leave it at that."

"I'll decide fer myself what to let go and what not, thank ye," Aunt Lois said in a huff. "And I'm only trying to help, Mamma," she said, looking with those no-nonsense eyes of hers at Granny. "Figure he ain't coming, and if'n he do, then it'll be a big surprise."

Granny pushed her glass away from her, setting down the spoon she just licked clean. "Help me clear up the table, Lois," Granny said. "I want you to help me with somethin' afterwards." Daddy picked himself up and went out to sit on the porch for a spell. He and Uncle Henry talked about gardening, which for me meant talking about nothing much. Liz and Becky went out back and down to the springhouse, sitting in the shade of the willow trees that kept the sun off the little rock building. Mildred and I sat ourselves down at the bottom of the front porch steps, letting our stomachs settle a bit.

About the time full-stomach laziness had set in, we heard some racket from inside, and Granny's voice came out through the screen door saying, "Be careful, Lois." We got ourselves up and peered through the screen door. Granny and Aunt Lois were setting up Granny's quilting frame in the living room.

"Ain't no use in this, Mamma. Joey ain't coming."

"Now I told you, Lois, he is. And I'm gonna make the nicest present I can fer his Christmas present. You and Robert and Doris always git a little something ever' year. I've stitched and sewed and poked my fingers with needles 'nuff over somethin' of yores year in and year out. So don't go begrudging Joey something nice."

"Why, Mamma, I ain't a-begrudging nobody nothin'. I'm a-trying to save you trouble with yore hands and trouble with yore heart. 'Sides, you ain't even started on the quilt. No use setting up the frame yet."

"I want it there and waiting fer when I do need it," Granny said.

And that's the way it went. Mildred and I stood there watching and listening until Granny and Aunt Lois had things all set up and both had had their say. Then Lois let it be known that it was time for her and hers to go home, and they did.

I went and grabbed a leftover biscuit and came back out on the porch. After everybody had left, in the cool of the June evening with a breeze blowing off the hills, I sat and rocked, watching the dusk turn to darkness, seeing stars pop out and light up. Daddy played his guitar, and Granny hummed along.

IV

BOBBY AND I rode into town with Daddy the next day. I came all bleary-eyed to the breakfast table, still not awake good even after doing chores. Practically early enough to set off deer hunting if it had been fall. Daddy'd been working longer days, and some Saturdays. The sock mill had some sort of government contract to provide socks for the military boys, and Daddy reckoned that as part of his contribution to the war effort. Daddy'd been in the big war back the generation before, when afterwards they said there weren't going to be any more wars. Daddy never said too much about his army time. But when someone at church had made a crack about the socks going out from the mill, Daddy let him have it. "Ever been in a war? Ever been stuck in a mud hole fer weeks with shells screaming down from the sky? You know what you worry 'bout next to keeping yore head on yore shoulders? Yore feet on yore legs. Ain't 'til yore feet have 'bout rotted off that you 'preciate a good, thick, dry pair of socks." Daddy took the socks for the boys seriously; after that church-day talking to, everybody else who was within hearing distance did, too.

Daddy dropped Bobby and me off at ol' man Bridges' and went on to work. We planned to work half a day making apple crates, go pick up a dinner pail at Aunt Lois's, then meet Daddy at the mill for dinner. Then we'd swim until Daddy's quitting time. Looked like the makings of a fine day.

We found ol' man Bridges back behind his house. A shed full of tools sat next to an open work area sheltered by a tin roof. Ol' man Bridges greeted us with a satisfied grunt and nodded his head over toward the slats we'd need to make apple crates. He had two hammers out waiting for us. We went over, grabbed an armful of slats, came and turned a couple of crates over to sit on, and started work. We got a penny a piece for each crate we made. Bridges owned a fair-sized apple orchard, and we knew, come August and September, we'd have jobs picking apples. But before the picking, the crates needed making. Not just Bridges needed them. A couple of middling to good-sized apple orchards dotted the county, and Bridges provided crates at a good price. Every now and again he'd ask Bobby and me to come help for half a day. I think the old man liked having someone to talk to as he worked.

Maybe in his youth ol' man Bridges' face had been nice and

smooth. But working out in the sun all his life made him all dark and wrinkled, his face a long oval punctuated by such deep wrinkles that he looked like a raisin. His mouth was no more than wrinkles run wrongways across his face, a mouth sucked into itself a bit because the ol' man had no teeth. Permanent tobacco stains sat on his lips; he always had a chaw in his cheek. He'd work a plug from the time he got up until bedtime. I've never seen a man that could talk, spit, and hammer in such a rhythm as ol' man Bridges. Almost musical.

"How's that brother of yorn, Bobby?" he asked.

"He's gittin' 'round better'n he did," Bobby said. His brother Paul had gone off and joined the army just as soon as he'd heard about Pearl Harbor getting bombed. Paul was right proud when he left, talking how'd he'd set things right, like a seventeen-year-old has any notion enough of what's wrong with the world to set it right. Bobby's daddy just said, "You be careful, hear." About broke up Bobby's mamma to see Paul go off. Things went bad, though. After just a few months of training, the army sent Paul off to join MacArthur's forces in the Philippines. His leg got shot nearly plumb off in early April. Course, maybe it saved his life. Philippines fell in May with heavy casualties. After a couple of months at Walter Reed in Washington, they sent Paul back to Smoky Hollow.

"Still, in some ways, he ain't no good," Bobby said. "Has all kinds of bad dreams at night, and he sits and broods most all day. Mamma says leave 'im alone and he'll git better."

"Can he git 'round at all?"

"Some," says Bobby. "Has to use a crutch, though. Took his leg off at the knee. Doctoring folk said 'tware too much of a mess to save anything below the knee."

"Mighty hard going fer some'un like Paul," Bridges said. "Always a-going, that one was. I 'member when he stood about yore size. He'd a-come up to the farm, scamper 'round the trees and up gathering apples, and nary ever letting one fall and git bruised. Lordy, he'd be at it all day and then be out all night with yore daddy coon hunting. It's gonna be hard."

"Yep, reckon so," Bobby said.

After a respectful spell, all of us keeping quiet remembering Paul's service, I said, "Uncle Joe's a-promising to come home fer Christmas."

"Don't say," Bridges said, spitting juice out just as his hammer buried a nail in the wood on the way down, his shirt sleeve passing his lips on the way back up. "I 'member 'im, boy, do I! He was one of the first boys ever worked fer me when I first got into the apple business. Purt' good worker, but his heart was sommers else. I had pickers whose whole purpose fer living was picking apples whilst they was a-picking. Not Joey. Worked hard with his hands, but kept his heart and mind to hisself. Onct told 'im, 'Joey, put yoreself into it, boy.' He just looked with this funny look of his you'd git sometimes. 'Ain't 'nuff in apples to put myself into 'em,' he said. Reckon he was right, eh?"

"Like Daddy always has said," I repeated Daddy's oft-said words,

"Uncle Joe's made fer bigger things than what's in Smoky Hollow."

"How's things up in Dee-troit fer 'im?"

"Good, good," I said. "Courtin' a Ford relative. Reckon he's big 'nuff in the company now that his head and heart can turn that way without gittin' bit off. That's what Granny says."

"Well, if'n you ask me," Bobby piped in, "if'n yore Uncle Joe was so smart, he'd a-been climbing the ladder over at Chevrolet. Them's the real vehicles."

I reached over and shoved Bobby, and he shoved back. Then we both laughed because that's just what we always did. I looked over at ol' man Bridges. "Reckon you know which'uns the best, don't ya, Mr. Bridges?" Daddy'd just bought our '39 Ford not more than a month before from Bridges.

"Aw, boys, I ain't a-gonna git caught in the middle of yore bickering. 'Bout anything that'll move up and down the road is better'n used to be with them horses. Right purdy thangs, but lots of work compared to an auty-mobile. Roads a lot cleaner, too, eh?"

Bobby and I both laughed. Then we listened for the rest of the morning while ol' man Bridges talked about when he was a boy up in Cherry Log, northeast of town several miles, and about running around with some Cherokee boys when he was our age, and talking about Chief White Path, and his daughter who had up and run off with a white man, a story from years before. Sometimes I thought ol' man Bridges liked having us around so he could get all his memories into someone else's head, so when he passed on someone else would know all that interesting stuff.

About dinnertime Bobby and I collected our money for the morning—more than enough to see us through the movies. We set off the mile or so to Aunt Lois's, kicking the same rock the whole way. Don't know why, but when you're twelve years old, and you still got the whole summer ahead of you, nothing seems better than kicking a rock along for a nice long distance. It means you don't have to get anywhere in a hurry, and when you get there you've got nothing more important to do than kicking the rock back the other direction.

We knocked at Aunt Lois's, and Mildred came to the door. Bobby had fallen sweet on Mildred, and I think she liked him, too. For myself, right then, never figured out why being sweet on someone drove all the words out of your head. I learned. Both Bobby and Mildred could talk the hair off a dog, but put them together and they forgot every word they ever learned but "Hey."

We went into the kitchen, and there sat three dinner pails all in a row. Aunt Lois looked at us, and without so much as a howdy do, she asked, "You boys wipe yore feet? Don't want no red dirt tromped all through the house." We had to show Aunt Lois the bottoms of our shoes before she'd give us our dinners. "Here's yore Uncle Henry's dinner," she said, handing it off to me as I took mine. "Reckon he forgot it this morning. Now go on so he don't git hungry waiting." And with that, we took off, clean shoes and all.

The sock mill lay about a ten-minute walk south of town, so we kicked along the same rock we'd brought with us. We got there right about eating time. Wooden tables sat under the shade—folks liked to eat outside when nice weather allowed. Preacher sat at the end of one of the tables, munching on a piece of day-old chicken and reading his Bible. Before we could steer clear, he looked up and saw us. "Come 'ere boys," he called. His face wore darkness like a thunderhead in August.

Preacher's gaze sat hard on us. "Read yore Bible today?" he asked.

"No sir, not yet," we said. Preacher figured everybody ought to read the Bible every day.

"Well, go home today and read about the Day of the Lord," he said. "Gonna be preaching on it Sunday. Might as well know what's a-coming."

Bobby and I sat there and squirmed a bit. I kept an eye out on the main gate, waiting for Daddy or Uncle Henry one to come out so we could scoot off.

Preacher saw my wandering eye and said, "A wandering eye's a sign of a wandering mind and heart. God knows how to deal with thems as wanders off. Read yore Bible. God won't be mocked. No sir! Wanna know what's it gonna be like when the Day of the Lord comes?"

Bobby and me sat dumb, two lambs led to the slaughter.

"Listen here," Preacher said, "right outa the good book of Micah. Here's what God says: 'Hear all ye peoples; hearken, O earth, and all that is in it; and let the Lord God be witness against you, the Lord from his holy temple. For, behold, the Lord cometh forth out of his place, and will come down, and tread upon the high places of the earth. And the mountains shall be melted under him, and the valleys shall be cleft, like wax before the fire, and like the waters that are poured down a steep place.'"

"Don't sound good, do it?" Preacher asked.

We shook our heads no.

"It gets worse. Listen what the prophet Zephaniah says: 'The great day of the Lord is near, it is near, and hasteneth greatly, even the voice of the day of the Lord; the mighty man shall cry there bitterly. That day is a day of wrath, a day of trouble and distress, a day of waste and desolation, a day of darkness and gloominess, a day of clouds and thick darkness.'"

Preacher looked up from his Bible and asked, "You boys want to be caught in the darkness? When these here mountains melt like wax 'fore His approach, you think you can hide? The day of wrath comes. Look at the world 'round us, boys. Wars and rumors of war. The day of wrath is near. So I want you boys to think hard—you wanna be on the side of the Lord, or agin 'im? Light or darkness? Sin or salvation? Life or destruction? You boys are of the age of accountability. The day of the Lord comes, his wrath approaches. Yore responsible fer yore sins 'cause you ain't babies no more. Are you?"

"No sir, we're not," I said. My eyes strained at the gate, willing Daddy to come through.

"Well think over this here passage I read to you today. Go

home and read it tonight. And see if'n God don't put it in yore heart to come to the altar this Sunday. Let God save you from the coming wrath."

Just then, Daddy and Uncle Henry walked out together. Bobby and I jumped up, me saying, "Gotta go. We got Uncle Henry's dinner pail." Not having learned the etiquette of a respectful exit, we tore off, leaving Preacher to mull over Sunday's sermon. I didn't rightly know when the Lord's day of wrath would be, but I had a feeling Sunday would see Preacher's, when he looked over a congregation not nearly as scared as they ought to be to his way of thinking.

In one of their many run-ins, Granny had told Preacher that God was good and loving as well as all the things Preacher talked about. Preacher just looked at her and quoted the Psalmist, "'The fear of the Lord is the beginning of wisdom.' Just trying to wise folks up a mite."

Granny spat back, "The beginning but not the end. Jesus is the end, 'cause Paul says that Jesus is the wisdom of God. And to my mind, I reckon 'im up on the cross saying, 'Father forgive 'em' moves us outa fear into love. And how's 'bout 1 John? 'Perfect love drives away fear.'"

Not much use those two talking. They saw everything different. I don't know who was right; maybe both of them. Maybe it took the both of them to make up the whole truth. Granny did tend to ignore all those things Preacher read about in the Bible, and they're in the Bible. But Preacher almost never read Granny's favorite Bible verses in church, and they are in the Bible, too. But I did realize, that day eating with my friend Bobby, my daddy, and Uncle Henry, that Preacher ate alone. From what I remembered, even then, Jesus always had a crowd to eat with, and Granny did, too.

Daddy's broad smile welcomed us, as did Uncle Henry's appetite. We ate under an old oak tree, away from the tables a bit, sitting cross-legged on the ground. Daddy leaned back against the broad trunk of that great shade tree, letting out a contented sigh. I nibbled on the last of my biscuit, wishing I had a bit of preserves to add. Bobby and I told how many crates we'd built that morning, and that we planned to stop back by Aunt Lois's to get Mildred and then go swimming. Even with Uncle Henry sitting there, I called it "Aunt Lois's." I know it was Uncle Henry's house, too, but sometimes he seemed more like an occupant than an owner. But that was just Aunt Lois's nature—everything she touched was hers. Including Uncle Henry. Daddy told us to be sure and be back at Aunt Lois's (he called the place hers, too) by six. He'd drop Uncle Henry off and take us on home.

Bobby and I picked up a rock on the way back to get Mildred. Sometimes we'd kick it back and forth, watching it roll slow. Then we'd give it the boot and see it pop along the road like water across hot grease. Mildred was waiting for us when we got there. Her face hung longer than that of a dog that had just been whipped.

"Can't go," she said.

"Why the heck not?" I asked.

"Mamma says it ain't ladylike, me going off with boys to go swimming. Says I'm gittin' too old to act like some tomboy girl who'll scoot up a tree, dress or no. I told her I ain't never done that." Then she put a look on her face that looked just like she'd stepped in a cow pile, directing that disgusted look at her mamma through the screen door.

We three stood around on the front porch, mulling over this turn of events. Long as I could remember, Mildred always went along with me when I did stuff. Dang, I hardly thought of Mildred as a girl at all. Why in the world would Aunt Lois care if she ran off with me to swim?

"Want us to stay here?" Bobby asked. "Reckon we could figure out some fun to have."

About that time, Aunt Lois came storming through the screen door. "No, you ain't a-hanging 'round here, causing trouble and stirring up dirt and tracking it into my house," she said. "You two run off."

Bobby started to say something, but then Aunt Lois gave one of those looks that everybody always said would cause a bull to think twice about charging. With a hasty good-bye, we ran off to the river that ran along the east side of town, not more than a couple hundred yards from Aunt Lois's.

Playing in the creek at home was fun, but the town river ran deeper, and it had a bridge running across it. Part of the under-belly had some steel cables running from one concrete pillar to the other. Right over the middle of the river it was deep enough that we could shimmy along the wire and then drop off into the water. We could do that for hours and not get tired of it. And we did. Couple of other boys came and joined us, and we had a good time of it. Wet and happy we slodged back to Aunt Lois's. Six o'clock had come and gone, but Daddy didn't much mind.

We sat in the back of the truck going home. The wind dried us off good. Since we'd been out of most of our clothes while swimming, we were delivered home as dry as when we'd left. I walked in the front door, but even before I got to the door I could smell Granny's cooking. We were having biscuits and ham for supper, and I sat down with a good appetite, half day of work balanced off by half a day of fun. Even the prospect of tending the garden a bit after supper didn't make me feel none the worse.

Granny'd read me about Tom Sawyer when I was little. When I got old enough, I read him for myself. Looking back on days like that day, a summer day when I faced the prospect of one just like it the next day, I figured even ol' Tom himself would have been jealous of me.

V

THE FIRST FINE hot Saturday of July meant blackberry picking. We'd pick from early morning until late afternoon; then we'd all head down to the creek. Granny would put some of the berries aside to make us a week's worth of cobblers, and the rest went into making blackberry jam. We'd keep a lot of it, but some of it would head off to Smoky Hollow's General Store, where Granny's cousin Michael Mullins would set it out with a fancy label plastered across it, letting people know it was homemade. Course, lots of folks in Smoky Hollow made their own jam, too. But the General Store sat off a main road that came over Fort Mountain, and passersby, especially if they came from down Atlanta way, thought it special to buy something homemade, and so Granny's jam always sold. I wondered, if they liked homemade, why didn't they make it in their homes. Maybe they didn't like picking the berries.

Like about everything, Bobby went with me to help pick, and Aunt Lois let Mildred come out and stay the weekend with us to help Granny a bit. Granny's cough had grown worse, and she seemed a little slower than usual. So Lois sent Mildred to help with the jam fixing and anything else that needed to be done. It promised to be another gift of a summer day.

All kinds of berry thickets ran along the road by our house, and in one place around the bend and down into a little cleared-out hollow grew all kinds of blackberry vines. The three of us carried our tin pails and picked and talked and ate as we felt like it. Even being careful, sometimes you'd get a too-ripe berry that burst with plumpness as soon as you touched it. Didn't take long to get your fingers all purple. And if you weren't careful, the thorns that gave the berries a bite would prick your fingers so that purple stain would mix with a little blood, and after a few hours you'd have the dangdest stains on your fingers you'd ever seen.

We'd fill our pails then run back to the house, where Granny had a great big metal tub to pour the berries in. While we picked, with Daddy off getting his share, too, Granny had out her iron kettle over the wood stove, cooking the berries down to a jam. Granny'd say the same thing every time we brought in a load. "What takes ye so long? Eating more'n you pick? All these here jars ain't gonna fill themselves." Then she'd give herself a private little smile and say, "Better git some water 'fore ye pick anymore. Can't work mules in this heat without water, and I reckon none of you's tough as a mule. Not yet."

Instead of pumping water behind the house, we ran to the little stream that flowed through the springhouse on its way down to Smoky Hollow Creek. Course, a pipe ran from the stream to the back of the house—that's where the water came from for the pump. We'd throw our faces down into the cool stream waters— protected from the sun by shade trees for the short distance it had to run from the side of the hill from where it came to the spring-house. Because it ran from the ground like that, the water always felt nice and cool. After the water melted away the summer dust from our faces and sent downstream the heat of our faces, we picked our heads up. Water dripping from the ends of noses, we partook of that drink that tasted better than anything I've had since.

We scampered up the hill where the spring gushed forth, took to the road, and looked for the last vine we'd stripped clean. It'd been a while since the last rain, so the red dirt of the road rose up around us like fog around the hills in fall. Our clothes had already taken on the reddish hue of the clay that folks thought either the prettiest or ugliest thing they'd ever seen. Aunt Lois despised it because she couldn't keep it out of her house. Uncle Joe had been run off by it. Granny and Daddy loved it. We kids just enjoyed it. Don't know why children like dirt, but they take to it like pigs to mud, so we kicked up the dust and joyed in its existence. Long as

I wasn't on my knees with green sprouts looking me in the eye, that red dirt was fine.

Daddy headed our way. He had a lot bigger pail than we had, and he was a fast picker. By late morning he was good and wet with sweat. Water formed like great beads on his face. They'd sit there not moving. Then, like a salamander that sits still on a rock in the creek and all of a sudden takes a notion to scamper off quick as lightning, those big beady sweat drops would take a notion to make a run down Daddy's face. You'd look and they'd be there. Then, all of a sudden, off and running and they'd drop off. Summer sun agreed with Daddy, so he always looked happy when working out in it.

"Reckon we orta take a dinner break here soon," Daddy said, sitting down near where we had been picking. He looked over at our near empty pails. "Been to the house?"

"Yep," I said. "Took us a little water break. Granny said to. Then we come right back."

"How's Granny seem?"

"Hacking a bit," I said.

"Tell you what," he said, looking at Mildred. "Why don't you let these here fellers do the picking this afternoon, and you help yore Granny."

Mildred's face fell a little. Mildred liked buddying around with me and Bobby. "Sure," she said.

"Just fer part of the afternoon," Daddy said, seeing the start of a hang-dog look. "I'll come in and help 'bout midafternoon. That way you can pick a little while longer with the boys 'fore it's time to go down to the creek and wash the chiggers off." Mildred brightened up at that and said, "Okay."

We picked about half an hour longer, Daddy helping us fill our pails. Then we took up with the road toward the house. All three of us kicked up red dirt like it was our job in life to make red clouds of dust. Daddy's long strides took him ahead of us so he wouldn't have to follow in the dust. "Go below the springhouse and wash up," Daddy said.

The three of us went out to where the noonday sun shone above and stuck our feet in the water. We splashed around a bit before washing up our arms and hands. I lay back a minute, then I shouted, "God drives a Ford!"

"What are you talking 'bout?" Bobby asked.

"Looky over yonder," I pointed. "The clouds. See it?"

"Nope. Ain't no danged Ford up there," Bobby said.

"Where?" Mildred asked, lying back, shading her eyes from the sun and looking where I had pointed.

"Just up over'n the trees," I said. "See the cloud there that looks like a rabbit?"

"Hey! I see it," she said.

"Go over two clouds and back one. See it? Looks just like one of them new Fords."

"That ain't no car," Bobby said. "That's a giant's face with a big nose."

"Ain't neither," Mildred said. "I think it's a Ford, too."

"Maybe so," Bobby said, "But it don't mean God drives no danged Ford. Don't you 'member Preacher saying God knows ever'thing. If'n God's that smart, he knows better'n be driving 'round in a tin-heap of a Ford."

Course, there was no way to respond to that but to roll over real quick and jump on top of Bobby. We tussled a bit, laughing. Finally Mildred dropped a handful of spring water on our heads. "I'm hungry. Let's go eat." Bobby jumped up and started off for the house. Mildred followed. I'd noticed that lately Bobby seemed to do about whatever Mildred said, making it plain how sweet he was on her. I tore off after them, not wanting to be the rotten egg.

We all hit the back porch within a step of each other. We were about to bang into the screen door, causing a ruckus to see who was getting in first, until, of course, we remembered what would happen to us if we tore into Granny's house that way. We could be just as rambunctious as we wanted outside the house. Granny'd always tell Aunt Lois, "Let 'em run off some steam, good fer 'em," every time Aunt Lois would holler at us for playing rough outside. "One of 'em'll fall and hit their heads on the porch steps or something," she'd argue. "No matter," Granny'd say. "Childern falling ain't ever stopped the world. Let 'em play." And we would.

But inside different rules applied. And if we dreaded Aunt Lois's tirades, we hated Granny's sharp look and soft-spoken words more. Her words could be like snowballs with rocks inside—soft on the outside but with a hardness on the inside that'd crack our skulls. Bobby opened the screen and held it for Mildred. He didn't hold it for me.

The kitchen stood empty, but we saw through to the dining room where Daddy stood over Granny, her all bent over in a chair, elbows on her knees and head between them. The three of us ran over to where they were. "What's wrong?" I asked.

"Hush a minute," Daddy said, his voice tense. He reached around and half rubbed, half patted Granny's back. She looked up a little, her eyes gone all red and teary—she'd had another hacking fit. All the color had run out of her face. Her head drooped back down as she said, "I'm alright."

"No, yore not," Daddy said, a hint of what I'd call anger if he'd been talking to me. "Yore sick. Alright people don't faint away onto the floor. Alright people don't cough up 'til the lack of breath chokes 'em."

"I said I'm alright," Granny said, but weak sort of. "I just got too hot over'n the stove. Got too hot and got to coughing and my head went a little light, that's all."

"That ain't all unless Doc Miller says it's all," Daddy said. Before Granny could say anything, Daddy turned on us and started giving directions. "Mildred, take care of what's up on the stove. You know how to cook down the berries, don't you? Then pull 'em off the stove, put 'em in the jars, and let 'em cool. I'll take care of the rest when I'm back."

Looking at me, Daddy said, "You make sure ever'body has somethin' to eat. Granny had some ham frying when she fainted.

It's over on the table there. Git some of this morning's biscuits, and that can be dinner.

"Can you git up now?" Daddy asked Granny.

"Reckon so," she said.

"Let's go on out to the truck, then," he said. "And all of you. When yore done with dinner, follow the creek down to the river and git good and wet. I don't want to have to worry 'bout no chiggers after berry picking. You'll itch plumb to death."

I always thought of our swims after berry picking as a reward because it was fun for the three of us to go the quarter mile down Smoky Hollow Creek to where it ran into Mountaintown River. It ran deep enough for us to get good and wet from head to toe, deep enough to swim underwater. The creek was just good for wading and fishing some. Course, Daddy thought more practical, I guess, but his practicality ran into our fun, and I mostly remember it as fun.

I watched Daddy help Granny up and step real slow with her to the truck. She looked bad and started coughing again. Daddy looked at us and said, "Be shore to do what I've told you." I nodded my head and watched them drive off. My belly hurt as I turned toward what Daddy said to do.

Mildred already stood over the stove, tending the berries so she'd know when to pull them off. Bobby sat in a chair close by that he'd pulled in from the dining room. I started getting the fixings for dinner; then I grabbed a jug to pour some milk into, which I had to get from the springhouse. Mildred pulled the berries off and started spooning them into pint jars. I set out the plates and glasses, and about the time I finished, so did Mildred. We all sat down, kind of quiet.

Granny and Daddy always made certain we said grace before meals, and I knew I ought to do it now, though I was missing them something fierce, wishing Daddy sat there to pray for me. His prayers always sounded natural, like he and God were sitting there talking. I bowed my head, and so did Mildred and Bobby.

"Dear God," I prayed. I thought a minute, trying to recollect how Preacher would always relate to the Bible when he prayed. "Help Granny git better, just like you helped all those people in the Bible git better." There. That included everybody and was a lot shorter than when Preacher would think up every instance of somebody sick. "Amen."

I opened my eyes, and I saw Bobby was about to take a bite of biscuit. "Thanks fer the food," I said real quick, before his teeth munched down. "Amen again."

We didn't talk too much while we ate. My belly still ached a little. Granny's spell had scared me, and my belly shrank in on itself, like it was trying to hide from any hurt my heart might get. Without too much hurrah we finished up and cleared the table.

Stepping outside into the sun seemed to work a spell on us. The notion of splashing in the water for a spell set our feet going, and before any of us knew with our heads what we were fixing to do, our feet took off to the creek. Mildred ran fast, and I ran fast, but Bobby ran fastest.

Bobby hit the creek in full stride, wheeled around and scooped up the water in his hands just as Mildred and I got there in a dead heat. He sent a spray straight up into our faces and then took off down the creek, fast paced but not running. Mildred and I took off after him. Cool waters washed across my feet and legs as we chased after Bobby. Finally, we all waded together. The three of us kicked up our feet big as we walked along, sending showers out in front of us to tell of our approach.

Each of us, one after the other, lay down right where Smoky Hollow Creek emptied out into the Mountaintown River, letting the water carry us a bit downstream. We moved down to where a bridge spanned the waters and listened to the occasional car drive across.

The water at that point came up about to our chests, the deepest part, really, in this stretch of the river. We'd jump up, catch our breaths, and hit the water with our feet moving out horizontal, so we'd go under water and be carried a ways downstream. Then we'd come back to the bridge and do it all again.

We squirted water through our hands, made waves with our arms, and generally threw as much water up into each others' faces as we could. We had contests to see who could stay under water longest. We had races across the river.

Once Bobby started dunking Mildred, and when I came over, for a second, I didn't think he wanted me interfering. Their eyes played off one another's, and right before I thought it might get embarrassing, Mildred let Bobby have a good soaking, throwing water up in his eyes then giving him a shove so he fell backwards into the water. He came up all spluttering, with Mildred already moving upstream. Without a word, we all knew the time to go had come. The sun hit the top of the trees, and the shadows deepened.

We didn't say too much going back. Our arms hung heavy in that good sort of wet way, water-logged muscles that have had a pleasant day starting to ask for a bit of rest. We splashed our feet a little going back, but not like when we'd first come along. We headed back to an uncertain situation, and we all knew it. We'd had fun, and we'd splashed. But that quarter mile back was a slow go, and the water we kicked up seemed to have lost its sparkle.

When we came out of the creek onto the path up to the house, I already knew things weren't quite right. Daddy's truck rested in its usual place, but there sat Aunt Lois and Uncle Henry's car right beside it. Mildred was supposed to stay the night, so I couldn't figure anything good of that car sitting there like a bad omen. Bobby reckoned how he ought to go on home. Mildred and I walked on into the house, for all the world looking like we were walking into a funeral.

VI

DECORATION SUNDAY CAME in the middle of July every year. This made for all day church. There was lots of singing in the morning, along with prayers and a good sermon, followed by a better dinner. It was a time to catch up with folks, enjoy the best of everybody's cooking, and lay wreaths around the graves, along with doing any tending needed to spruce up the cemetery. Granny and Daddy had to take care of Granny's folks' graves, Granddaddy's, and Mamma's.

Decoration Sunday was also called Homecoming Sunday because folks who had moved off would come home to tend the graves. In honor of the folks who had come back special, the church always brought in a preacher from years past so they could have church with the preacher they remembered from their days in Smoky Hollow. Preacher Arvil Stiles spoke God's word that morning, and after a spell of eating, talking, and resting, he'd preach an early afternoon service after some more singing. Then we'd march out to the cemetery.

The morning preaching sounded a right deal softer than usual. The church packed with folks singing the rooftop off, Daddy play-ing some guitar, and Preacher Stiles's good prayer set a joyful mood. Preacher Stiles preached about where Jesus told his disciples, "I go to prepare a place for you." Preacher Stiles allowed how that place was heaven, the home of all who loved Jesus. He said just like our homecoming in church, where we got to see old friends and join in the fellowship of the table with each other, so it'd be in heaven.

A right good sermon, it was, and a right fine service. Except for Daddy telling everybody at prayer time that Doc Miller was send-ing Granny down to Marietta for some doctoring stuff, it was about as nice a church time as I can remember. Everybody else seemed to think so, too. They all told Preacher Stiles what a good job he'd done by preaching so nice a sermon. The old, silver-haired man smiled, accepting compliments and giving them back like he'd never been gone.

Bobby and I gathered up our fried chicken and biscuits and went to sit on one of the long benches underneath the tin canopy. All our outside eating was done under this contraption, posts set in the ground supporting a tin roof, ready to keep off sun and rain without cutting out the fresh air. The narrow canopy covered five long wooden tables with long wooden benches, about a foot and a half between tables to allow folks to move about without having to go all the way to one end or the other. We started a new table, waiting on the rest of the family to join us. As I bit into a chicken leg, I looked up and saw Preacher sit down on the other side. He didn't look as happy about Preacher Stiles's preaching as everybody else.

"How you boys doing?" he asked, picking up a chicken breast and biting into it.

"Good," we both said at the same time.

"Like the preaching this morning?" he asked.

I didn't ever like to lie, and so I said, "It was a right good sermon, I reckon."

"People like nice sermons," Preacher said, putting a fork into some green beans that'd been cooked for hours with bacon grease and onions. He seemed thoughtful.

"Reckon so," Bobby said as he looked around for somebody to come and sit with us. But by the immediate look of things, we had the Preacher to ourselves for a bit. We were cornered prey.

Preacher looked hard at Bobby. "Been to the altar yet to be saved?"

Preacher knew he hadn't. Bobby stumbled around the words in his mouth a bit. "Uh, no sir."

"Well, what's the use of painting purdy pictures of heaven if'n some of the people sitting there ain't ever gonna see the real thing?" Preacher asked.

Bobby fiddled with his biscuit. The tips of his ears turned red. Bobby wasn't as good as me talking with adults. So I said, "Maybe talking 'bout how nice heaven is will make people want to go."

Preacher turned on me and held me in his gaze, like a cat about to spring on a rat. "How many folks did you see at the altar today?"

"None."

"Reckon why?"

"Dunno."

"I'll tell ye why," Preacher said, putting his fork down and leaning over his plate. "Bobby, yore daddy raises bees, don't he?"

"Yes sir," Bobby said.

"And it's the job of bees to make honey, ain't it?"

"Yes sir."

"So will the bees give you their honey just fer the asking?"

"No sir," Bobby said.

"That's right," Preacher said, "they don't. They want to keep what they reckon is theirs. Just like us. 'Cepting with us, God says we got to give our lives to 'im. And let me tell you, ain't no sinner wants to give up his life to God anymore'n any bees want to give up their honey fer you to pour on yore biscuits in the morning. Ain't that right, boys? Ain't it?"

A weak "yes sir" came out of our lips. Preacher had caught us up in his logic. We were flies caught in a spider web.

"Bobby, now you tell me," Preacher said, staring hard down on poor Bobby. "How does yore daddy git that honey outa them hives?"

"Well," Bobby started, "first he gits the smoke pot ready, then . . ."

Preacher jumped on Bobby there. "The smoke pot! Yes, indeed, the smoke pot. Those honeyed insects have to be smoked from their hives. And don't you ferget," he said, fire burning in his eyes, "hellfire is God's smoke pot. There's lots of purdy things in the Bible," the Preacher continued, "but they don't mean nothing 'til God's smoked us out."

Preacher picked up his fork then and ate some beans, savoring the taste of spiritual victory sweeter than any dish on his plate. And it may not have been salvation, but it was surely a relief when Granny and Daddy, Aunt Lois and her brood, and Aunt Doris's family all headed our way. Some polite conversation followed, but Preacher never had as much to say when Granny was around, though he asked polite like after her health. Granny gave as good as she got, and I don't think Preacher was usually in the mood to take on Granny's piece of mind.

Thank the Lord that a breeze kicked up in the afternoon. After dinner, everybody filed back into the church, looks of satisfied bellies being worn on everybody's face. We had quartet music for near on an hour. Joe Harper's daddy sang tenor. He was the leader of the quartet, most of them coming from Pleasant Gap church on the other side of Gilmer County. He could sing higher than any girl in our church, and he could hold his notes so long his face turned red and puffy like a blown up red balloon. After a number, he'd take a handkerchief from his pocket, wipe his face off good, and say, "Praise the Lord, that was a good'un." Everybody else thought so, too.

Daddy sang between the quartet and the preaching, to cool

everybody off, I suppose. We'd all got worked up, clapping hands, some folks stomping feet to the rhythm of the quartet music. But with Daddy up there everybody leaned back and relaxed, using the fans with pictures of Jesus knocking at the door to cool their faces, helping the breeze do its job. Things got quiet as Daddy reminded them all why they were there. "I was standing by my window on one cold and cloudy day," he started. Folks just nodded at the chorus. "Will the circle be unbroken, by and by, Lord, by and by?" It was like Preacher Stiles said in the morning service. There'd be a homecoming in heaven to match the one in church, though the in-between time until then could be a hard wait. Thinking about my mamma, I knew it to be so.

Preacher Stiles gave another fine sermon, not the less so for being a good deal shorter than the morning sermon. So after hearing how the prodigal son finally came home to the open arms of his daddy, we went to take care of the day's real business. We all fixed the graves up real nice. We pulled weeds and trimmed the grass around the tombstones. We decorated the graves real pretty. I laid one of Granny's roses on Mamma's grave. Granny spoke a right nice prayer at her folks' graves, and Daddy talked to God about Granddaddy and Mamma. Womenfolk cried softly after all was said and done, Daddy knelt down at Mamma's grave, head bowed under silent pain, and me choking back the tears with the fierceness of a boy who didn't want any of his friends to see him cry. Going back home, everybody was real respectful and quiet.

Sitting outside on the porch—adults in rocking chairs or on

the swing and us kids scattered up and down the porch steps or dangling our legs over the end of the porch where we sat—Aunt Doris tried to get Granny to talk about what Doc Miller had told her. She tread softly, but determinedly. She had all intentions of knowing everything Daddy and Aunt Lois already knew. Her living off out of county and being the baby of the family put her at a double disadvantage.

"Don't reckon they know anything yet," Granny said, while Daddy and Aunt Lois stole looks at each other that flat contradicted Granny. "It's just a precaution, Dorrie, so don't worry none." Granny hacked a bit. "Lordy, church plumb wore me out today," she said. "Though it was awful nice to see Arvil back up in the pulpit." Course, what she didn't say that everybody knew was that it was good not to see Preacher there. "Preacher wasn't giving you boys no hard time, was he?" she asked me.

"No ma'am," I said, not wanting to get Granny all flustered. If she knew what Preacher had said, she'd be upset. I figured it wasn't a lie; Preacher thought he was helping us, not giving us a hard time. Besides, between what he said, what Preacher Stiles had said, and thinking about Mamma in heaven had put me in a mood to think more than talk.

Daddy sat in his rocking chair, looking at the Thursday's *Times-Courier*. The Ellijay paper came out once a week, but it carried news for the whole county. Aunt Lois always brought it out for Daddy to read on Sundays, though she reckoned she didn't know why. "Mostly gossip 'bout who went where," she said.

I guess she was right, in part. There on the front page was the headline "East Ellijay." East Ellijay was across the river from Ellijay, though the two of them together weren't big enough for one town, much less two. The nature of the news from East Ellijay could be gathered from the first couple of lines. "Messrs. H. E. Painter, Cecil Hipp, and Ralph Smith have gone to Akron, Ohio, with hopes of securing employment." I knew Mr. Painter's daughter the way I knew a lot of children from East Ellijay—met her at the swimming hole, part of the river that separated the two towns. The news went on from there. "Mr. and Mrs. Newman West and family spent Sunday with relatives in Calhoun. Mrs. S. I. Purdue has as her guest her granddaughter, Mrs. Lewis Loovern and children." I figured all this stuff for silliness. All the folks we knew best, we could find out at church what they'd been up to; no need to print it in the paper.

"Bought any war bonds, Henry?" my daddy asked Uncle Henry. Beside the East Ellijay column, the front page carried an advertisement for war bonds. The American Legion was selling them, and the paper had a picture of an older man with a snappy salute and well-trimmed mustache looking out at you. "Not yet, going to though," Uncle Henry said. Right below the war bonds stuff sat another headline—"Corp. Milton Pratt Killed in Solomons." Bobby's brother'd had a headline about him too when he came back shot up, but it wasn't on the front page because he hadn't been killed.

"Listen to this, Mamma," Daddy said. "Electricity's to be run up here in Smoky Hollow it says."

"What in the world do we need with 'lectricity?" Granny asked. "We got kerosene lamps to see by at night. The springhouse keeps stuff cool we need cool. 'Tain't no use fer it, far as I can see."

"I don't know," Daddy said, "I reckon it might be useful. An icebox like Lois and Henry's 'twould be nice."

"Aw, Mamma, you'd like it if'n you had it. I know we do, don't we Henry?" Lois said, waiting for Uncle Henry's response to what wasn't a question.

"Uh-huh," Uncle Henry said, words Uncle Henry used a lot when talking to Aunt Lois.

"I just love it," Aunt Doris volunteered. "Mamma, it'd save you trips outside to the springhouse. You could keep a whole lot more stuff longer."

"Ever'thing keeps fine the way it is," Granny said. "'Sides, too old now to learn things over. Reckon as long as I'm here, might as well do things the way I'm a used to doing 'em." I saw from the faces of Granny's children they all thought that might not be as long as they'd like. Or me. I missed Mamma fierce, even though I was little when she died. If something happened to Granny, I knew it'd be bad for all of us, but it'd be especially hard on Daddy and me. I heard him tell Granny once that he reckoned he'd had his fill of hurt.

Granny got up from her chair and made to go inside. "Lois. Doris. Let's git supper together." Lois and Doris followed Granny inside, and I got up, just wanting to watch them move inside. I stood with my face to the screen door, and as they moved to the kitchen, Granny stopped and ran her hand over the quilt that was partly made. "Maybe after supper you girls can help me some," she said. "I orta git going on this thing so it's finished." By the way Lois and Doris exchanged looks, and from the feeling in the pit of my stomach, I knew that it wasn't the Christmas deadline that bothered her. Uncle Joe might get there after Granny had left, but she wanted that quilt to be waiting for him.

So, after we finished supper, I sat in the corner, listening to Daddy play the guitar out on the porch, watching Granny, Aunt Lois, and Aunt Doris quilting. Granny wore a determined face as she worked, making it look like she sat in a factory like Daddy's rather than in her home. For all the world that it was a gift of love, the quilting took on the grim aspect of a job that evening, like Daddy's, where so many socks had to make it out on time or everybody was in trouble. Maybe that was it. As Granny worked, the usual peaceful air she had when quilting was gone; trouble dogged her face.

VII

A July Tuesday blazed its way through my open bedroom window. The curtains hung limp, not a bit of breeze to stir them. Already this early sunshine had heated up everything it rested on, and it would make for fierce hot work that day.

I heard stirring in the kitchen. I slipped out of bed, pulled my overalls up, and walked into a room full of activity. There Daddy stood, looking over the papers that he needed to take with Granny to Marietta. He looked real tired. He had worked an extra shift at the sock mill to make up for missing work that day. Good thing the war effort needed so many socks, or else he would have just lost the pay. Granny hovered over the table, packing up dinner pails. Aunt Lois had the dish towel to the last of the breakfast dishes.

"'Bout time," Aunt Lois pronounced, seeing me fidget my way into the kitchen. "All this gittin' ready to do and you a-sleeping yore life away." She turned to Daddy. "Don't know why you let 'im sleep in today of all days. Why, he orta already had morning chores done and be a-helping us."

I looked around, hoping to see the one possible redeeming feature of Aunt Lois's presence: Mildred. Weakly, without hope, I asked, "Is Mildred here?" I hoped maybe she was outside.

"No, Mildred ain't here," Aunt Lois declared. "Home with her sisters. No use bringing her here just so you two could worry us to death." Aunt Lois gave me the up and down. "Put the two of you together and there's more than twict the trouble either of you could git into on yore own. One and one makes three when it comes to you two messing 'round with what don't need messing with."

"Lois, leave the boy alone," Granny said, looking at me with a kindness worn wrinkly from its constant expression. "Hungry, son?"

"Let the boy git his own breakfast," Lois interjected. "We got to git on the road. Lord knows it'll take hours as it is to git down to Marietta. We're ready, so let's go."

Daddy gave a resigned sigh. "Reckon we orta git on," he said to Granny. He pushed himself up from the chair like a great weight hung on him. Daddy looked plumb beat. Placing a hand on my head, he said, "Get yoreself some breakfast, son, and be shore and do yore chores." Like an afterthought, he added, "And don't fer-get to weed the garden."

"Don't ferget, indeed," Aunt Lois added. "Place is run over with weeds, if'n you ask me. That boy ain't got the heart fer gardening, but he's got the back. I'd put 'im to it harder than you do. Keep 'im out of trouble, too." I sat at the table, trying to figure out how I had got Aunt Lois in such a bad mood by just getting out of bed.

Granny put a hand on Aunt Lois's arm. "I said leave the boy alone." Granny's voice carried a quiet authority. Lois shot a look my way, but she didn't say anything. Looking at Lois and Daddy, Granny said, "You two git on out to the truck. I'll be there d'rectly." The way Granny turned her back on them, they knew to go on.

Granny pulled down a clean plate, then opened the stove door. Heat pushed out, mixing with the hot day. The fire was out, but not so long ago that all the warmth had fallen off the metal. Several still warm biscuits, with their open-your-eyes smell, appeared before me.

"You'll need to fetch some milk from the springhouse," she said, "but we've not put up the butter or preserves yet." Both were quickly set before me from their spots on the counter. "You be a good boy today," Granny said, holding me with her eyes, eyes weak and watery looking from weeks of coughing now. "And don't you mind yore Aunt Lois. She's scairt, and so's yore daddy, though like with ever'thing else he don't shoot his feelings out his mouth like Lois."

"Ain't you scairt?" I asked Granny. We'd all been anxious since Doc Miller said she should go to Marietta. My thinking about my mamma had been all mixed in with being scared something would happen to Granny, too.

Granny heaved out air, making a puttering sound with her lips. "Ain't no use in being scairt," Granny said. "After yore granddaddy died, I coulda been scairt of living, and was fer a spell. But God wanted me alive, so I reckoned I orta do the best living I could. If'n God wants to call me home now, I reckon that's okay, too. I'm tired, son. A spell of rest, rocking by yore granddaddy, would suit me fine. So, no, I ain't scairt. Worrit 'bout all you young'uns, mostly." Granny looked me in the eye and said, "Always 'member this. In life and in death, God saves his childern. He's been taking real good care of yore granddaddy, and he's been taking real good care of yore mamma. And he'll take good care of me if'n I gits called home." After a pause, she added, "And he'll take good care of you, too." Then she turned and walked out, and I heard the screen door slam shut, and I sat at the table and cried until my biscuits turned cold.

Crying drove off my appetite, but, out of habit, I put some preserves on the biscuits (no use putting butter to them as cold as they were) and ate my breakfast like Granny and Daddy told me to. I figured I'd milk ol' Bess first, then gather in the eggs. After that, I reckoned most of the day I'd have to spend splitting wood and working in that danged garden.

The day seemed to drag on forever. I didn't mind the milking and egg gathering—didn't seem much like work. But I'd put off splitting wood, and I knew I needed to spend a goodly amount of time on that. So, all morning long, with breaks for some cool spring water and sitting under the shade, I split a ton of wood. And all we had was the stuff I hated to split—oak and pine.

Danged oak was so hard I couldn't hardly do anything with it. I'd swing my axe down, trying to make a dent that'd hold the iron wedge in place, but it always took a bunch of times. Finally, getting a groove just deep enough to hold the wedge up, I'd switch to the sledge hammer, swing it over my head and come down hard. Had to come down hard, else nothing would happen. But my skinny arms served as unsure guides, and sometimes—more often than not—the hammer wouldn't come down center solid and would just graze the wedge, knocking it out of place. Then sometimes I'd have to try to sling the ax down on that old hard wood some more, trying to cut a place deep enough to hold the wedge good. If I could get a groove deep enough, and if I hit the wedge center solid, then the wood started to split, and a few more hits and it'd all be over and done with. But that's a lot of "ifs" in the hot July sun—aggravating as could be.

Well, not as aggravating as the pine. Danged pine was so soft it was no trouble getting a groove to hold the wedge, but the wood sometimes just gave rather than splitting, and the wedge would be buried up to its head in the sappy wood without it splitting. Then I'd have to try to dig the wedge out and try another angle. I got so aggravated that I thought I'd heave off and split the wood with just the ax. I bent backwards and then swung the ax over my head as hard as I could. I hit the wood a glancing blow, and the momentum carried the ax on down so that it buried itself deep into the red dirt next to my foot.

It took a second for me to realize that I'd plumb nearly cut my foot off. I was always good to wear my work boots when splitting wood. Thing was, I saw a perfect little oval over on the right side of my right boot. Right where the foot is widest, just below where the little toe is connected, the oval outlined my red-dirt-tinged flesh. I looked around in shock for a second, thinking of going and telling somebody. But I was there by myself, so there was nobody to tell.

So I went down to the springhouse, lay on my belly, looked at my red-headed expression of disbelief, then dunked my head into the cool water, hoping to cool off, both inside and outside my head. That was best, I reckoned. I needed a cool head to split the kindling that needed splitting next. If I made a danged-fool mistake like I just did while holding the wood in one hand while slivering it, I'd lose a finger.

After my cooling-off spell, I finished up on the wood. Plenty of kindling now to start the stove, and some nice solid chunks to keep a good fire going awhile. I decided such work should get a reward. I went inside to the kitchen and grabbed a left-over fried apple pie from the night-before's supper. Granny made the fried pies. Simple enough to make. She took flour, then added some lard and sugar and a little milk to make the shell. Then she'd dip some homemade applesauce into each one. I'd helped with the applesauce back the fall before. Real easy, really. Just peeling the apples, coring them, then cooking them down, adding a little cinnamon and sugar. A little grease heated up real good browned each side to tasty perfection. A perfect treat to take down to the creek and eat on while I waded around, cooling off and fixing my mind to the gardening chores. I wanted to go ahead and weed so I'd have a goodly part of the afternoon to go see Bobby.

I sloshed upstream a bit. Trees hung over the creek, making for a cool tunnel of green. I munched on my fried pie, thinking about nothing and everything, picking up little rocks with my toes, kicking my foot out trying to see how far I could throw them. A goodly sized rock split the water just upstream, and that's where I headed. Made a nice place to sit and think on a hot day, just a little water rolling over the top, which kept you real cool as you sat.

I reckoned that, if I ever got big enough, I'd probably go off to live down around Marietta or on down in Atlanta. Shouldn't have to be gone all day just to go see the doctor. Once in a great while, every few years, we'd head down that way. Since Daddy'd been in the army he had privileges down at Fort MacPherson in Atlanta. We'd go and do some shopping at the Post Exchange. My boots with the new hole in them came from there, though I hadn't got to go that time.

Yep. Doctoring, shopping, they had it all down there. More than one movie theater. I thought that'd be a real good thing. Best of all was that there wasn't a danged garden at every house like in Smoky Hollow. I was going to grow up, move away, be rich, and go buy vegetables if I ever wanted them. That's what Uncle Joe did, I bet. Probably had somebody to go buy them for him with all his money. He jumped up off his red-dirt knees to make money so that they wouldn't ever have to have red dirt on them again. Me and Uncle Joe. We saw eye to eye on that one.

Finally, I dragged my carcass up off the rock and splashed on to the bank. Little streams of water flowed from my pants to mix with the red dirt, turning it from orangey looking to something deeper colored. I stood still for a minute, letting the water run off and pool up; then I took my big toe and started stirring, making a nice little bit of red mud. I squished it between my toes, making them feel all cool and gooey.

I then went on to the garden with an attitude that would have made Aunt Lois self-satisfied with her opinion of my worth. But, dang it all, how are you supposed to be any good at something you hate so much? But work I did. "You eat it, you help tend it," my daddy would tell me. Made me wish sometimes that I could live just on biscuits or corn bread. But somehow or another I figured even if I didn't eat it, I'd still end up tending it. So I plopped down on my knees beside a row of white half-runners, the green beans Daddy so loved to eat, and I went to weeding.

I had to laugh. I couldn't ever start weeding without thinking about that time when I was still little that Daddy sent me out to weed. Aunt Lois and Uncle Henry had come for some reason, can't rightly remember why, and she stopped off to look at my work. "Lordy have mercy," she said and stomped off to the house.

I followed her, wanting to know what was wrong this time. Even at a young age, there was always something wrong with what I was doing, to hear her tell it. She no more than hit the front porch when she started calling out, "Mamma, Robert, come out here and look what that boy is doing. Danged if'n he ain't pulling up all the tomato plants." And I had. Daddy gave me a good talking to. Granny tsk-tsked me. Lois figured I had a whipping coming because she said I had to have done it on purpose. But I didn't. They were green and they were little and they looked like weeds to me. Didn't mean anything by it. Looking back, kind of funny. Everybody should have known then that gardening didn't suit me.

I weeded a spell; then I decided it was time for a little dinner. I went to the springhouse, got the milk, and poured myself a big glass. Then I got some of the night-before's corn bread and broke it all up like Granny did. That was about all I wanted. I ran and put the milk back up, and then I rested a spell. No use weeding in the middle of a July day. A nap was just the thing.

When I woke up, I stretched my boney self out and looked out the window at the garden. I'd done a good job, and I reckoned I could finish after suppertime. So, I took myself up to the road and headed off to see if Bobby wanted to go wading or something.

I was disappointed by Bobby's mamma. She told me he had gone off to spend a few days with his aunt, uncle, and cousins up around Turniptown. Dang! I remembered that he was going sometime, but I didn't know it was supposed to be that week. Being sick to death of waiting for everybody to get back from Marietta, I took off on up the road. Reckoned I might go up to the trestle and drop rocks off. Always seemed a nice peaceful thing to do.

Railroad tracks ran along the mountain up a little ways from the road, maybe fifty feet. It ran that way from just past Bobby's house till it got to Crooked Creek. The mountainside turned one way but the train track just kept going over the creek. The trestle always made my mouth hang open. A huge timber bridge spanned the creek, great big creosoted posts anchoring the thing. Get that danged black stuff on you and there was no getting it off.

The July midday haze made for a hot climb, but it didn't seem nearly as hot as it would've been if I'd been weeding. With a fun sweat on my face, I finally reached the top. I plopped down on a railroad tie and looked around. From up there I could see Bobby's house, but not mine, though I could see the curve in the road right before my house. I liked being up where I could see everything.

After a while, I gathered myself up and walked out over the creek. The trestle probably spanned sixty yards or so, and I liked to get right in the middle—that's where the middle of the creek was, and it was deepest there. The rocks made a mighty good splash, and the "kerplunkt" sound the bigger rocks made came up sounding nice and loud.

So I laid myself out, my belly over one of the rails, my chin propped up on one fist as I looked over down at the water. Lazy sort of, I dropped one rock, then another. I liked making out the different sounds the different rocks made. The sun beat down on me as I went through my lazy motions, and I watched the water, figuring it to be about as lazy as me as it slowly moved along. Heat and laziness, and slow motion. And me all tuckered from my splitting wood, despite my little nap.

Books say you hear things before you wake up, or that your hearing wakes up first. Not so for me. Feeling came first—the vibrations. At first, a little rumbling made for a nice feeling, gently shaking me from head to toe, but jiggling my tummy especially. I know it was the shaking that first woke me; but finally the sound caused my head to snap up.

Trains make awful noise. There's all that metally sound of wheel on track. But then came the whistle, warning off danged fools like me as the trains come close to the trestles. Many a time Bobby and I heard that whistle, train barreling around the side of the mountain. We'd skip on over to the other side, take a few paces off the track, and wave at the conductor as he passed by. Seemed like they all had the same face—big, round, red faces looked out at us, cheeks fat as squirrels with nuts from all the tobacco. They'd spit out as they went by, their way I suppose of saying howdy.

Course, this time, there was no me and Bobby, and we weren't already up and ready to run and fudging a whole bunch toward the opposite side from where the train was coming. It was me still half asleep and scared and seeing the train with no fudging head start.

Running a train track is funny business. My legs weren't long enough to take the crossties two at a time, and taking them one at a time felt like taking baby steps. I knew I'd better not trip, so I had to be careful. Running baby steps is hard, though, and I had to concentrate real hard and not pay attention to the sound coming up behind, whistle blaring away.

As soon as I came within a couple of feet of solid ground, I jumped hard as I could. I hit the ground solid and rolled. With a scared face I looked up as the train went by. A big round red face spit out on my side, and the conductor laughed. So I was embarrassed as well as scared, and with a face red from being mad and embarrassed, I scooted down the hill, crossed the creek, and headed home.

The shakes had almost stopped by the time I got home. About that time, everybody drove up. I stopped and took in the scene: Aunt Lois fluttered like a danged chicken as soon as her legs swung out; Daddy got out like he'd just come off another double shift at the sock plant. They got Granny out, and they helped her walk to the house. I'd never seen them help Granny walk before. I'd never seen Granny walk the way she did—she walked, for the first time, like an old lady. I didn't need a doctor's report to see bad news written large all over her body. The shakes started up again.

VIII

"RECKON UNCLE JOE will bring us something nice?" Mildred asked.

"Don't rightly know," I said, "but if'n he has as much money as I figure, we orta git a little something, don't you reckon?"

"Mamma says he's not coming," Mildred said. "Mamma don't seem to like Uncle Joe none too much."

I knew what she meant. Every time Granny mentioned Uncle Joe's visit, or every time she worked on the Christmas quilt, Aunt Lois's face took on a few more wrinkles, her eyes got beady, and her mouth puckered up narrow. But she didn't say anything. Granny had told her not to say anything about Uncle Joe not coming. Granny had her heart set on a visit, and she said that a mother knew her son's heart, too. He was coming, and that was all there was to it. So Aunt Lois had to keep her mouth shut for once, but I swear I thought sometimes all those unsaid words might turn her head inside out.

"She's just jealous," I said. "Uncle Joe's off'n doing something big. Going off'n some big place. Probably living in a big house, driving a big car."

"Mamma says yore just like 'im," Mildred said. Course, that was something I already knew. Aunt Lois always carried on about how my mind was off wandering like Joe's. "Put the boy's feet to the fire," she told my daddy. "Better he gits burnt now than later. Mark my word, life'll burn 'im if'n you don't. You ain't doing 'im no favors indulging his ways."

I never quite knew what Aunt Lois meant by that. Daddy and Granny always pretty much let me be myself. But since being myself went against what Aunt Lois thought made for best, she wanted me remade. "It's easier to mold the clay while it's still soft," she told Daddy one time. "Wait till he's older, when his dang fool dreams makes a nobody outa 'im," she said, "and it'll be worse. He'll have to be broke and restarted. But that never really works." Granny told Aunt Lois to hush up, and she did. Thing about Aunt Lois, though, was that her eyes talked as loud as her mouth. Nope. Mildred didn't tell me anything I didn't already know.

"Welp, I'll tell you one thing," I said. "There's gonna be one way I'm gonna be just like 'im. Ain't hanging 'round here forever.

Going someplace to be somebody, I am. Can't do that here. Uncle Joe knew it, and he did something 'bout it."

We swung on the swing in silence a while. Thing I liked about Mildred was that you didn't have to say anything if you didn't want to. Quiet was always right comfortable with her. She let out a big sigh.

"What's the matter?" I asked.

"Still thinking 'bout Uncle Joe. Mamma told Daddy that'd it kill Granny if'n Uncle Joe didn't show up, and she said it'd be just like 'im, thinking of nobody but hisself."

"He'll come," I said.

"How do you know?" she asked. "Mamma says he's said he was a-coming 'fore and didn't. Mamma says that if'n Granny wasn't sick, she'd know, too. Just a bunch of wishful thinking."

The screen door swung open, and Granny shuffled out. Her steps fell slow, and she made careful not to wind herself. Mildred turned all beet red; you could always tell when Mildred felt embarrassed. She knew Granny had heard her. When we'd last checked, Granny had been napping a spell. She must have woken up hearing us talk about Joe and Aunt Lois.

"Git out into the yard you two," Granny said. She didn't sound mad or anything, but she didn't sound like she wanted to see us sitting there when next she spoke either. We went out a few steps off the porch.

"Sit down. No, lay down," she said. Mildred and me looked at each other. This seemed passing strange, but we did as we were told.

"Now, close yore eyes." I closed my eyes. The midafternoon July sun beat down on me. We might have storms a little later on, but right now the clouds hung off a ways, so the sun attacked my freckled skin like it would burn it off if it had the chance. With my red hair and fair skin I always burned easily.

"Now, you two smart'uns, tell me this—is the sun shining or is it behind a cloud?"

Seemed like a strange question. "Well, Granny," Mildred said, "we know'd the sun was shining 'fore we ever set foot off the porch."

"Alright. But maybe some clouds come up real fast. So, I put it to you agin, is the sun shining?"

"Well, shore, Granny," I said.

"How do you know? You can't see it with yore eyes closed," she said.

"Well, dang," I said, "I can feel it. Don't have to see the sun to feel it. Like when it's behind you, when yore sitting right still fishing or something. You can feel it heating up yore head even if'n 'tis behind you. You know it's there."

"That's right," Granny said. "Now you two git up and come keep me comp'ny a spell."

We clambered back up on the porch and took our places on the swing. After a minute or two, Granny told Mildred, "Honey, don't you ever talk back to yore mamma, and don't ever sass her and tell her she's wrong. That's not fer you to do." Granny paused, gathering her thoughts. Granny didn't let every thought she ever thought slip out between her teeth like Aunt Lois. "Whatever yore mamma says, Joe's a-coming. And the reason I know is that I can feel it as shore as you two could feel the sun on you." With that, Granny smiled at Mildred and said, "Go fetch me my sewing box. Gotta work on the patches fer the quilt some."

Mildred jumped up, then came back in no time. Granny pushed her chair into a slow rock. She had started doing everything slow; that's what the doctor had said to do. Granny's heart was give out; that's what the doctor in Marietta had said, and I figure that's what Doc Miller had said, too. Just that Daddy wanted to make sure. Losing Mamma made him worry a mite more about doctoring stuff than most people seemed to, and he wanted to make sure Doc Miller diagnosed right. Dropsy's what most people called what was wrong with Granny, though Daddy said the doctor in Marietta called it congestive heart failure. Not much anybody could do about it.

Daddy didn't say too much, but it sounded like Granny'd be okay probably for a while, but as her heart got weaker and weaker she'd have more and more problems. Lots of rest was about the only thing the doctor said she could do right then. If she got short of breath, she should sit up; maybe try sleeping sitting up as much as she could, too. Also told her to keep her legs up. Drinking tea did her good, too. Only learned second hand from Mildred why: tea made you pee, and Granny needed to pee a lot. Something to do with getting rid of water in your body because the heart couldn't beat hard enough to keep water out of the lungs. Least ways, that's as best as I understood it then. I later learned a whole lot more.

Daddy and Aunt Lois didn't want Granny by herself, so I was to watch her. Cut into a lot of my summer playtime—had to wait to fish, play in the creek, climb trees, run in the woods, and all the things that make summer fun. But it also cut into my daytime garden chores, and that was okay with me. The garden stood off a bit from the house, so I had to wait until Daddy got home. Cooler then. Aunt Lois would come and check on Granny sometimes, too. She also figured Mildred ought to be worth something helping out around the house. So I started seeing more of Mildred than usual.

"Sing me a song," Granny said to the two of us. I had a good voice, though it hadn't decided yet exactly what pitch it was going to settle on. But Mildred had a right pretty voice, one that sounded older than she was. Folks at church always beamed at her when she sang, giving their approval with a right many amens when she finished up. Sometimes Aunt Lois would play the piano for her; sometimes Daddy would play his guitar.

"What you want to hear?" Mildred asked, always glad to be invited to sing.

"I dunno, something nice, something 'bout Jesus."

Mildred and me thought a moment, then started singing a good ol' Wesley hymn.

Jesus, lover of my soul, let me to thy bosom fly!
  While the nearer waters flow, while the tempest
    still is high.
Hide me, O my Savior, hide, till the storm of life is past.

And so we sang until the hymn was done.

"That feller knew a right smart 'bout Jesus," Granny said. "Now, sing my favorite." We knew Granny's favorite. And as Granny rocked slowly back and forth, she put her scissors down and closed her eyes. Mildred and I swung gently, singing in our churchiest voices,

In heavenly love abiding,
  No change my heart shall fear.
And safe is such confiding,
  That nothing changes here.
The storm may roar about me,
  My heart may low be laid.
But God is 'round about me,
  And can I be dismayed?

After a spell of silence, Granny said, "You two 'member that. Things change. Hold on to that which don't. Love don't change. God is love. Says so in the Bible. When you two grow up, wake up ever' day reckoning to yoreself, 'God don't change. Love don't change. Nothing else much matters.'"

Mildred and I just swung for a spell. I closed my eyes, and next
thing I knew felt like a danged spider had fallen on my head. My
eyes popped open, and I swatted at my head. I saw Mildred
pulling her hand back to herself, and she started giggling. I gave
her a friendly punch on the arm, her knowing how I hated spiders
and all. Everybody's afraid of something. Don't rightly know why,
but spiders scared me plumb to death. I hated spiders.

"Know who you two young'uns remind me of?" Granny asked,
her voice in that remembering place in your mind that makes you
sound far away because you talk soft like.

"Who?" Mildred asked.

Granny looked us over real good. With the saddest smile I'd
ever seen, where the lips are turned up but the eyes are cast down,
she said, "You two are just like Lois and Joey used to be." Mildred
and I sat right still, both knowing we'd hear something we hadn't
heard before if our tongues didn't get in the way of Granny's
thoughts. The bridge in her head connecting her words to her
memories was fragile; we knew our voices would make the bridge
collapse.

"Yep, just like Lois and Joey growing up. Those two were thick-
er'n thieves. Always played good together. When they got a
might older, looked out fer one 'nother. Joey loved Lois, and Lois
adored Joey. He'd sit and dream dreams out loud, a-talking big,
and she'd sit acrost from 'im, bigger eyes, taking it all in, thinking
'im the smartest thing ever was just to be able to talk 'bout things
the way he did."

Granny closed her eyes again. She stopped rocking, and her head hung back a bit. She took in a big breath and blew it out slow. I wanted to say, "What else?" but I knew not to. She looked almost like she had fallen asleep, but she hadn't. She was sitting and remembering, remembering and reliving, reliving and enjoying. After what seemed like forever, she opened her eyes and gave us that sad smile again.

"Things change. 'Cause God don't change, love don't change. I feel so sorry fer Lois sometimes," Granny said. Her head wagged back and forth a bit. "She never dreamt he'd actually take off and follow after where he thought those big ideas was a-taking 'im. Broke her heart. Not like he was a courtin' feller taking off on you; 'tware deeper'n that. Like a part of her walked off, the part she thought the best. She ain't never forgiven 'im fer that. He tried writing her at first, but it just made her madder'n ol' wet hen. After 'bout a year, Joe tells me that she wrote a letter, her first and only one, that told 'im that he should come back or quit writing. She shoulda known he wasn't a-coming back. So he quit writing her. I think that way 'tware easier fer her to figure he didn't care 'bout her."

"Things changed fer Lois," Granny said. "Don't mean love changed. She's never been able to rightly grasp that. Just hope that when Joey gits here she'll finally 'member that."

After we sat a while, Granny slipped out of her chair and shuffled inside, leaving the two of us to chew over what she had said. Mildred spoke up first, and she surprised me.

"Do you really hate it here so much?" she asked. "I mean, you ain't ever been no place else, and all you know 'bout other places comes from what you see in books."

"Well, heck no, I don't plumb hate it," I said. "But it ain't enough. I want to see more. I want to do more. I got all these places in my head I've read 'bout, and I want to see 'em."

"What 'bout yore family?" Mildred asked. She might as well have asked, "What 'bout me?"

"Oh, I reckon I'd visit more'n Uncle Joe does," I said, though I always wondered why he didn't ever visit. Never been back once since he left. Granny said he worked all the time and couldn't get away. I'd heard Daddy say once that when Uncle Joe went away, he went away for good. Might not seem right—and by the sound of Daddy's voice that's what he thought—but that's the way it was. Now that Granny said what she did, it hit me for the first time how as everybody missed Uncle Joe. Made you wonder, since he never came back, if he missed any of us.

I looked over at Mildred, and I reckon I thought she sat thinking the same thing, and I reckon she wondered, if I left, would I miss her or anybody else left behind? "I may be like Uncle Joe, but I ain't Uncle Joe," I told her. "'Sides," I said, "If'n I don't go off, what reason will I have to bring you back something nice?" She laughed at that, and we started back talking about if Uncle Joe might bring us all something from the city, and what in tarnation that might be.

IX

REVIVAL MEETING CAME the first week of every August as if the Lord God Almighty himself had written it on a stone tablet. I couldn't ever figure it: August was the worst month of the year in Smoky Hollow. The heat burned fierce, and the humidity made it worse. Sweating itself became a chore, and it plumb wore you out. Yet there we all were, bunched up in church every night for a week, everybody sweating, everybody flapping the church fans in their faces to make pretend that that made it a little cooler. And if we all sweated just because of sitting, Preacher looked like a danged fountain, drenched from head to toe. Despite the open windows, more likely as not no wind blew through. Once I said what foolishness I thought it to be to hold meeting in August—

why not fall or spring? Nice weather, everybody would enjoy it
better. You'd have thought I was talking about breaking all ten
commandments. It'd always been in August, and it'd always be in
August, I was told. So it was.

We'd go from Sunday to Sunday. Preacher'd get us ready
Sunday morning, talking up the revival, talking up the Lord's
doing great things and bringing sinners to the altar. Then revival
proper would start Sunday night and go every night through
Saturday night. We always brought in a guest preacher, somebody
from one of the other churches not too far away, and that
preacher would bring singing with him. Same as when our
preacher went off to do meeting; he'd have Daddy come and play
his guitar and sing all week long. Just the year before, Preacher
had asked Mildred to sing, too.

Sunday morning, after a week of preaching every night, marked
the most important day of revival meeting. That's when everybody who got saved was baptized. That day always stood out as
my favorite church day of all. Right special, it was. The guest
preacher and singers were gone. Our preacher would do the baptizing. We'd all meet at the church at the regular hour; then we'd
march, singing hymns, down to the Mountaintown River, right
about at the place where Smoky Hollow Creek ran into it. When
we were all there, we'd gather on the bank where it was washed
down smooth, gravelly river rocks making a scrunchy floor, cool
to the bare feet when bare feet were allowed—not during baptism, but later on. Then, we'd all start singing, "Shall We Gather

at the River," and then Preacher'd talk about Jesus being baptized in the Jordan River, and how lucky we were to have such a nice river and such a nice spot by the river to do our baptizing. Talked like Jesus himself picked out where our church would be just so we'd have a right proper baptizing place. And it was.

Then all the saved folks went out to meet Preacher, one at a time. Preacher'd hold his right hand high, and he'd say in a real loud voice, "I baptize thee in the name of the Father, and of the Son, and of the Holy Ghost." Then he'd place his left hand behind the person's back, and his right hand always went over the face, and his thumb and index finger'd meet at the person's nose, closing it off so there'd be no water getting up the nose. Saw a baptism once over at another church; went because a grandchild of one of Granny's friends was getting baptized. That preacher must not have done it right, because the boy came up all spluttering like he danged near drowned. Children started giggling, parents started hushing, and a right solemn moment seemed a mite funnier than church usually is.

After the baptizing, we all went back to church; those who'd gotten baptized changed into dry clothes, and we had preaching. After that came dinner on the lawn, and that was something— baptizing Sunday was almost as good as Decoration Sunday food-wise. We'd eat until popping, and while the grownups rested and talked, us children got to go back to the river and swim. What was right quiet and reverent in the morning became a ruckus in the afternoon. Always made for a good Sunday—

Preacher was happy, the saved ones were happy, the adults were happy, and us children got to be children for part of the time, so we were happy.

Ol' Preacher Jenkins from the Nine Mile Church, not too far away, came to do the preaching this meeting time. By trade a carpenter, he'd been all browned by the summer sun. He was a wiry man with big hands and big forearms that looked like they belonged to a different sort of feller. He had little eyes behind thick glasses that sat on top of a nose that was straight but ample in its width, kind of like his arms—didn't really fit the wiriness of the rest of him. He had a right deep voice, the kind a young'un always figured God probably had when he went to talking to Moses.

The amazing thing about Preacher Jenkins was the way he could hold an open Bible. He called the Bible God's word, said it was the only thing worth paying attention to, and said any preacher that didn't preach from the Bible was no preacher at all. And to prove his point that he relied on that Bible, it stayed in his hand, open, the whole time he preached, which could be a considerably long time. Sometimes he'd bang his fist on the pulpit; sometimes he'd raise his hand up to heaven; sometimes he'd swing down, jumping over the altar steps to pace the aisle, slapping people on the back as he went by them. And the whole time, that open Bible lay perched in his hand, like it had been glued there or something. Thing was, Preacher Jenkins never looked anything up in his open Bible—it just lay there for everybody to see.

He quoted chapter and verse for about everything he said, but he did it all from memory. Found out later that Preacher Jenkins couldn't read; he'd memorized verses he'd heard growing up. But reading or no, he was always a right fine speaker with that deep voice of his and his moving around like he was in the great drama he kept talking about. I reckon he was, really.

He was, I think, a kind man, and one who had some hidden sorrow. I once heard him talking to another adult, talking about children, and how his were all grown up. He paused a minute and said, "Yep. When they're young they step on yore toes; when they grow up, they step on yore heart." That was one of the first times I ever remember hearing bone-deep sadness.

Preacher Jenkins brought two groups of singers with him for this meeting. One was a quartet of men who called themselves the Gospelteers. They sang good, especially the good ol' foot stomping favorites. Then there was the Garrett sisters. There were three of them, and one, Joyce, was just a year older than me, though we were in the same grade at school. That Sunday night in August, they started off meeting with a three-part, high-spirited version of "Higher Ground." And as the words, "Lord, take me up to higher ground," came out of Joyce's mouth, I swear I thought she appeared the prettiest girl I'd ever seen, all sweet and nice looking, a big smile on her face. I thought it'd be nice to hold her hand maybe, or sit next to her.

All during that first night of meeting, I couldn't get Joyce out of my head. The sisters sang again, right before the sermon, and the sweat running off the side of her face looked like a glistening crystal to me. I wondered if I put my hand up to wipe it off for her if she'd care. Maybe she'd like for me to; maybe she'd like me. Then my thoughts got all jumbled, and I started thinking things you ought not think in church.

I tried paying attention to Preacher Jenkins. He told me about God's love, but he also had a thing or two to say about people who didn't love God. But somehow or another God's love and people's love and me and Joyce all got mixed up in my head, and I kept looking at the back of her head, her sitting up in the front pew, wondering if she had noticed me while she sang. She always treated me nice at school, and the last few months I had started thinking more and more about girls. My head was turned toward Preacher, but my eyes strained off to the right-hand side of the front of the church, thinking, thinking about Joyce.

Finally, Preacher Jenkins wound down. The altar call came, Preacher asked those that would like to be saved to come up, to cheat the devil, and make God and all God-fearing men and the angels themselves happy. Everybody stood up to sing that final song; all that felt called to walk forward would step up to the front, talk with Preacher, and then kneel down at the altar, Preacher praying a prayer with them, then leaving them to their own praying when another stepped forward.

Problem was, my mind was set on Joyce. My boy's body was slowly growing into a man's, and sometimes that meant embarrassing situations when I thought too much about girls the way I thought about Joyce. Daddy looked down at me, and his eyes said to get up, so I knew I had to. I hesitated for a minute though, fixing my thoughts on the singing that had started. Tradition dictated that we start the first night's altar call with the same song every year, so we did this year.

We'd already gone past the first couple of lines. I joined in on "I once was lost, but now am found, was blind, but now I see." Then I started paying good attention to the words, trying to drive Joyce from my mind with the words of the song. It worked like a charm. I sang the last verse real loud.

> When we've been there ten thousand years,
>   Bright shining as the sun,
> We've no less days to sing God's praise,
>   Than when we first begun.

By then my body had calmed down, and I could move about without shame. Daddy even looked down at me and said, "Right good singing, son, right good singing."

After meeting, I went up to Joyce and told her how good she'd done. She smiled and said thanks. After looking at our feet and figuring they weren't coming off, we both shuffled off in different directions. She had a pretty smile.

We got home and Granny seemed tuckered out. Daddy told her she ought to go on to bed, but she said she wanted to sit a spell on the porch. Daddy went and got a couple of apple crates and set them up so Granny could sit out with her feet up. She was wheezing a little, but she told Daddy she was fine, just needed a little cold water. I jumped up to run get her some, but she told me to sit, motioning Daddy to go get it. "Want to talk to the boy," she said. That was her way of telling Daddy to take his time getting a glass and going out to the water pump.

"Good preaching tonight, that," Granny said. I reckoned how it was. "Purdy singing, too, 'specially those Garrett sisters. Right purdy voices." I reckoned how that was true, too.

"Ever thought 'bout answering the altar call?" Granny asked. The question surprised me. We'd always gone to church, and Granny and Daddy loved it, and they said Mamma and Granddaddy liked it, too. And heck, I liked going. But I hadn't ever thought about going up to the altar.

"Ain't ever felt rightly called," I said.

"Strong preaching tonight," Granny said. "Figured just 'bout anybody'd hear God's call tonight that'd been a-listening."

But I hadn't been listening much. I'd been thinking about Joyce. I had only the vaguest notion of what Preacher Jenkins had said. The words had hit my ears, but my thoughts about Joyce mostly drowned them out.

Granny looked me up and down, a kind but concerned look on her face. "I've watched my young'uns go up and answer that call, and I seen 'em baptized afterwards. Yore my young'un, too. It'd do me a right world of good if'n you'd answer God, too. Yore gonna be thirteen soon, and so you're gittin' to be at the age of account-

ability 'fore the Lord. I ain't telling you what to do, son, 'cepting
that you orta listen. See if'n you don't hear God's call in Preacher
Jenkins's voice. And if'n you hear it, don't be afraid to walk up
there. Listen, son, listen. There's more of God in Preacher
Jenkins's words of love than yore likely to hear in our preacher's
words of fire. It's there in both, I reckon, but I think you'll hear it
louder and better in meeting this week than you usually hear it on
Sundays. That's all I'll say 'bout it. Listen."

Daddy came back with the water, and I chewed over what Granny
had said. "Go git yore guitar and sing me a spell," she told him. In
the house then back out, Daddy sat down and strummed a bit. He
looked over at Granny and asked, "What you wanna hear, Mamma?"

"How's about that nice song you made up special for Easter.
That's right purdy," Granny said.

Daddy had made up a fine song back in the spring. Told all about
Mary being sad that Jesus was dead and about her going to his tomb
and finding him missing. Then it spoke of the joy she felt when the
person she'd mistaken for the gardener turned out to be Jesus. Lots
of folks told Daddy they thought it a right proper song and all, and
I reckon it was. He started off in his sweet tenor voice:

With head bowed down low, and a step mighty slow,
    She walked through a garden to be with her Lord.
He was buried and dead, cold cave for a bed,
    Still she had to be close to the one who had called
    her friend.

Then he sang through the sad parts until he got to the happy ending, when Mary recognized Jesus:

> And with a heart that rejoiced, and a voice that was moist,
>   With the tears that spoke gladness and shouted with
>   love,
> She drew near.

The song was about being with the people you love, and how that love overcomes everything. When she first heard it, Granny told Daddy that she reckoned he'd hit the gospel square on.

After smiling a bit, Granny announced she was headed for bed. Daddy told me to get on, too, because I had a bucketful of work to do the next day. August was time for gathering and canning and putting away, and it made for long, hot work. So I went off to bed, wishing for the world that tomorrow'd wait.

I tossed and turned a bunch. I think Granny wanted to see me baptized because she thought she'd miss it if I waited much longer. She didn't have to say that, but I reckoned that's why she brought it up. So I lay there and thought about Granny, and her telling me to listen for God. Then I heard Daddy's voice again in my head, singing his song. Words and phrases from Preacher Jenkins came to me, but they seemed to issue from Joyce's smiling lips. I tossed and turned and struggled with my waking man's body, my Granny's God, Preacher's admonitions, and Daddy's singing. Everything got all mixed up in me, and things that felt good to the touch felt bad to my soul, and I couldn't sort out sin and God and Joyce and Preacher and baptism. Most of all, I didn't want to disappoint Granny, and I knew that if she knew what'd I'd been thinking while I should've been listening for God's voice in Preacher Jenkins's words, she'd be real disappointed in me. So I went to sleep trying to think of higher things, singing myself the words to "Amazing Grace" so that things that were lower would quit stirring and let me be.

X

SOME FOLKS GO to sleep peaceful, then have a nightmare. The rooster crowed and I woke up to one. Aunt Lois stood over my bed, and as I sat up she hollered out, "Mamma, this boy's gonna sleep his life away." She looked at me and said, "Git on up now. Yore daddy's gone off to work early, and I'm here to see to it that you git a good start on that garden. Time to start bringing stuff in, and me having to do all the canning 'cause yore Granny ain't up to it. So git on up, and let's git a-going."

Waking up to Aunt Lois put me in a bad mood. "I can't git up with you standing right over me."

"Why not?" she asked.

"I ain't got no clothes on," I said, stating what should've been obvious. I never slept with anything on in the summer. Too dan-ged hot.

"You ain't got nothing I ain't never seen 'fore," she said. But then she turned on around and headed out. "Just make shore to git on up. If'n I'm a-gonna work all day, you are, too." She sounded flustered. Heading out of the room, she said, "Mildred's here to help, if'n you two will work instead of play."

With her gone, I got up and stretched a bit. I reached over to grab a pair of overalls and had just got 'em up when I heard a knock at the door. Mildred whispered in, "You dressed yet?"

"Yep, as dressed as I'm a-gonna git," I said, which wasn't exactly true. I'd have to put on some work boots before going out. I didn't figure it to be a down-on-your-knees weeding day. I reckoned I'd be hoeing potatoes at least part of the day, and I didn't want to take any toes off. But I was ready to come out for breakfast.

Mildred slipped in and closed the door behind her. She closed her eyes and let out a big breath, like she was trying to blow out the bad. "Mamma's in a terrible fierce mood today," she said. I didn't need to be told that. "All she talked 'bout on the way out here was how Uncle Joe was letting ever'body down, being gone and all. She said somebody needed to write Uncle Joe and tell 'im to git down here and help, or at least send some money if'n he was all that rich. She said she was a-gonna write and tell 'im Granny lay a-dying fer all he cared. Didn't care fer her whilst living, why care if'n she died? That's what she said she was a-gonna do. She's awful sore."

"You young'uns come eat or see if'n I don't send you out with no breakfast," Aunt Lois hollered. That got me moving toward the door. Without Daddy there and with Granny not being her usual self, I figured it'd be me and Aunt Lois, nobody to stand in her way. Mildred tried in her way to let me know as much. She figured if her mamma was so mad at Uncle Joe, after what Granny'd said, she might have a mind to take it out on my hide. So we took ourselves on into the kitchen.

Daddy would sometimes talk about this drill sergeant he had in the army. Said he barked orders out in such a way as he seemed like he was nothing more than a mean ol' ornery dog baring its teeth at you, barking to warn you that it meant to tear into your flesh. Practically didn't hear the words after a while, Daddy said. Just the barking and baring. Didn't want to get bit, no sir, said Daddy. Weren't no lady soldiers, didn't reckon, but if there were, I figured Aunt Lois would be the top drill sergeant. That's what I figured when I sat down at the table and she started in barking at me. Told me after I did the milking and bringing in the eggs I could start in the garden, as if I didn't know my own danged chores.

First thing she said to do in the garden was to cut okra. Nasty stuff. It tasted good fried up, coated in cornmeal, but the danged stuff canned tasted awful. If it got hidden in soup, that was okay, but Granny would make this tomato and okra dish that I plumb hated. The okra would be all slimy. I don't even know why we planted the stuff, not for canning, anyway. I had to wear gloves to cut it, else the danged prickly hairs seemed to get in under your skin. I reckoned Aunt Lois wanted me to do the job I hated the worst first, just to show she'd make me do it. But I didn't give lip. I downed my biscuit and blackberry preserves and off I went. That's the dangdest thing, I thought to myself. She'd worked herself up into such a state that I'd rather be out working the garden than be around Aunt Lois.

The sun had barely broken good over the hills, yet the heat already beat miserably. I took my knife and my basket, I slipped on some old work gloves, and I went to work on that garden. I'd show them, I thought. I'd do a good job. That's what they didn't get. Even when I tried hard, seems I didn't do a good enough job. But I planned on showing them. Even if my heart wasn't in it, I'd make myself work like Daddy himself. Those danged okra plants would be stripped bare in no time.

Mildred came out a bit after me, wondering, I reckon, why I hadn't waited for her. But I couldn't bear to be in that house with Aunt Lois. She hovered like a black cloud over my day, and there wasn't anything a boy my age hated worst than a black cloud on what should've been a fine summer day for swimming or some other such good thing. Mildred took her basket and went over to the tomato vines. We'd been eating good on them all summer, but now the time had come to bring in a bunch for canning. Mildred started singing to herself.

You could've knocked me over with a feather. There she stood, singing "Higher Ground"; must've been on her mind because of the service. But just hearing it made me go fetched in the head, it seemed. All of a sudden, Joyce came to my mind, and church, and Granny's talk, and my using "Amazing Grace" to settle my body. Revival and saving came at me, as well as living and dying. Those things got mixed in with my resentment about how Aunt Lois treated me, and how in the world could Mildred come out with her mamma, listen to her goings on about Uncle Joe, warn me off her bad mood, and come out singing? Singing? Sure, Daddy'd sing in the garden, and Granny, too, but they liked that danged plot of turned-up red clay. I didn't. I hated it. I wanted to be away, far away, away with Joyce, living somewhere else, didn't care where, just so it didn't have a two-word name like Smoky Hollow. Uncle Joe had been right; everybody else was wrong. Get out while the getting's good. Even with Granny dying, I thought. And me not saved yet.

"Quit that singing, dang it!" I shouted at Mildred. She looked over at me with a hurt and confused look. We practically never yelled at each other, and we didn't really much fight. "What's the matter?" she asked. "It's just singing. Makes the time go faster."

"Nothing'll ever make this time go faster," I spit out. "Smoky Hollow time. Garden time. Like Joshua telling the danged sun to stand still." I could tell this really shocked Mildred. Saying danged while talking about somebody from the Bible didn't usually sound right. "I hate this," I said, "so don't try making it seem better by singing and all. It don't work. It just don't work."

I turned my back and started in again on that okra. I sliced through the stems like I was slicing off my life, trying to cut it off from Aunt Lois and red clay and danged vegetables I didn't even like but had to bring in. Then I felt bad and turned my head over my shoulder and said at Mildred, "Go ahead and sing." At the time, I was slicing particularly hard on that okra, just to make it feel like that okra didn't stand a chance over against the likes of me, me all mad feeling and bad feeling and going to show them feeling. Thing is, pull that blade back hard enough and it'll go through a glove same as it'll go through an okra stem. It took a second for me to realize I'd cut through my glove into my thumb.

"Now look at what you made me do!" I yelled at Mildred.

"I didn't make you do nothing!" she snapped back. Then she saw that something was wrong and came over. It didn't take long for her to tell what had happened.

"Go wash off in the creek, yore hands all dirty from gardening and the inside of those gloves and all," she said. "I'll go git Mamma."

"No," I said, panic sweeping over me. Not the drill sergeant. She'd think I was like those people I heard Daddy talking about, people who, to get out of combat would go and shoot their danged legs, hoping to be sent back to the hospital and then on home. He thought it a crying shame that some folks got out on account of that while poor ol' Bobby's brother lay in the shape he was in, doing real fighting for the country and all. Sergeant Lois would figure I just went and cut myself to get out of the gardening. Right then and there I reckoned I'd cut my whole hand off rather than listen to her get on me. No. I had to think.

"Mildred, listen," I said. "I'll go wash off a bit. You go see if'n you can git in and outa the house without nobody noticing." I looked at her basket—lots of pretty tomatoes in there. "Go take yore basket in. Then git me something to wrap this up in. If'n you can git to the kitchen, there's some iodine in there in one of the cabinets. Bring it, too. Go on now and don't let on that nothin's wrong."

Mildred wore a worried look. "Please," I said. She knew as well as me what Aunt Lois would end up saying, so she said she would. She picked up her basket and took on off toward the house, and I set my feet toward the creek.

I kicked my boots off and waded in a bit. I squatted down on my haunches and pulled off my gloves. My thumb seemed a bloody mess, and a dark blood stain covered the glove's thumb.

I stuck my hand down into the water, cool even on this August day. Water swirled around my hand, and blood ran off downstream with the water. I thought sometimes that that creek water ran in my blood, so I reckoned it proper that my blood ran in the creek water now. The water calmed me, and I peered through it at my thumb and I figured for all the bleeding it wasn't cut too badly. The creek had done its job, had swept the blood away, water diluting it along its course so that just a little way down stream the blood disappeared, like it'd never been in there to sully it. The water being kind of cool also slowed the bleeding some.

Mildred rushed up behind me. "Couldn't find nothin' much,"

she said. "And I couldn't git to the iodine. Granny and Mamma's already in there a-working." She handed me a scrap of fabric, and I knew it'd come out of Granny's quilting basket.

I started to wrap my thumb in the material, but then I thought Mildred might do a better job, able to use two hands and all. So I asked her to wrap it up, not too tight but tight enough to keep it from bleeding. She did a right fine job, but with the passing of time and the pressure my thumb started throbbing.

After putting on my boots and fetching my gloves, Mildred and I walked back to the garden. "Thanks," I said. "Sorry I hollered at you like that."

"It's alright," she said. "I know how sore you git gardening and all." Then she gave me a big smile. "Just think. When yore grown you'll be rich like Uncle Joe and never have to do any gardening again. Ain't that right?" she asked.

"That's right," I said. I knew she was trying to make me feel better, to make me think about how being grown up meant no more doing what I didn't like to do, being my own man, not having to answer to the likes of Aunt Lois. And so I went on and cut okra best I could, being a lot more careful, but also being slowed up a bit because of my thumb. But I worked at it, hard and steady, and daydreamed the dreams of a country boy made big.

Dinnertime came and we heard Aunt Lois calling us in. I made a stop by the shed to get another pair of gloves so nobody would see the blood on them. My bandage shone red with blood, but not so much that the thing was sopping. I pulled a glove over my right hand and stuck it in my pocket. I stuffed the other glove in my left pocket and went in.

I tried sauntering up to the table like I had nary a care in the world. Course, about that time Aunt Lois turned around. "Get those hands outa yore pockets," she said, "or I'll fill 'em with sand." I pulled my left hand out, but I was real slow pulling out the right hand, and I didn't get it all the way out until I had sat down, where I could hide my hand under the table. I'd have to figure out how to eat with just my left hand.

Aunt Lois served up leftovers from supper—fried chicken and corn bread mostly. If Lois had ever paid any attention to me really she'd have known that something was up. Usually I'd take a leg in my right hand and a piece of corn bread in my left, and I'd take turns taking bites out of each. But on that day I mostly ate all my chicken at once, then I ate my corn bread. After downing a good-sized glass of milk, I let out a contented sigh.

"Don't be gittin' none too comfortable," Aunt Lois said. "I want corn got in this afternoon; then after supper you can work on those 'taters 'fore we go to meeting. I want a big mess of corn so Doris can start helping git that ready when she gits here."

"Oh, Lois, let the boy rest a minute," Granny said. She'd been sitting at the table all quiet while Aunt Lois did all the work. I don't think she liked Lois taking over the way she did, directing Granny's kitchen and all, but that was the way of it mostly with Granny sick. "Keep on and you'll worry the freckles off'n his face." She said that with a smile.

Mildred giggled at that. I don't know why, but she found my freckles to be funny. Mildred's skin ran clear, not like mine. During the summertime, after I'd been out in the sun some, I was one big freckle, all my little ones getting bigger and running together and all.

"Well, reckon it won't hurt none to rest a spell, let the sun git outa the middle of the sky. But don't stay in here 'cause I've got to git back to work. Why don't you two young'uns go with Granny out to the porch. Be a mite cooler I bet." Aunt Lois herself looked like she could use some cooling off. Her face beamed redder than some of the tomatoes Mildred had brought in.

"Let's go, childern," Granny said. "Lois is a-running us off."

"Mildred," Aunt Lois said, "clear off this table first, 'fore you go out."

So Granny and I made our way to the porch. She plopped down in her favorite rocker. "Son, why don't you fetch something fer me to set my feet up," she said. I brought her a basket, and we sat in the shade of the porch, hoping a breeze would kick in. Mildred came out, and we got on the swing and swung slow, making our own little breeze. Eyes half shut, Granny said, "What's wrong with yore hand, son?"

I stammered. "Ain't nothing wrong, Granny. It's alright."

"That so?" she said. "How come when you set this here basket down you had a glove on yore hand. Same hand I reckon you kept under the table whilst you ate." I guess Granny had noticed, so there wasn't any use trying to fool her.

"It's alright," I said again. "Just a little cut. Wasn't paying no 'tention whilst cuttin' that okra, and I sliced myself a little."

"Let me see," she said.

I hopped off the swing and walked on over to Granny. Took my glove off, and she saw where Mildred had wrapped the thumb up. She undid the fabric and peered at the cut.

"You put any iodine on that?" she asked, knowing I hadn't because there wasn't the stain that iodine would have left.

"No," I said. "Just washed it off and bandaged it up. You and Aunt Lois was working in the kitchen, and I told Mildred not to bother you none, barging into the kitchen and all, looking fer iodine."

"'Twouldn't be no bother to me, though I reckon I can hear Lois gittin' all bothered," she said. "Mildred. Go in the kitchen and git the iodine. If'n yore mamma asks what it's fer, just tell her I'm a-wanting it."

Mildred took off and came back in a snap. Granny put some iodine on the cut. "Don't look too awful bad, but let's keep an eye on it," Granny said. "Mildred, run fetch 'nother piece of material outa my quilting basket. Little bigger piece this time."

So, by the time Aunt Lois came out to run us off to the corn, Granny had patched things up, making a fuss but not too big of one. I put my gloves back on. In a strange sort of way, that made Aunt Lois take notice. "That's right," she said, a hint of approval in her voice. "Reckon yore right ready to go. Mildred, fetch yoreself some gloves, too. I want you two to bring in plenty of corn fer Doris to shuck."

And by the time Daddy came home and they called us in for supper, Mildred and I had done a right smart work. My thumb ached, but it was worth it. Lois didn't say anything about me being a lazybones to Daddy, least not that I could hear. And I reckon we'd keep Aunt Doris busy a spell with what we'd done. Even Aunt Lois said so, and she smiled, sort of. Maybe it hadn't been such a danged bad nightmare day after all.

XI

Aunt Doris spent the night with us after she got in. Said she'd work hard a couple of days, and then she had to get back to her young'uns and husband. Aunt Lois and Mildred went home, Lois saying they needed to do some of their own work. So, I didn't see much of Mildred or Aunt Lois for the few days Aunt Doris stayed.

Bobby's mamma came down to help out some for a day. She took over Granny's kitchen, doing the really hot work of canning. Granny sat out on the porch mostly with Aunt Doris, who shucked the corn best she could, though you could tell she couldn't do it as good as Aunt Lois. Aunt Doris seemed fragile compared to Aunt Lois, personality-wise as well as body-wise. Don't know why, but I stayed a bit quieter around Aunt Doris, afraid a real loud noise might cause her to break or something. I think Granny enjoyed the peace with Aunt Doris after having had Aunt Lois whirlwinding through the house.

Granny worked on quilt patches, making big patches out of a bunch of little ones. I didn't know how Granny thought up those designs in her head, but she did, and it seemed that each little scrap she sewed she knew exactly where it fit in the quilt. Granny made unusual quilts; right pretty compared to most. Lots of folks just did big squares, one sewed to another, but not Granny. Seemed she worked a danged jigsaw puzzle sometimes, with as many pieces. Don't rightly know anything about quilting, but I knew Granny did hers like nobody else in Smoky Hollow. So she'd sit and sew, and Aunt Doris would shuck, and they talked quietly together.

Bobby came with his mamma. We talked some about me being up on the trestle and nearly getting runned over. I hadn't told anybody else but Mildred; I knew the grown-ups would just end up hollering at me. So we talked, me on one side of the corn row plucking, him on the other. We always grew a lot of corn. Granny would cream and can it some, but we also had to have plenty to dry out and take to the mill to make our cornmeal. When you ate as much corn bread as us, you needed a lot of cornmeal.

"Reckon on picking apples this year?" Bobby asked. We'd built a bunch of apple crates, making our movie money. We'd also been picking apples the past few years. We could scamper up the trees to get some of the apples, and when we had to use the ladder, we hung lighter than the men, so seemed to work out better us getting the higher-up apples.

"Reckon so," I said. "Though reckon it depends on Granny and who's here to watch her. If'n Daddy's at work and Aunt Lois or Mildred or nobody's here, I figure I'll have to stay."

"Good money," Bobby said, stating the obvious. We worked a while longer in silence. I began to think Bobby brought up the apple picking to start talking about something else, but then he shut up, like he was thinking real hard on something.

After a while, I asked, "Going to meeting tonight?"

"I reckon," he said. "It's so danged hot and stuffy in there I can't hardly stand it."

Another pause.

"Ever thought 'bout going forward?" I asked.

"I don't know," Bobby said. "Reckon I orta, but just hadn't seemed right. I don't know why ever'body makes such a big deal outa it."

"Nope, me neither," I said, but without much conviction. Granny thought it to be a big deal, and I knew it would be a big deal to Daddy. "But I like going," I continued. "I 'specially like the singing."

"Me, too," he said. "Though I think Mildred sings as good as them Garrett sisters."

"Yea, but they sing purdy, too," I said, not wanting to seem too obvious in taking up for Joyce. Must not have seemed that way, because Bobby continued on.

"Not as purdy as Mildred. I think I'd rather hear one real good voice, and Mildred's got a real good voice," he said.

We worked on a mite more, sun beating us like two of the worst young'uns ever, except instead of bleeding from the beating, we sweated. Still, felt like bleeding, for all the energy it took out of me. Sun stood at midmorning, but I felt more inclined to do what I wanted with Aunt Lois gone and all. "I reckon we deserve a break," I told Bobby. "Why don't you head down to the creek, and we can cool our feet a spell. I'll run fetch us a couple of gourds by the springhouse, and we'll drink our fill right outa the creek."

So Bobby took off for the creek, a bit more hop in his step than one might have thought from the way he went about gardening, like he was all worn out. He was worse than me for gardening, I think. I walked toward the house, deciding to go say howdy to Aunt Doris and Granny, just to let them know we were getting water and not goofing off or nothing.

Aunt Doris's red face looked all funny. You didn't see Aunt Doris all in a sweat very often; seemed to mess her face up. Hers wasn't a working face. Maybe that's the way Aunt Lois saw me. Granny rocked back and forth ever so gentle, her eyes closed, her sewing in her lap.

"Looks like the sun's gonna eat you alive, boy," Aunt Doris said. Unlike Aunt Lois, Aunt Doris said it like it might be a bad thing.

"Yep. Fierce hot," I said.

Granny opened her eyes and gave me a half smile. "Reckon it's time fer to rest a spell?" she asked.

"Yep," I said. "Reckoned I orta stop and ask if'n 'tware alright fer me and Bobby to take a break down by the creek and git us a drink and cool our feet a bit."

"Better git while the gittin's good," Granny said, chuckling to herself. We both thought, I reckon, the same sorts of thing about Aunt Lois and how she'd take to me asking to rest a spell. "But 'fore you go, could you fetch me some water?"

"Me, too," Doris said. "This heat's 'bout to melt me away."

I think she meant it. Aunt Doris's face did sag, like the flesh stood ready to run off the bone. "Be right back," I said.

I ran off to the kitchen and grabbed a couple of glasses and headed for the springhouse. I could have pumped the water back behind the house, but I had to get the gourds, and anyway I always thought the water tasted cooler straight from the spring. So, I filled the glasses full, grabbed the gourds that hung on a nail on the springhouse, and took the water to Granny and Aunt Doris. Before they could as much as say thank you, I was off to the creek.

Bobby already had his boots off, feet in the water. He had moved a couple of sitting stumps out into the creek a bit, just far enough to get your feet good and wet.

"Hey," I said. "I'll be shore to git my water upstream from those stinking feet of yorn."

"Hey, the stink's done washed off," he said, grinning. "I got myself some purdy smelling feet now." I popped him on the head with the gourd before giving it to him. Thirst had gotten him down so bad that he went and filled the gourd with water instead of popping me back.

I sat down on the stump beside him. These hollowed-out gourds with their long handles made perfect drinking utensils. So for a few minutes we mostly sat there and scooped up the water, drinking God's refreshment to our hearts' content, letting the creek water do its job inside and out. It didn't seem quite so hot after a few minutes of sitting and dipping feet and scooping water.

"Yep, Mildred's got a real nice voice," Bobby said, picking up our conversation from the garden. "Reckon she'll come to meeting again tonight?" he asked.

"Don't know," I said. "Aunt Lois acted all high and mighty about needing to git things done 'round her house, so I don't know if'n they'll be making any trips in from town whilst Aunt Doris is here. How come?"

"Just wondering," Bobby said.

After another couple of minutes, he started up again. "Reckon yore daddy will be going into town Saturday? We could go to the movies."

"Don't rightly know," I said. "With all the gardening and taking care of Granny and all, don't figure so. But I can ask."

"Maybe Mildred would want to go, too," he said. I finally figured out where in tarnation all this talk was coming from. Just a few months before, I might have given Bobby all kinds of grief for liking a girl. But if I told him about Joyce, I didn't want him laughing at me, so I decided I ought not laugh at him.

"Probably," I said. I waited to see what else Bobby would say, how far he'd take the conversation. Whatever else I was, I could be patient and listen, and that always served me well, then and later.

"Reckon she'd let me sit with her?" he asked, looking downstream away from me like he was asking whether or not I reckoned it might rain or something unimportant like that.

"Don't see why not," I said. "If'n yore good 'nuff fer me, reckon you orta be good 'nuff fer her." He turned his head right quick to see my eyes, to see if I talked good-natured or not. He figured me for being good-natured, which I was, and I reckon he felt grateful that I tried to make the conversation a mite lighter.

"Oh, yeah," he said, shoving me at the shoulder, "that orta make ever'thing just peachy. Good 'nuff fer you," he snorted. "Why ain't nobody else got the patience fer you. Reckon I'm the one that's some sort of danged angel fer a-putting up with the likes of you."

I got to snort at that one. "Hey, all I'm a-saying is that Mildred and me are family, good family, and what I like she's not gonna turn her nose up at. Family, I say. Can't you see the 'semblance 'tween me and her?" I put my hand up over my head, took my middle finger and pulled up on my nose to make a pig nose, and used fingers on either side of that one to pull up on my eye lids, exposing the pink. I started to pucker up and say "kiss me," but I broke up laughing just thinking about it. Bobby thought I was laughing at my own face, and he started in, too. "Naw," he said, "ain't much of a 'semblance. I reckon Mildred got all the good looking parts, and you got the spares."

Now, nobody can take that kind of insult sitting down. So I slowly stood up and said calmly, "Well, if'n that's the way you feel . . ." then I ran my gourd through the water with one swift motion, scooping up and slinging with the same motion, soaking Bobby good.

By the time we finished, we were both sopping from head to toe and laughing until our sides about busted wide open. There's nothing like being at the age where you laugh just because it feels so good to laugh, where you laugh so hard it about breaks you apart. We stumbled out of the creek and threw ourselves on the long grass a bit from the river bank, just off the side of the path. We just lay there, sun trying its best, despite the humidity, to suck out some of the moisture from us. For a few minutes, it felt right good. I knew we'd feel sticky soon, wet clothes gathering up red clay dust, too humid for the sun to do its job proper, dragging out the drying out process. But for that moment, it felt like a right friendly sun, and we were at the age to just lie back and take the gifts that came to us without complaint or thought for what would happen next.

Finally, I said, "Reckon we orta git on back. Better to have something to show 'fore dinnertime, else I'll be working through without no supper fer being a lazybones." So we got ourselves up and drug ourselves back to the red-floored prison house.

Don't rightly know why I didn't say something about Joyce.

About did a few times. Somehow just knowing Bobby was sweet on Mildred made me reckon that it was alright for me to be sweet on Joyce. I figured us for two of a kind.

We put in a hard day's work; even Daddy said so himself when he came dragging home from the sock mill. He seemed right glad to see Aunt Doris and gave her a kiss on the cheek, something I don't think I ever saw him do with Aunt Lois. He always acted tender toward Aunt Doris, and I think it suited his personality to be that way. Everybody always said he treated my mamma with a kindness rare in a man, but Daddy treated everybody with kindness, seemed to me. He was a good man, my daddy. I think he'd have been more tender with Aunt Lois if she hadn't had a danged brick wall thrown up around herself, like she didn't need anybody to be nice to her.

Daddy told Bobby's mamma thank you, and he told Bobby the same. He patted me on the back and said, "Good work, son." It was a day where you figure if you have to garden, then maybe it was alright on days like that day. At suppertime, Daddy said grace and thanked God for the good life we had; then he remembered Mamma and asked God to help us all remember her good. I didn't really remember too well. Despite that, I figured Daddy was right to say thanks for the good life. It was good.

XII

SATURDAY NIGHT CAME, along with time to go to meeting. The last night of revival had arrived, and folks expected big things. Preacher Jenkins had preached strong all week; everybody said so. The singing raised the rafters, and the prayers were long and heartfelt. Everybody reckoned God ought to bless such a fine meeting time as we had. So, with a feeling of things coming to a boil, we all walked into church that night. I was eager to see myself.

All the fans wagged back and forth, trying to push the heat back from faces red from working outside all day. Our preacher stood up to welcome everybody to the last night of meeting. He was raring to go, seemed like.

"Ever'body had a good time this week?" he asked. Lots of amens answered him. "Ever'body enjoyed the singing this week?" he asked, pointing a hand to the quartet and to Joyce and her sisters. Louder amens greeted him. "Ever'body likin' the heat?" A few chuckles greeted Preacher, but not many. "I'm a-serious. Raise yore hands if'n you liked sitting here all week, sweat pouring down yore body. C'mon now, raise yore hands." A boy sitting near the front with his family, little Lester Quarles, raised his hand long enough for his mamma to slap it back down. Preacher stood there, waiting for hands. No more rose up.

"You know, compared to the fires of hell, this is a January freeze," Preacher said, saying it so mad all of a sudden that I figured smoke might snort out his nose. "It's alright to enjoy the good preaching. It's alright to listen to these fine singers. But it ain't alright," Preacher said, raising his voice, "to listen to a man of God preaching the gift of salvation and to sit back and spit in God's face!" Gasps escaped the lips of a few people. Spitting in God's face was serious business.

"That's right," Preacher went on. "If'n God's laying out the gift of eternal life to you, if'n God provides this here man to be His voice, the voice of one crying in the wilderness, then to ignore that voice is as good as spitting in God's face, 'cause it means you ain't got no fear of God and you ain't got no respect fer God. God's a-calling somebody. He don't send His Word out to return empty. But somebody's a-spitting. Just 'member that. Somebody's spitting 'cause that person's saying, don't need what God wants me to have." Preacher paused a minute, wiping the sweat from his brow with a handkerchief. In a short time he'd worked himself all up. Then he seemed to collapse all over the pulpit, falling on it practically and leaning out as far over as he could. In a quiet voice, one where you had to try real hard to hear, Preacher said, "God ain't gonna be mocked. Yore gonna be saved or yore gonna be damned. Listen to Preacher Jenkins tonight, and you decide which one you think's best." With that, Preacher moved away from the pulpit, motioning to the singers to commence the singing for the night.

The quartet sang first, like they did every night. They'd start off with a song, and then the congregation would sing. As I sat back, taking in the heat of Preacher's words—August words, them— the piano player starting thumping keys, and soon the music was off and running, and meeting proper for the last night of 1942 revival started.

I'd heard the song they sang once or twice, but I'd never paid attention to the words. That night, I did. I listened good. The words carried the same kind of smoldering power Preacher's words had.

The song told about hell. The verses sang all about despair and pain and suffering. But it was the chorus that stuck with me, the chorus that seemed to be sung over and over again.

Brother if you're walking and talking with Satan,
　　　Think of all the trouble and sorrow that's waiting,
Ever'body's gonna have a terrible time down there.

That last line had a real low note, held out long by the bass singer, real low like the note reached down to hell itself.

Then all of us sang. I don't know why, but everything seemed to be hitting me hard that night, making me think, making me see things in my head. The pianist played upbeat as we sang along.

> Are you washed in the blood,
>> In the soul-cleansing blood of the Lamb?
> Are your garments spotless? Are they white as snow?
>> Are you washed in the blood of the Lamb?

Thing was, the whole time we sang, I kept thinking back to when I cut my thumb. As much as that hurt, I thought about Jesus, and how those nails must have felt. And I saw blood.

Next came time for Joyce and her sisters to sing, right before preaching time. The oldest Garrett sister, Elsie, started out by herself, "What can wash away my sins?" Then Joyce and her other sister answered, "Nothing but the blood of Jesus." Then I figured Jesus' blood must be like the creek. I stuck my bloody thumb down in it, and all the blood got washed away and disappeared. I'd heard Preacher preach a passage that said that our sins were as red as blood, but Jesus went and made us white as snow. I started thinking about how that clear creek worked its wonders.

Joyce looked awfully pretty that night. But I tried not to let my imagination carry me away. Instead, I closed my eyes and listened to the words.

Oh precious is the flow,
    That makes me white as snow,
No other fount I know,
    Nothing but the blood of Jesus.

Then time came for Preacher Jenkins to speak. He preached sort of like our preacher that night. He reckoned there were people out where we all sat who needed to be saved, but we sat too stubborn to walk forward and dedicate our lives to Jesus. So, he said he and Preacher picked out songs just to bring home that Jesus' blood saved us, and that without that blood we'd be mired in sins like hogs in mud. And he reckoned that to be bad. We stunk with sin, he said. These were powerful words from Preacher Jenkins, but he decided, he said, as how he needed to stir folks up some. Better to step on toes now so as those selfsame toes didn't burn in hell none, he said.

Then he started in on the book of Revelation, the last book in the Bible. And he talked about the judgment day, how we all would be judged. God had a book of life with everything recorded in it we ever did, he said. I sat listening. Then he got me, I reckon.

"How many of you love yore mammas and daddies?" he asked. About everybody raised their hand. "How many of you got yore mammas and daddies in heaven, right now, as we speak?" Some of the adult hands went up. I sheepishly raised mine, knowing my mamma lived in heaven.

"Ever want to see 'em again?" Preacher asked. That hit home with me. Course I wanted to see my mamma again. Granny used to tell me all the time that I'd see her again in heaven. Mostly when I was little, but I'd still hear it now and again as I got older.

"Think 'bout all yore loved ones," Preacher Jenkins went on. "Yore mammas and daddies, yore sisters and brothers, yore sons and daughters. All of 'em, all of 'em I tell you, gonna stand 'fore the judgment throne." Amens rose out of the crowd.

"Listen to this here book of Revelation," Preacher Jenkins hollered. "There's gonna be a raising, and there's gonna be a judging, and then fer some there's gonna be rejoicing and singing and praising God!" Amens came louder.

"But listen to what else," Preacher said, voice getting lower, reaching down to hell itself to raise the damned. "There's gonna be a crying, and a suffering, and a gnashing of teeth, 'cause this here book says that some won't be in the book of life. Some, it says," and he paused for what seemed like minutes, wiping a tear from his eye, he was that caught up with emotion, "some, it says, will be thrown into the lake of fire with the devil and his angels."

Silence. Preacher Jenkins stood with one hand holding out the Bible, the other on the pulpit, hanging on like he was hanging on for life itself, like he was hanging on to keep from slipping into that lake of fire. His knuckles tensed white, his jaw set, and he looked up, like he was looking up to heaven. And he just stood there. Finally, one of the men Preacher Jenkins brought to meeting from his own church said, real quiet like, quiet as a prayer, quiet because it was a prayer, "Help 'im, Lord."

God must have heard, because Preacher Jenkins took off again.

"Brothers, sisters, listen, think, and pray. Do you want yore loved ones' last sight of you, the last sight they'll ever have of you fer all eternity, to be that of God casting you into the lake of fire? Do you want to break yore mamma's heart, or yore daddy's heart, do you want to break yore God's heart by being condemned to burn in the flames of hell forever? Do you?"

Silence again. I'd always figured on seeing Mamma again. But now I fidgeted—worried maybe Preacher was talking about me. Maybe God told him to get after me so I wouldn't cause my mamma heartache.

"Don't think you need God's mercy?" Preacher asked. "Don't reckon you need to walk these here aisles and fall on yore knees here at the altar, begging God's forgiveness?" Preacher Jenkins had everybody now. He pulled out his handkerchief and wiped down his face good.

"Listen to the good book," he said. "Listen to the words. There's gonna be a book of life, and it's gonna have us in it, and everything we ever done. And this ain't no school book we're talking 'bout. This is God Almighty's book, and I reckon that makes it more special and more wonderful than we can imagine."

He picked up the glass of water that always sat beside the pulpit. Our preachers always talked so long and loud they needed something to wet their throats so they could keep going.

"You know what I reckon it's like?" he asked. I wanted to know. What would it be like? For the first time I could remember, I sat on the edge of my seat at meeting.

"Reckon it'll be like the movies we have nowadays," he said. His tone turned calm. "Ever'body here been to the movies? Raise yore hands if'n you've seen a movie." Most folks raised their hands.

"Right enjoyable, ain't it?" he said. "Sitting back, watching them pictures up on the screen so ever'body in the whole theater can see. Where ever'body can see," he said again, and then his narrow eyes narrowed even more. His voice took back its hard edge.

"That will be judgment day," he thundered, slapping his hand on the pulpit. I noticed that Susie Watson jumped plumb nearly out of her seat. "That will be judgment day," he said again. "Yore whole life, up fer ever'body to see. God will be showing movies, 'cepting it won't be no movie stars. It'll be yore life he's showing ever'body, and it'll be there fer ever'body in the whole of creation to see."

"Think that might be fun?" he said. "Don't reckon it will be. Oh sure, there's lots of things fer each of us to be proud of. But 'member, God knows our hearts, God knows our thoughts. Ever'thing will be up on that screen. Ever'thing we do, ever'thing we think, ever'thing we feel." He stopped long enough to sip a bit more water.

"Won't no cover of darkness cover what ever'body sees on that screen," he went on. "Ever' bad thing, ever' filthy thought, ever' deed of evil 'twill be there. So think to yoreself: 'Has I done anything I don't want my mamma to see? Has I done anything I don't want my daddy to see, or my wife, or my husband, or brothers or sisters?' All our secrets, up on the screen of judgment. Now let me tell you something. They ain't none of us wants that." Preacher paused a second, and then he said, almost to himself, "No, ain't none of us wants that."

He let us all sit and simmer a while, thinking about that big heavenly movie screen and what would be there for all to see. Then he went on.

"Know what? I don't want that. Y'all don't want that. What's a feller to do? What's a feller to do? What's a feller to do?"

Then Preacher went to waiting again. Seemed like an eternity, and I think everybody wanted to know the answer. Then, all of a sudden, Preacher Jenkins started thumping on the pulpit, but not like he was mad. More like getting a beat down. After three or four slaps on the oak, he started singing, real soft at first, then getting louder.

> What can wash away my sin?
> Nothing but the blood of Jesus.
> What can make me whole again?
> Nothing but the blood of Jesus.

Then he looked out at us all, and he said, "Now, all you good folks join me." And we all did, and that little church grew loud with singing.

> Oh precious is the flow,
> That makes me white as snow.
> No other fount I know,
> Nothing but the blood of Jesus.

"That's it," Preacher Jenkins said. "The precious blood of Jesus. If'n you want something good up on that screen, trust in the blood of Jesus. If'n you want all yore bad deeds wiped off so that nobody sees 'em, trust in the blood of Jesus. God promises us," Preacher Jenkins went on, "that if'n we turn to 'im, if'n we trust his Son, if'n we let ourselves be washed in the blood, then it'll be Christ who lives in us. Instead of us up on that screen, it'll show Jesus hisself. He's given hisself fer us, so that we might become righteous."

Preacher Jenkins stopped, took a long drink of water, and emptied the glass, which meant he had nearly finished up. "Don't matter what you've done. Don't matter what you've thought. Don't matter what you are. God'll take you just as you are, and he'll put Jesus' picture up in front of yorn. Just as you are, if'n you'll trust 'im. But it's up to you. Won't you come? Won't you come now? I know God means fer somebody to be saved tonight, to have the embarrassment of a wicked life taken away. Won't you come? He's a-waiting. He's a-waiting. What are you a-waiting fer? He'll take you just the way you are. You don't have to wait fer nothing. Come now. I'm a-praying fer you."

With that, Preacher Jenkins dropped down to one knee. Seemed the weight of everybody's damnation and salvation lay on his shoulders. Softly, the piano started playing, playing a song while Preacher Jenkins prayed. Then he stood up, looked out at us, looked straight at me it seemed, and said, "Sing with me now."

And we started in with the song that ended every week of revival meeting I ever went to growing up.

Just as I am, without one plea,
    But that thy blood was shed for me,
And that thou bidst me come to thee,
    Oh lamb of God I come, I come.

Don't rightly know what came over me. Everything that Preacher Jenkins had said hit home that night. Thinking about Mamma and that movie screen and things done in the dark, thinking about my cut thumb and the river washing the blood away, making it clean, thinking about my feelings for Joyce and how they just popped in my head and me not able to control them, and wouldn't that be awful for everybody to see because I was confused enough to think such thoughts were evil instead of natural. With a light head, I heard the words:

Just as I am and waiting not,
    To rid my soul of one dark blot,
To thee whose blood can cleanse each spot,
    O Lamb of God I come, I come.

At first, people stood all around me. Then all of a sudden they stood mostly behind me, as I moved to the front to talk to Preacher. His eyes bore into me as he asked, "What you want, son?" And I, for all the life of me, I started tearing up, and my throat got all tight, and the room seemed spinning, and all I could do was whisper the words, "I wanna be saved, Preacher." My preacher came and knelt beside me at the altar rail, and he motioned me to get on my knees, too. Then he prayed for God to save me, and when he asked if I trusted Jesus, I said yes, though I reckon I always had, but saying it right then seemed to make all the difference to everybody.

According to custom, I stood at the back with the preachers after meeting so everyone could shake my hand. Some of the old ladies gave me a hug. My daddy beamed pride. Maybe it was me, but Joyce's eyes seemed to sparkle as she took my hand and said, "I think this is wonderful."

And it was wonderful. If God left the ninety-nine sheep to find the one, I guess I felt like the one. Everybody made a fuss over me, like I had done something special, like no one else had ever done what I'd done before. Granny was too choked up to talk, and she hugged me, and I held her frail body, for the first time reckoning it frail, happy to make her so happy.

There were things wrong with our little church same as things are wrong with all churches. But one thing they did right and one thing you never forgot if you went there was your saving. And the baptism the next day, with me in the river I loved so much, with all the food and good times, made it seem like God Himself had come down and thrown a party just for me. And it's something I've always tried to be grateful for.

XIII

WE'D BEEN PICKING for a couple of weeks, but only about the first of September did the golden and red delicious apples come in good. A fine Saturday looked down on us, and Bobby and I sat in the shade of one gnarled old apple tree, one of the oldest in the orchard, and ate our dinners. Didn't matter how many times I had cold fried chicken and biscuits, always tasted good washed down with spring water.

Daddy had taken Granny into Marietta, so I had to stay with Aunt Lois and Uncle Henry. Better anyhow, because the apple orchard lay near town. As I sat there munching on my biscuit, I had a hankering for some preserves, but there was none to be had.

"Why does yore daddy take yore granny into Marietta fer?"

Bobby asked. He tried to make it sound like he was just asking, but I'd heard some of the folks at church talk sometimes when they didn't think I stood close enough to hear. Some thought it a waste of time and money. Ain't nothing to be done for dropsy, they said. They talked like Daddy was doing foolishness trying to help Granny out.

Even Granny seemed to think it a bit foolish, but Daddy allowed as how he'd had a daddy to die and a wife to die and danged if he wouldn't at least try to do something for his mamma. That seemed to pacify Granny well enough, though she acted like she was doing him a favor by going to the doctor rather than him doing her one by taking her. Daddy said he just wanted to be up to date on the condition and to know what the doctors, the good doctors, knew. This didn't mean he didn't like Doc Miller, just that he'd been in service and been a few places. He knew that the first and best of everything having to do with doctoring didn't hit Smoky Hollow first. The one time Granny asked how Daddy paid for these special doctoring trips, Daddy just said he was taking care of it. He seemed a little peevish, so Granny let it go.

"Reckon he just wants what's best fer her," I said.

"How is she, anyway?" he asked.

"Oh, I dunno," I said, and I really didn't. She didn't seem to be getting worse, but she didn't show any signs of getting better, either. As long as she took it easy, kept her feet up, and all that, she did okay.

Sometimes at night she'd have a hard time, especially if she had sunk down in the bed. She'd been told to sleep propped up to help her lungs stay clear. But sometimes she'd get off her pillows, and then she'd end up every now and then having a bad spell. Seemed like the bad spells came mostly at night. Daddy would sit with her and help best he could, and he always hollered at me to get up, usually to fetch a little water so Granny could wet her mouth some because it'd go dry.

During the day, while she quilted a bit and slept and quilted then read from her Bible, she didn't seem all that sick—if you didn't remember too much how Granny always was up and about doing chores. I think just sitting around wore her out more than anything.

Bobby closed his eyes, letting his dinner settle while resting. Then he asked, "Going to the movies after picking, ain't we?" And then I knew we had arrived at his real concern. He'd asked about Granny so as not to appear too anxious about the movie. But he was.

Bobby had been staying in town like me. He had an aunt and uncle that lived in town, and so some days he just stayed with them so as not to have to make the trip from Smoky Hollow. His relations lived on the other side of the town square from Aunt Lois and Uncle Henry's, about a five-minute walk, just behind the courthouse on the road up to Corbin Hill. When we both stayed in town, we almost always tried to get to the movies, especially when we were making apple money.

"Don't rightly know," I said. "Aunt Lois woke up in one of her moods this morning, and she reckoned as how when I got off work here I should work 'round her house, since she did so much work fer me and Daddy at Granny's." To be fair, she was right. Aunt Lois had been a danged workhorse.

"Ah, c'mon. Shorely you can wiggle yore way into going. We's got to git out and have some fun." A note of desperation hung in Bobby's voice. If Aunt Lois had heard it, there for danged sure wouldn't have been any movie going. Bobby was sweet on Mildred, and Mildred didn't mind it, Bobby being a little older and it making her feel like she was getting older, too. Mildred went to the movies with us lots of times, but just the time before, Mildred sat with Bobby. Course, we always sat together, but normally it'd go Bobby, then me, then Mildred. That way I could talk to my best friend and my favorite cousin. But this last time, Mildred jumped into the row first, and Bobby quickly followed. So I sat on the outside of Bobby, but even so I could tell, when I looked over out of the corner of my eye, that they held hands. I reckoned it'd go on this way until Aunt Lois caught on, and then I figured it'd stop. But she didn't know yet.

"Better gather up some apples if'n we're gonna leave right after work," I said. Ol' man Bridges allowed us to pick up a sackful of apples off the ground. They'd be bruised, and some had worms, but they were mostly alright. We'd pare them, cut out the wormy parts and the bad bruises, and use them to make applesauce, canning enough for the winter. I'd been helping a lot with that because it was easy to do. Granny'd sit there and supervise and keep me company, but I'd do most of the work.

So I stood up and stretched a bit. September warmth had dried my boots out good, having been soaked earlier by the morning dew. I folded up my dinner sack and stuck it in one of my overall pockets, same one that had some penny candy in it, so I pulled out a couple of pieces of hard candy, stuck one in my mouth and flipped the other to Bobby. He helped me fill up a paper poke full of apples, and then we went back to work.

We worked hard, Bobby and me, or least as hard as a couple of boys our age could while thinking about going to the movies and not totally ignoring the sunshine and figuring that the day shone nice enough that it needed to be enjoyed and not just ignored. But we did good, I figured, and with a sense of having earned our money, we headed out for Aunt Lois's.

We got to the house, and Bobby said bye and said to be sure and make it to the movies, me and Mildred, and not to be late. Then he took off to his aunt and uncle's, running because I reckon it just felt good to run. I was a good runner, but Bobby was the fastest of anybody I knew.

I went into the house careful like—Aunt Lois hated having her screen door slam shut. A neat little writing table sat in the corner of the living room. It had little drawers for papers and pens, and there Aunt Lois sat. I started over toward her, just to say howdy and be friendly, not just because I wanted to go to the movies but because I reckoned it polite, me staying at her house and all.

I guess it wasn't polite, but I stopped after a step or two and stood there, watching Aunt Lois from behind. There she sat, her straight back up tight against the straight back of the chair. She plainly was writing a letter or something because she had out her supplies, and she had a pen in hand. But she just sat there, quiet like. Aunt Lois was a lot of things, but quiet didn't figure into it much. Slowly her hand reached out, and I saw her pick up an old piece of paper, yellow with age. Then I realized that she held Uncle Joe's letter, the one that Granny had spoke of, because I saw the Ford emblem on the paper. It didn't look exactly like Granny's letter, but it looked enough like it that I recognized what it was.

Aunt Lois sat and stared at the letter for a spell, like she was try-ing to cipher it out or something, but that didn't make sense. All of Granny's children could read good—it made her real proud, because lots of folks couldn't read at all. Aunt Lois looked and looked at the letter. Then her hand started going all trembly, just a little at first, then more and more. It seemed like an eternity between when that shaking started and when she put the letter down. Her strong shoulders picked up, and then she heaved out a great big ol' sigh, like the first sigh she ever sighed. It held all the built-up sighs of her life. There seemed no end to that downtrod-den breath escaping out of her. But then came a worse sound.

If it had been wintertime, or if I knew from when I left the house that morning that Aunt Lois was sickly, I might have mis-taken that noise for a nose that had a cold in it. But Aunt Lois didn't have a cold, I knew that. Her sniffing her nose like that meant she was crying, and it scared me worse than if somebody had pointed a loaded gun at me. I stood glued to the floor, scared to move, scared to breathe, scared to give myself away.

I'd have never thought Aunt Lois would cry about anything; she didn't seem the type—too dadburn stubborn and ornery I reckoned. And when a noise came from her mouth, a stifled and broken cry that punctuated her sniffle so that there was no mistaking it, I thought I was dead. I reckoned nobody in the world had ever seen Aunt Lois cry, not as a grown-up anyway. And here I was, probably the last person on the face of the earth she'd want to see her cry, and me wishing the face of the earth would open up and swallow me so I could get away.

I slowly stepped back, trying my best not to make that old floor creak. Might have taken ten minutes to retrace my few steps to the door, that's how slow I went. I tried putting down the weight of each step real slow like, easing myself into my steps. My muscles all tensed up, and I felt like I would explode.

I finally made it to the screen door. Here came the hardest part. I slowly pushed, slowly, slowly, trying not to make a sound. Aunt Lois put her pen down and laid her hands in her lap. Her head fell back, and I heard her neck pop. She must have been tenser than me. I could tell she was fighting the crying spell. She'd let a little out; now, by golly, she was out to whip the rest of it. I think her struggle with herself kept her from noticing me.

I made it outside and started the process of slowly closing the screen door. A little creak sounded at the very end. Her shoulders stiffened up a mite, but she didn't turn around. I never figured out if she didn't really hear me or if she didn't want anybody to see her red eyes. Either way, she didn't turn around, so I snuck quietly off the porch. Shaking by the time I got on level ground, I gave off a danged big sigh of my own. Then I went around to the back of the house.

When I got back there, I saw Uncle Henry puttering around. I think he pretended to work on something, mostly to keep out of the way. Liz and Becky sat all huddled up on a bench, talking away. My eyes surveyed the yard, and I finally spotted Mildred back by the shed, sitting in the shade.

"Hey," I said as I walked up to her. She looked up at me with eyes that said, "I'm glad you're here."

"Hey," she said back. Then quickly her expression changed. "You didn't go into the house or nothing, did you?" she asked.

Didn't know exactly what to say. "Well, I started to, but yore mamma looked busy, so I didn't." I reckoned that to be the truth, more or less.

"Good," Mildred said, letting out a sigh of her own. "We ain't none of us allowed back in the house 'til Mamma says so," she said. "She's in a black mood today, I can tell you that. Finally, she just sorta blew up at ever'body and told us all to git out and not come back in 'til she told us to."

Mildred glanced over at her sisters, then said to me in a hushed voice, "Said she was gonna write that no-good Joey and tell 'im all 'bout Granny and ain't he ashamed that ever'body's carrying the load but 'im and ain't he a fine one fer taking off from his family and see what it's led to now. She was gonna tell 'im, she said. You know Mamma. I reckon she will. If'n she blisters his hide in that letter the way she did ours with her looks, figure he'll not hardly be in no shape to make the trip. You know how Mamma is when she's mad."

"Yep," I said. I knew I couldn't tell Mildred what I had seen. No mad-as-an-old-wet-hen mamma sat in there at the desk, only a lonely sister trying to figure out how to ask her brother to come home without sounding like she was begging. "Yep," I said again. "I know."

"I reckon you orta stay outa sight if'n you can," Mildred said. "She's got you and Uncle Joe figured fer birds of a feather, and if'n she can't clip his wings she'll shore try cutting yore's."

So we sat there in silence for a spell, and it surprised me a right bit when Aunt Lois came to the door, calling everybody in for supper. She must have been fixing it while doing her letter writing. And even though everybody crept in like danged mice making their way into the cat's house, Aunt Lois herself didn't seem to take much notice of anybody. She had everybody sit down, and she served us up a right nice supper of corn bread and vegetable stew. Nobody talked much, but not because of how Aunt Lois acted. She didn't make anybody talk, but she didn't seem to object to it either.

Maybe it was because I'd seen what I'd seen, or maybe it was because I'd seen what I'd seen and she knew I'd seen, but Aunt Lois seemed right nice to me. She even patted me on the back of the head once as she went around the table, asking me if I'd worked hard that day. The question startled me, and I don't reckon as how I'd ever heard it from her before; she always supposed I didn't hardly work at all, and usually she couldn't figure out why anybody'd want to waste good money on me picking when about anybody else could probably pick a whole lot faster. But she asked, and I answered that Bobby and I both had worked hard, and I also told her that I remembered to bring home some apples to take to Granny for the applesauce making.

And it was with a look of astonishment that Mildred looked at me when I asked Aunt Lois about going out to the movies. Reckon she expected the house to fall in, but all that happened was that Aunt Lois let out a sigh—a little one this time—and said she reckoned she didn't see any harm in it.

And so Bobby and I got to spend some of our apple money on a movie, and from what I could tell, Bobby also spent a little of his apple money buying popcorn for Mildred. She had her own popcorn money, but Bobby wanted to buy it, and I reckon Mildred wanted him to buy it. So we sat there, us three, in our new seating order, Mildred and Bobby seeming to enjoy being with each other as much as being at the movie. I mostly thought about the Aunt Lois I'd snuck in and out on. I wished that Uncle Joe would come home for Christmas like Granny said he would, not just for Granny, but for Aunt Lois, too. I figured, in one of my first real feelings of compassion for another human being, that she deserved that much.

XIV

MISS STOVER'S MOUTH always turned down, but not like a frown. I've noticed that sometimes when people go to thinking real hard the corners of their mouth will turn down as they push their lower lip upwards. Maybe Miss Stover, being a schoolteacher, had to think real hard. But even if it wasn't a frown, it still gave her a look of sadness about to creep out.

I always thought Miss Stover to be an awful fine teacher. She sat between Granny and Daddy's age. Her hair had grayed some, and her glasses sat across a nose that seemed just a little too small for her broad face. She wore her hair up in a tight bun on top of her head. I reckon if she was like most, when she took it down to wash, it fell way down her back. Her dresses, though threadbare, mostly like all of our clothes, always seemed neat, and she had an orderly way about her that caused her to be a good teacher for our school, because all of us with all our different ages sat in the same classroom.

Granny and Daddy both talked about her at times; them liking her made it easy for me to like her, even though I think I would have liked her anyway. We got along, and she helped me learn how to read all the stuff I found interesting and that Aunt Lois found to be nonsense.

She'd had at least a year of teacher's school, Granny said, which made her something. But her folks got sick, and she had to come home and take care of them. A lingering sickness, apparently, where they weren't sick enough to die but not well enough to do too awful much. So Miss Stover took care of them, and everybody said she had done a fine job of doing it.

She didn't ever marry because she didn't ever have time for courting don't reckon. When her folks passed on, both within a year of each other, Granny and Daddy both figured her to be too old and set in her ways to want to think of marrying, though they both seemed to think she could have gotten married if she had wanted.

Sometimes doing my schoolwork I'd look up at her, and she'd be staring off, lower lip pushed up, thinking up a storm. I always wondered if she ever thought about what life could have been instead of what it was, because sometimes not just her mouth but her eyes looked sad, too.

Whether sad or not, she didn't let her feelings interfere with

her teaching us, and she did a good job of that. So I never com-
plained too much about having to start school every September;
did it more just because I reckoned it to be expected and because
Bobby really did hate going, and I didn't want to spoil his bad
mood, being as that's what made it bearable for him to go.

I'd seen pictures of little schoolhouses in our books, but they
didn't look too awful much like ours. The pictures showed build-
ings that were always red with white trim, and they had a little
bell tower at the top. A nice green yard surrounded them, and
sometimes a white picket fence, too. They'd built our school with
just ol' clapboard, no paint on it much, and we had a tin roof, like
about all the houses, so I don't know if a bell tower could have
been put up even if we had wanted one. A few hardy weeds took
the place of grass. Again, like a lot of houses, our little school sat
about three feet up off the ground, stacks of rocks at each corner
serving as the foundation. Steps with no railing led up to the
door, and there was no real porch to the place.

It wasn't fancy, but then none of us were, either. Mildred's sisters thought themselves too good to go there. They'd tell me that
they'd just die having to go to a country bumpkin school like
mine. It was about the only time I wished they did go to my
school, if they held sure to the dying part and all. But it suited us
who went, and Miss Stover made sure we each learned as much
as she figured we could.

Of course, a teacher really couldn't teach a bunch of different
children of all different ages at the same time. So the best thing

about our school, I thought, was the way we helped each other out. Made us feel like our little Smoky Hollow community was more like a family. Miss Stover did help each grouping of young'uns, but she could only help a group if all the other groups stayed busy. The bigger children would help the smaller ones. Me being twelve almost thirteen, and being a good reader, I'd been more of a helper the past year or two, and it suited me. I had a patience for a person my age that made me right helpful—I could wait long enough for one of the little ones to work something out for himself instead of jumping right in like some of the older ones did just to show how much they knew. I guess maybe I didn't have to show how much I knew; schoolwork came easy to me, and everybody knew it. So I made for a good helper.

All that's to say, that as I met Bobby up on the road, I had settled into a right good mood; I liked school and I especially liked the first day because it was like starting a journey off somewhere. My reading took me to places in my head, and I enjoyed it. So, when Bobby's first "danged school" came out of his mouth, which is to say when I first stepped within earshot, I came back with a good-natured, "Yep. Danged school." And then I joined him in kicking up the red dust as we made our way the mile or so to the schoolhouse, Bobby kicking, trying to drag his feet and put off the whole miserable start of school as long as possible. I made dust fly, too, but more because I just liked to.

We were swinging our dinner pails when we walked past the Garrett place. I started to stare up at it when the screen door flew

open and out came Joyce and one of her sisters. The oldest didn't
go to school anymore. I quickly turned my head aside to make
like I wasn't looking up that way, and I found me a good rock for
kicking and started concentrating real hard on doing just that.

I hadn't really seen Joyce since the revival because I didn't
really have a need to walk toward her house—Bobby came from
the opposite direction, and most of the carrying on was between
our two houses. Also, Joyce's folks went up to the Nine Mile
Church, so I never saw her at church. It'd been a little more than
a month since my saving, and I'd tried not to think too hard on
her because sometimes I couldn't control my thoughts too well. I
knew Jesus washed me clean, but I was still a little leery about
that whole movie picture and judgment day stuff. So Joyce was
there in my head, but none too close to the surface, though I
thought about sitting with her when I saw Bobby and Mildred sitting together at the movie theater.

By the time it took Joyce and her sister to reach the road from
their door, we had gone about thirty feet on past their place.
Bobby talked about I don't know what because I was concentrating so hard on my rock kicking and all. Just as I got ready for a
good square kick, Joyce hollered, "Hey! Slow down and we'll walk
with y'all."

Bobby stopped and turned around right away. I waited a second,
taking in a breath, trying to figure out what in tarnation I'd say to
Joyce that wouldn't come out sounding real stupid. By the time I
got turned, they had come within just a few feet of us.

"Hey!" Bobby said. "Ain't this fine, having to go to danged school on such a purdy day," he started.

Joyce's sister, who didn't much like having to walk with us, I think, because she was older, though in the same grade, just looked at Bobby and said, "Well, you can't spend yore whole life playing like yore gonna be little forever."

"Ain't little," Bobby replied. "'Sides, didn't say I was gonna play none." He kind of shut up and looked like Joyce's sister now, like he wasn't too keen on having the Garrett sisters for company.

Joyce's sister sped up a bit and Bobby seemed to drag his feet even more, like he was digging a trough through that road all the way to school. That left just Joyce and me together to talk. I looked off to the side of the road, thinking maybe I'd get all inspired and have something to say. All I saw were trees, and right then they didn't seem none too inspiring.

Just as I felt myself starting to sweat from the heat of all the unsaid words, Joyce up and started talking. "How's Bobby's brother doing?" she asked. "Daddy said he wasn't doing no good."

"I dunno," I said, buying myself some time to think. I thought she might be going to say something about Granny, or even about seeing me at meeting, me being saved and all, when she sang as part of the service. I had hoped she'd say something about it so I could tell her how pretty I thought they sang.

"His leg hurts 'im some," I said, repeating what Bobby had told me. "Hurts where'n there ain't no leg. Reckon the army doctors said it would be that way some, but Bobby's brother thinks it hurts more'n it should."

Course, I think Joyce wanted to know more than that, but I didn't know what she had heard, and I didn't want to go and talk about Bobby's brother much because of the way it seemed to be making things in his home bad. So I just waited.

"Well, it's gotta hurt having yore leg gone like'n that," she said. "But Daddy said they was things wrong in his head, too, and that it worrit his mamma and daddy."

Now I knew the drift of the conversation. After Bobby's brother had been home for just a few weeks, he started acting all strange. Once, I guess, the family was sitting out on the porch. Bobby said he came out all in a run because that's the way Bobby moved. He blew out the door and flew off the porch before the screen door, which he had knocked wide open on his dash out, came slamming against the frame with a real loud "Bam!" His mamma started to yell at him for it, because she always told him not to go in and out of the house like a danged tornado.

All of a sudden Bobby's brother, hearing that "Bam!" jumped out of his chair with a scream and vaulted over the railing of the porch, hit on his one leg, and fell to the ground. Bobby saw him crawling on his belly away from the house as fast as he could go. His daddy came tearing down the steps and around to get him. Soon as his daddy got there, Bobby's brother reached up to meet his daddy's outreached hand and yanked him down to the ground.

"Get down, yer idjit!" Bobby's brother yelled. "You'll git yore damned head blown off'n yore shoulders."

It took a long time, but Bobby's daddy got his brother back in the house, where they got him calmed down. After that, seemed any loud noise would set him off. He thought he was back in the danged war sometimes. So Bobby's house had gotten real quiet, unnaturally quiet, and that sat hard on Bobby because he wasn't a naturally quiet person. Bobby's family did their best to keep his brother calm, but they couldn't control everything. One day, Bobby said, a car came by the house, and it backfired. Danged, he said, if they about didn't get his brother back in that day. Got real violent and all, he did. Reckon that was what Joyce asked after.

"Yep," I said, "I think they is worrit." I wondered how much I should tell her, but I reckon she'd probably heard plenty at home, so I just said, "I hope he gits better."

"Yeah, me too," she said.

We walked on a mite more, and we could see the schoohouse. Both of us grew quiet, and we were both flush I reckon, because I could see it on her, and I could feel it on me, and the day wasn't hot enough yet for flushing. So, screwing up my courage, I said, "You shore sing purdy."

Immediately Joyce turned her head to me with a smile and said, "You really think so?"

"Yep," I said, not figuring what else should go with the compliment. "Thought you sang right nice at meeting. Made ever'thing special." Only other thing I could think of was that she looked as sweet as she sang, but no way was I going to say that, not out there on the road and near school and all.

"Preacher Jenkins said we did right nice, too," she said. "I was glad to see you come forward the way you did. I told Mamma that I knowed 'tware Preacher Jenkins preaching the word of God and all, but that maybe our singing helped some, too."

"Yep," I said, and then I ran out of words.

So we walked along for just another bit, and then we were at school. "Reckon we orta head right in," I said, and she allowed as how that was probably so. I let her walk up the steps in front of me, and Bobby came up from behind me and gave me a shove in the back. When I turned around he wore a big grin like he knew some big secret. I just shoved him on the shoulder, and we walked on in.

XV

THERE'S DIFFERENT KINDS of hot, even if the temperature is about the same. September hot was always a good kind of hot. Not saying it couldn't be nearly as hot as August, because it could, and not saying it couldn't be humid, because it could be that, too. But usually the air lay just a little less hot and a little less humid, and nighttime temperatures fell a bit more. But mostly it was knowing that it was a heat that'd seen its better days, a heat that had some end in sight and you knew it wasn't all that long off. So there I sat in church on a late September Sunday morning, feeling a little hot but not resenting it like an August hot. A little breeze blew through the windows, so you didn't really need to work the fans.

You couldn't tell that it wasn't August hot with Preacher,

though. Sweat drenched him, and he worked as hard as I'd ever seen him work. There seemed to be some sort of urgency to him, but don't know why. Sometimes, if he wasn't too awful down on things, he made a good preacher. And that Sunday's preaching sounded right good. He preached in his sing-song preaching voice, and he beat the pulpit between the verses of his sermon to help him keep time. He preached on Jesus' baptism.

"And then Jesus went a-down to the water," he said, hitting the pulpit with his fist. Jesus came out as "Jeeesus."

"And then Jesus says—ah—gotta baptize me, John—yes Lord—gotta baptize me." Bam.

"Yes—ah—Jesus was in the water," bam, "that pure clean water," bam, "the water of the Jordan River," bam. Preacher took a long drink of his water. "Yes, in the waters of the blessed Jordan," he said.

"And then the heavens, they opened up," bam, "and God's spirit come a-flying down," bam, "and the spirit took the shape of a dove," bam, "and then God," bam, "Almighty God," bam "God hisself says . . ." And then he stopped. He looked at us all, drawing us in, keeping silence a spell so the congregation could give him help. Finally, a few men began in, "Help 'im, Lord, help 'im." And then I reckon the Lord did, because he started up again.

"God a-says," bam, "this is my beloved son," bam, "in whom I am well pleased." Bam. "This is my beloved son," he roared, "in whom I am well pleased." "Praise God, praise God, praise God. He was well pleased with Jesus."

"Now, how 'bout you?" he said, looking at all of us. "Is God well pleased with you? Is God a-well pleased, I say, with you?" He paused, wiped his brow, and finished up.

"If'n the dove came down, I say, if'n the dove came down, came down on you today," he asked, "would he say, 'You are my son in whom I am well pleased?' Think 'bout it. Think 'bout it."

Then Preacher started praying for all of us who sat out there, asking God to open our hearts so we'd hear the voice of the dove. No threats or anything. Just asking God to help everybody do right. Like usual, he lay all over the pulpit like he was about to collapse after the sermon, praying up a storm. He looked plumb tuckered after he finished up. During the last song I almost wished I had waited to walk forward so there'd be somebody to respond to his sermon. He stood up there, arms folded, head down, singing along with us all, hoping to look up and see a lost sheep come up. But nobody came, and I felt sorry for him because I think he tried real hard.

We all made our way out of church, real slow like, everybody else taking time to shake Preacher's hand and tell him he'd done good. Granny sat for a spell, until folks had mostly cleared out. Then me and Daddy and Granny and Aunt Lois and hers made our way to the door.

Daddy shook Preacher's hand right vigorously and said, "That made for a good 'un today. I 'preciate it." Preacher just looked back and said, "God is good."

Now when Granny got up there she surprised us all. Maybe Granny surprised herself, or maybe she'd planned it. Anyway,

instead of saying something nice about the sermon or the weather
or asking after his health and all, Granny up and said, "Come join
us fer Sunday dinner. It'd be right nice to have you and yore sister
visit with us a spell." I wasn't the only one surprised. I knew
Preacher got asked to Sunday dinner now and again, but, being as
Granny lots of time didn't like his preaching all that well, seems
like we didn't ask him much. Maybe the sermon set well enough
with Granny that she reckoned it deserved a good chicken dinner.
Under Granny's direction, Daddy and I had cooked up a nice-
sized apple cobbler the night before, so we'd have a nice dessert to
go along with the chicken and biscuits and gravy and beans and
all. Maybe some fried potatoes and onions.

Preacher looked at Granny; then he shook his head a bit and
simply said, "We'd be right pleased to join you."

"Well, why don't y'all come on 'long in 'bout an hour. Dinner
won't be quite ready, but we can set a spell on the porch and visit
whilst the childern git things prepared."

Once we left church and got home, Aunt Lois made it plain
that she didn't like it. "Why in the world did you want to invite
him and Edna Mae fer?" she asked. Edna Mae was Preacher's sister. "I reckon how he's alright, but she plumb gives me the
willies." Aunt Lois kind of shivered all over, and I don't think she
was pretending. "Ain't nothing nobody does is right with that
woman," she went on. "She's got the coldest look I ever seen, like
a January frost staring you in the face." I figured there must be
something to a person who could give Aunt Lois the willies.

"Edna Mae's not so bad," Granny put in. "She's had a hard life, like most of us, and she's always kept up her responsibilities in the face of it all. If'n she ain't all sunshine, that's alright. World needs the rain, too." Granny smiled, and I figured she was making a joke. Aunt Lois didn't catch on, though. I didn't think Aunt Lois ought to be talking about people not being friendly. Of course, that's the kind of thought you kept to yourself.

"I don't know, it's not just that," Aunt Lois went on. "She's so, well, reckon she's just so hard. I 'member onct little Billy Davis come to our Sunday School class, and Edna Mae was the teacher. Reckon I wasn't no more'n ten. Poor little boy wasn't wearing nothing but rags 'cause'n that's all his family had. Reckon he didn't know to take a Saturday bath, either. Still, he was just a little boy, and 'twas his first time and all. Don't reckon his folks came, and I figure he came outa curiosity to see what 'twas all 'bout. Reckon he found out. Edna Mae sent 'im home, saying he had to clean up to come to church, spouting out that cleanliness was next to godliness. Embarrassed Billy 'nuff that he didn't ever come back. Don't think he's darkened a church door since."

"Now, Lois," Granny said, "that's been a long time since. Edna Mae and me are just old ladies now, so give us some peace." Preacher and his sister and Granny were all about the same age, in their sixties or so. I did agree with Aunt Lois—Preacher's sister's mouth always seemed to be all drawn up, like her smiling muscles had all shriveled up from lack of use.

"You young'uns run on," Granny said to me and Mildred. "Lois and Liz and Becky are 'bout all we need here in the kitchen fer now. I'll stay to see they does things right. You two come tell me when Preacher and Edna Mae come along." So me and Mildred went on out, and we sat on the porch steps while Daddy and Uncle Henry sat and rocked in the rockers.

Walk into the middle of a conversation not for your ears and it seems the silence deafens you. That's the way it was when Mildred and I went out. About the time I got to the screen door, I heard Daddy saying, "She ain't gittin' no better, but she ain't gittin' no worse neither. Don't rightly know what to expect." Then I heard Uncle Henry say, "Well, how long they reckon she's got?" And then Mildred and I came out and took our place there on the steps, and the silence set in.

Nothing's worse for a young'un than silence. Grown-ups can sit and rock and think and do nothing and be quiet, but my nature didn't allow it, not yet. So I piped up and said, "Granny said fer me and Mildred to keep an eye out fer Preacher and his sister."

"Well, be shore just to set and look then," Daddy said. "Don't you two git up and do no running 'round or nothing. Keep yore Sunday shines that way, just setting nice and all." Granny had already told us to keep on our Sunday duds and stay clean.

Directly we heard a car coming. Preacher drove slowly down our road and parked under a big ol' oak tree. He stepped out of the car and waited for his sister, who seemed to take her own sweet time getting out. She swung her legs out, pushed up at the bun of hair on her head, smoothed down her dress up front, and seemed to get up slower than molasses. Then she stood and ran her hand down the bottom half of her dress, like she was wiping off dirt, though I didn't see any.

Preacher's sister raised her head to our house, and from the look on her face, I reckoned she and Aunt Lois had something in common—neither of them was too pleased for her to be there. Reckon she came because her brother said so, or maybe because anybody'd be crazy to miss a good Sunday dinner at our house. She was there, but she didn't like it. If I'd been old enough to care about stuff like that, I'd be figuring my dinner wouldn't be going down too good, but I was still young enough not to let anything like that interfere with my appetite.

Watching Preacher's sister had frozen me for a minute like one of those danged Gorgons I'd read about in my history book at school. It had some stories from ancient Greece, and I liked them a lot. If Preacher's sister had had a danged snakes' nest on top of her head, I don't think it'd made her look any less freezing. But then I got on my feet; Mildred did, too. Then we remembered to go tell Granny. Granny's face broke into that gentle smile of hers when I told her. Aunt Lois's face just looked like normal, only more so, which is the best I can say for her trying to hold back her comments.

Mildred and I came back out with Granny; I had grabbed the crate that was by her chair so she'd be able to prop her feet up. When we got outside and Granny had made her greeting, she turned to me and said, "Son, go git a couple of the straight-backed chairs from the dining table." So I ran off, got the straight-backed chairs, and then watched and listened as Daddy and Uncle Henry tried to convince Preacher and his sister to take the rockers while they sat in the straight-backed chairs.

I didn't think any of the four of them were ever going to sit down. There was sitting room for everybody without the dining table chairs, but adults didn't ever seem to want to sit on the swing while entertaining company. Mildred and I took to the swing, and that seemed right and proper. Finally, Preacher took Uncle Henry's rocker, but his sister wasn't going to take anybody's chair, she said, and so she sat in the straight-backed chair, and Daddy kept his rocker. Reckon the straight-back chair suited Preacher's sister anyway; stiff as she was, I couldn't imagine wasting a good rocker on her—she'd just see how still she could sit in it.

Preacher asked after Granny's health. Granny talked straight about things, and I think I got the answer that Daddy was about to give Uncle Henry when Mildred and I first came out.

"Oh, some days are better'n others," Granny said, "but that's true whether yore sick or well. I ain't got no reason to complain. I thank the Lord fer the good days, and I tries to thank 'im fer the not so good days. Figure if'n I complain too much He might do something 'bout it." She laughed a little at that, but nobody else did much. I could tell they didn't know whether they should or not. "Reckon I'll make it 'til Christmas at least," she said. Everybody knew she had her heart set on seeing Uncle Joe at Christmas.

Then Granny and Preacher mostly, with the odd comment

from Daddy or Uncle Henry and an occasional puff of air from Preacher's sister, fell into a conversation, and they fell into it so easy it surprised me. Guess I'd always known it, but Preacher and Granny grew up together, and they knew lots of stories on each other, and for this afternoon they decided to visit some of them old memories.

For about twenty minutes they talked, ending with a story about a little boy whose mamma had caught him swimming when he wasn't supposed to be. From what I could tell, they'd both seen him being run to his house by his mamma, who had a hickory after him, swatting at him every step of the way. They both laughed awful hard at that, like they both knew more to the story that they didn't tell out loud. Finally, Preacher up and said, "My oh my. Where do the years go? That seems like'n 'twarn't all that long ago, but it's been nigh on fifty years reckon."

"Yep," Granny responded. "Time gits away from you. Git up on toward our age, and the years pass by at a murderous fast pace." She got real quiet then said, "Yep. One day you git old 'nuff to know that if'n it keeps up, one day you'll be dead." And everybody else got quiet, because they knew Granny was talking about herself.

Might have been an awkward quiet, even for grown-ups, if Aunt Lois hadn't come out and announced that Sunday dinner had been set. She made polite greetings to our guests; then she held the door for everybody to come in. Everybody except me. "We're gonna need those chairs," she said. So I grabbed them to take in. Granny saw to it that everybody got settled. Aunt Lois poured tea, and it was time to eat. Everything sat out where we could pass the food all around; everything except the cobbler we'd made the night before. It rested on top of the wood stove, warming a spell. Then Granny looked over to Preacher and with the nicest voice asked him, "Buford, will you return thanks?"

I'll always remember that prayer. Not only did Preacher thank God for the food, but he also said right nice things about Granny and asked the Lord to be with her and help her and bless her. When he finished, everybody opened their eyes, and Granny said "Thank ye, Buford" to Preacher, and I reckon by the way she said it and the red around her eyes she meant it. And, except for the invisible high-tension wire that seemed to be strung between Preacher's sister and Aunt Lois, it made for a fine Sunday dinner. The meal was so nice that it seemed to make the day holy, so I reckon we pleased the Lord. I know it pleased Granny.

XVI

THE BEAUTY OF a Smoky Hollow October couldn't ever be beat. The colors on the trees made the woods look all special, and see-ing your breath for the first time in a year made for a seasonal rite of passage. My birthday's at the end of October, so that made it special, too.

I needed to get dressed and go do chores before running off to school, but we'd had a frost, and I loved spending a little time sit-ting by the window after a frost. There'd be real pretty crystal designs on the window, and I liked to look at them before getting rid of them. Not that I was special keen on getting rid of them, but I knew if I didn't the first peek of sun would. So I'd sit there, just enjoying the frost, and every so often I'd put my thumb up to the window and watch a section melt away. So, part by part, the nighttime frost artist's picture ran down the window in cold watery trails.

After getting in the milk for the day, gathering eggs, and putting out hay for our cows, I had a good breakfast and took off for school. Daddy had left by this time, and Granny expected Aunt Lois directly and said she didn't need a baby-sitter anyway, and so I went on. Daddy liked for me to wait and sit with Granny, because he didn't like having her there by herself, but it couldn't always be helped, and Granny, if she took it slow, didn't seem to have too much trouble. So she'd often send me on when I was ready to go. She said to get on and not be late for school on account of some old lady.

It seemed a dreamy day for me in some ways; don't rightly know why, but October days were often like that. Crisp air with a blue sky, high up wispy clouds, and the colors made me think of far away places. Sometimes if I'd just sit and stare at the surroundings, Smoky Hollow did seem like a far off place sometimes in the October air.

Sometimes, just sometimes, the October sky in Smoky Hollow looked a little like a picture I'd seen in one of our books. A feller named Maxfield Parrish painted it, and I paid attention to his name because he did the pictures for one of the old books we used to teach the littl'uns by sometimes—a book called *Mother Goose in Prose*. I can't rightly remember why the picture was there or in what book, but this Parrish feller had drawn a picture that looked

to me like ancient Greece, and I liked to read all those mytho-
logical stories about Zeus and Hercules. But reckon it was the
blue sky in that picture that made it look like a dreamland, or a
place so far away you just couldn't get to it, the kind of place I
always figured I'd like to go to when I dreamed about leaving
Smoky Hollow. And if the sky looked just right in October, I'd
sometimes think to myself that Smoky Hollow blue resembled
that Parrish blue, and maybe I already stood in some far off place
and just didn't know it.

So while I visited one of my far away states of mind Joyce came
up beside me—we often walked to school together by this time.
Sometimes Bobby joined us, but lots of times Joyce and I walked
by ourselves because it didn't take too long for Bobby's not liking
school to work its way down to his feet. He'd often come dragging
in late, acting like he'd just walked twenty miles to get to school,
all puffing and tired acting, disgusted and all. Maybe for him,
coming to school equaled a twenty-mile walk.

Anyway, Joyce and I walked to school together on a regular
basis, being sweet on each other but neither of us saying much
about it. I reckon I must have been looking up and dreaming
because I didn't hear her coming—heck, I didn't even know I was
by her house, that's how caught up dreaming I was. As Joyce's step
fell in with mine, she asked, "Whatcha thinking 'bout?"

By now Joyce knew me to be a bit of a daydreamer, and she
didn't seem to mind. Lots of times we'd talk about things I didn't
talk to anybody else about, not even Bobby. We conversed about

the inside kind of stuff that Aunt Lois always got so danged nasty about, so I figured most folks didn't want to hear it. And even though Bobby was my best friend, I knew he had no interest in the things I dreamed about—he liked it in Smoky Hollow, he liked the rhythm of country life, he liked everything about it. Except, of course, tending garden, which no right-headed boy would like. But with Joyce I could talk. She listened, then she talked, then she listened some more, and I always reckoned we thought alike on a lot of things. Talking to her had gotten easy. So I talked.

"Oh," I said, "just a-thinking 'bout places diff'rent from here and wondering if'n in some ways places diff'rent aren't 'bout the same somehow, too." Then I told her about the blue sky, and how it looked like that picture of a blue sky, and how it made me think about things I hadn't ever seen and places I hadn't ever been.

She just stepped right along with me, listening to my goings on, and then she asked me how far away I wanted to go. I said I didn't rightly know. Then she said something that surprised me, because it showed she had been thinking about us. Or maybe she was just making talk.

"Well, all this talk of yore's 'bout when yore all growed up," she said. "What 'bout next year?"

"What 'bout next year?" I asked back.

"What you gonna do 'bout school and all? Are you going?"

Now, I hadn't given that question too much thought, but she was right to think about it. Smoky Hollow's school just went through eighth grade, and Joyce and I sat that year in the eighth grade, even with her a year older than me. After eighth grade, you had to figure out what you wanted to do, or else your parents figured it out for you. Lots of folks only went through eighth grade and then stopped, taking on more responsibilities at home, helping the family earn a living until marrying time. Heck, eighth grade—lots of the children didn't ever go that far. Some folks needed their children at home to do chores, and they reckoned they didn't need much learning except being able to read a bit, write a bit, and cipher enough not to get cheated by other folks. By eighth grade, about half or more of the children I started with no longer attended school.

Bobby swore eighth grade would be his last. I knew Granny and Daddy wanted me to go on, but we hadn't talked it up or anything, so I didn't rightly know the plan. And danged if I'd never asked Joyce.

"I reckon I'll go," I said, "but I ain't shore or nothing." I figured the grown-ups would decide matters for me. Going on past eighth grade would be a big to-do. There was no schooling to be had in Smoky Hollow once you left Harmony School. You had to go into Ellijay and go to Ellijay Academy if you wanted to get your high school diploma. Not too many did out our way, not in 1942 anyway, because it made for a good deal of trouble. Lots of folks still didn't have automobiles, and most, even if they had them, wouldn't have wanted to drive young'uns back and forth every day to school—too much work to be done. Now Daddy and a few others worked in Ellijay at the mill, but by and large there wasn't any room for a bunch of schoolchildren to be hauled back and forth. It'd be a while yet before we got a county high school with a means to get there. No, if you wanted to go to Ellijay Academy and you didn't live near enough to walk, you had to board at the school, which I don't think anybody in Smoky Hollow had the money to do, or you had to live with a relative or something.

In talking with Joyce, I realized why I hadn't thought too much about schooling for the next year—if I went, it meant living with Aunt Lois. Knowing that Granny and Daddy were for me going on in school and all, it seemed silly that I hadn't ever thought through the consequences of what that meant, but now I knew what it meant, and it stopped me dead in my tracks.

"What's the matter?" Joyce asked.

"Nothing," I said, then started back on down the road, though with a good deal less good will than what I had when I started. Danged! Living with Aunt Lois. Don't reckon I'd ever look at an October blue sky living with her—she'd find a way to make it gray. Danged!

"My Daddy's a-thinking I might orta go on and all, since I do good at schoolwork," Joyce said, obviously proud that her Daddy thought enough of her schoolwork to send her to the academy. "Means I'd have to live with my cousin Louise," and she made a face when she said it, probably close to the way I looked when I said "Aunt Lois." "But I want to go. How 'bout you?"

"Reckon so," I said. "But I ain't shore what I'll be doing, Granny sick and all. Daddy needs me to help out, and he don't like leaving Granny by herself none, and I kinda help out by being with her before and after school or when Aunt Lois can't come, though sometimes Granny sends me on to school anyway."

And as I said "school," there we were. Joyce and I walked in together, as was getting to be the custom, and took our seats. I looked outside at that October blue sky again and wondered where I'd seen that Parrish blue sky. It wouldn't be too hard to find—our school didn't have that many books. And I spent the day thinking about blue skies far and near, strange and familiar, and wondering if I'd ever see anything but Smoky Hollow October blue to take me away in my dreams. And so the day passed, me half in a dream state, half with an eye out for that book, which I found and looked at a bit, and then leaving time arrived. And as I walked from school to Joyce's house, then from Joyce's house to mine, the pretty blue sky started graying up like we could expect to get a soaking fall rain that night. And then I saw a strange car near the house, though it wasn't strange when I saw Aunt Lois on the porch talking to Doc Miller.

"Well, I reckon yore brother done 'splained it to you," Doc Miller said. He stopped when I stepped onto the porch. Aunt Lois's eyes said "Git," so I just kept on walking into the house. Granny wasn't in the front room, and since Doc Miller stood there I figured maybe she had taken to bed because she felt poorly. I leaned up against the inside of the door frame and listened. I figured it didn't make for eavesdropping—she was my Granny and I reckoned I ought to know what was going on.

"Like I was saying," Doc Miller went on, "the doctors down in Marietta 'splained the situation to yore brother, and I've talked to 'im myself. Now Lois, there ain't a thing in the world we can do 'bout this. Yore mamma, bless her heart, just ain't gonna be 'round much longer."

"But she has good days and bad ones," Aunt Lois said. "And 'cepting fer occasional bad spells, she don't seem too awful bad."

"Well, that's the way of it," Doc Miller said. "I bring her this here medicine, but it ain't gonna make her well, Lois; it's just helping her 'long 'til things go bad in a way ain't no medicine gonna help. That's the way of it with this dropsy stuff, and most folks don't even fool with the medicine 'cause of the money and all they don't have. I don't know how yore brother's paying fer it, but he is." He left open a question there, but Aunt Lois didn't offer up an answer, so he went on.

"Now this dropsy, it's about the heart not beating strong 'nuff, and yore mamma don't git 'nuff oxygen. We know that. That's why she's short of breath and shouldn't ever overdo. And it causes fluid on the lungs and all. Don't rightly know why she has it—could be any number of things. Maybe she was sick when she was little with scarlet fever; that can hurt a heart. Maybe it's her blood pressure—whenever I've taken it, it's been high, and they say if'n it stays high all the time then that can cause dropsy when a feller gits older. But whatever the case, Lois, her heart's just plumb wore out, and you can't fix that."

Aunt Lois stood quiet for a minute. Then she said, "Well, what's this medicine fer then?"

"Well, it helps right now," Doc Miller said. "It's got something called digitalis in it, just the right 'mount. Heck, comes from common foxglove. Kill ya if'n ya git too much, but a little bit helps the heart beat stronger and more steady. But it don't work forever, Lois. Just makes her more comfortable right now."

"How are things gonna turn out, then?" Aunt Lois asked.

"Well, two ways this thing can work itself out," Doc said. "She may just keep a-gittin' sicker and sicker, going down some sorta steady over the months. If'n this happens, I'll fix her up with some morphine—it'll help her sleep some and lessen the anxiety of not being able to breathe good. And let me tell you, it can git right bad, ever' ragged breath you figure will be the last, and it goes on like that fer days, maybe even a couple of weeks. Morphine'll help her."

"What's the other way this thing could go?" Lois asked.

"Well, sometimes it's right sudden," Doc said. "Heart goes all bad, rhythm's all shot, and thing'll just shut down. That's the quick way it could go." He stopped for a minute. "That's the good way to go."

So, for the first time, I heard Doc Miller be blunt about Granny. I guess nobody thought I should know too much about things, so they all just talked generally about Granny's bad heart.

But everything I heard Doc Miller say sounded so settled, so like Granny for sure was going to die, and die soon. And I figured if I was going to stand there and listen to grown-up talk about grown-up things, I'd have to be more grown-up like to deal with it. But it was hard, awful hard, like seeing an October blue sky go all gray.

XVII

THE LAST SATURDAY in October broke over Smoky Hollow, and I just lay there enjoying my comfortable bed. After late-October corn-shucking, when we brought in the last of the corn, all dried out for feed and making cornmeal, my mattress had been restuffed. Granny and Daddy slept on feather mattresses, but, like most young'uns in Smoky Hollow, I slept on a corn husk mattress, made from the thin, tender sheaves closest to the corn kernels. Since it was only me, we usually had husks left over, and we saved them for families with bunches of children. But I made sure that the most tender, thinnest sheaves were kept for me. And on this cold October morning it felt good to be snuggled down under my bed coverings, mattress making a place for my body and holding it there, warming it.

I don't know why, but I woke up all excited. I was thirteen. Thirteen years old. Seemed like that had to be a special year, and I was trying my hardest to make it start off special by being all cozy and figuring myself for Mr. Stay-in-the-Bed. I didn't expect a present—I hadn't gotten one for a couple of years. Most us young'uns got maybe a little something up until we reached ten or so, but after that the grown-ups figured children were big enough not to get birthday presents. Still, Granny and Daddy always made my birthday a special day. Granny'd make me fried apple pies and let me eat as many as I wanted. I loved fried apple pies, and I could eat a whole mess of them.

Directly, I heard Daddy calling—"Git up, boy! Yore Granny and me ready fer breakfast, and we want some eggs this morning to fry up."

Now Daddy didn't usually have a mean tone to his voice—he didn't need to. Things got done when he said so and that was it. He didn't have to say something twice because I always got to it the first time as best I could. But this voice sounded strange. So I got me out of bed, threw on some trousers, and walked out to the kitchen where Daddy sat at the table with Granny. There they sat, talking quiet like. No frying pan sat on the wood stove, and they didn't seem to be in a hurry for breakfast. Then Daddy put on a mean sort of face and said, "Go git some eggs, son." I was puzzled by the way he acted, but I figured maybe he was tired, staying up with Granny sometimes and working hard and all. Danged, maybe he just felt ill, though I mostly thought that Aunt Lois held that job in the family.

I walked on outside, feelings hurt a mite. Reckon they were hungry, but they could have said something about my birthday, I figured. So I scuffled along, thinking myself a danged fool because I just then realized I'd walked out without a shirt or shoes, and danged if the air didn't nip at me. So I picked up my feet and ran on to the barn, figuring on grabbing a few eggs so they could have fried eggs—and knowing I'd get some, too, but not dwelling on that too much because it might take me out of my hurt feelings mood. But I stopped in my tracks at the barn door.

I just looked over at the little chicken coop we had fixed up inside the barn. A shotgun leaned against the wall by the coop! And it wasn't some old shotgun or used one or one of Daddy's—it was brand spanking new. My feet finally followed my eyes, and I hurried over to the gun, picking it up and looking at it and all. It had a little bow tied on the end of the barrel, and I knew that meant it belonged to me.

A shiny thing, it was. A shotgun—a twelve-gauge by the looks of it. Looked around for shells but didn't see any. I cracked her open, looking to see if she was loaded, but she wasn't. But danged if the inside barrel didn't shine, too. Then I picked my feet up and headed for the house, making it from ground to porch in one big leap over the three back steps.

Daddy and Granny probably thought I blew into the kitchen like a wild banshee. I didn't have words, which was unusual for the likes of me. But I didn't have any. I didn't know what to say. I hadn't figured on a present, and I knew Daddy worried about money and all, though he didn't hardly let on. Still, you could tell. But there it was, a shiny new shotgun and me thirteen and all and Granny and Daddy sitting there smiling like all get out. And then I saw a box of shells on the table wrapped up in a bow made out of a strip of Granny's quilting fabric. All I could do, since cat had got my tongue, was hold out the shotgun for Daddy and Granny to see, like they hadn't ever seen a shotgun before, or like they hadn't been the ones to put it out in the barn. But I wasn't thinking. I just held it out, proud as a peacock.

"Well, looky there," Granny said. "Where'd you up and find that?" she said.

"In the barn, Granny!" I exclaimed, knowing full well she knew it was in the barn but proud to say so just the same.

"Now that don't look like no little boy's birthday toy," Daddy said. "Must be 'cause they's gittin' to be 'nother grown-up in the house."

Again, I just beamed, seeing if my arms would stretch out any farther to hold out the shotgun. Daddy got up and gave me a right friendly pat on the shoulder. "Hide those eggs in the barrel?" he asked.

Then I remembered about the danged eggs. "That's alrighty," Daddy said. "I'll fetch 'em. You can sit here with yore Granny and see if'n you can figure out how that thing works." He laughed as he said that, heading out the door, because he knew full well I knew how it worked. Daddy had taught me all about shooting.

He came back with the eggs, and then he started in pulling out the mixing bowls. Instead of fried eggs he made slapjacks. I loved slapjacks with lots of butter and covered with sorghum syrup. That rich, dark, gooey liquid on golden brown slapjacks was like having a danged cake for breakfast, if you asked me. A good start to a good day.

There's nothing better than having a birthday on a Saturday. No school to mess with, and no church either. It was a day that was all mine, and excepting for a few things that always had to be done, I had time to enjoy it. And with no little pride I announced to Granny and Daddy that they'd better just figure on having fried rabbit for supper because I planned to go hunting with my very own gun and danged if those rabbits hadn't better watch out!

On toward evening was a good time to get rabbits—they sat out feeding then. So I spent the afternoon getting ready for them, holding my shotgun and aiming it and all. I'd taken the shells and a pencil along with the gun to the hay loft in the barn. Cool October air felt good. With a rain the night before the smell of fall was full in the air, and I sat there enjoying my day. I sat on a bunch of hay, looking out over the field. Some of the leaves still hung on to the trees, making a picture-pretty scene, surrounding our little pasture area that made its way down to the creek.

Danged! What a difference a few months made. I remembered back to the last haying back in August, scorching heat, sweat coming off slicker than snot. Ol' man Withrow had brought out his team of horses, two of them with a blade rigged up on a con-traption they pulled to cut the hay. Daddy and I followed with the

hay cart, pulled by the nag Withrow had also brought. We pitch-
forked like crazy, slinging hay everywhere until you felt hay all
over you, itching you to death. Finally, we finished up. The hay
had been pitched up into the loft, Withrow took his toll—a good
wagon load—and we were done. I hated hay pitching on hot
days, but I had to admit that nothing beat sitting on the stuff in
late October, cool, smelling like a barn ought to smell, like the
land had been put in the barn so that nature didn't stop at the
door. It was nice. I wasn't sitting on top of the hayloft; I sat on
top of the world, least ways as much as a barely thirteen-year-old
boy can.

I had a pencil, and, with a serious outlook, I took every shot-
gun shell out of the box. With pencil in hand, I started labeling.
On the first one I wrote, "Rabbit #1." On the second one I wrote,
"Rabbit #2," and so on until I had done all of them.

About an hour before the sun touched the tops of the mountains, I climbed out of the hayloft. I stuck about six shells in my
pocket, and I went and put the rest in my room. As I walked out
the front door, Granny and Daddy were sitting on the porch.
Granny liked being outside, even if a bit of cold hung in the air.
They had their sweaters on. Granny smiled at me. "My heart's set
on rabbit, son," she told me. "Me, too," Daddy said. And with
that said, I took off over the field to the creek, hopped across,
surefooted on the rocks I knew by heart, and started off up the
other side. I knew where there was a clearing about quarter mile
from the creek, and I figured it made for a good place for rabbits.

I walked a few minutes then stopped to load my shotgun, loading my single shot into the barrel chamber, then snapping it shut like the fiercest hunter that ever lived. Then I walked real quiet to the clearing, going careful, trying not to make a noise to scare off the rabbits.

Three or four rabbits sat there munching. I made out the biggest one. Bringing the shotgun to my shoulder, I closed my left eye and ran my right eye down the barrel to the sighting bead at the tip. I stopped breathing whilst I pulled real slow on the trigger. With a "kablam" and a kick, the shotgun went off, and I saw a rabbit go down. Rest of the rabbits scattered, and I knew better than to try to unload, load, and shoot again—it'd be wasted effort. They scampered off to the safety of the thicket, all except the one. I ran into the clearing and picked up the rabbit—a goodsized one. It'd make for good eating, since the start of cold weather had just started—rabbits fattened up good in the fall for the onset of winter.

I'd brought along an old burlap sack, and I scooped the rabbit up and put him in, tying a knot in the top. Then I cracked open the barrel of my shotgun and popped the shell out. I reached down and picked it up. The side of the shell told the whole story: "Rabbit #1." I put it in my pocket to take home and keep, and I still got it in a box that'd look like junk to anybody else but me. But it's a great box—full of reminders of days like my birthday.

After going to another clearing I reckoned it time to go on home. I didn't figure I had to keep the second shell that said

"Rabbit #2" because I had no rabbit to go with the shell. My streak had already been broken, but danged if it hadn't started off with a bang!

Granny and Daddy saw me coming back home, them looking like they hadn't moved a muscle since I'd left, and looking like there was no reason in the world for them to have to. Porch sitting's an art form, and it took folks with the time to perfect it to make it look right. They looked comfortable, contented, rested, and satisfied. And they looked like they deserved to be—good porch sitters never looked lazy, just rewarded for, not a day of hard work, but for a life of hard work.

When they saw me heading their way, they looked at me right proud, and I looked back at them right proud. Daddy said, "Well, let's dress it so we can eat." Daddy and I went about the task of skinning and cleaning, digging out pellets and cutting up. Like most times with Daddy and me, not much got said. We were happy enough to be in each other's company without having to comment on it or make it seem like we had to talk to make the time pass; Daddy had no interest in making time pass. He enjoyed what he was doing and he enjoyed doing it with me, and I reckoned it was about the best day for a birthday I'd ever had. Only thing said much was when Daddy started in cutting the rabbit up into frying parts. "Yore Uncle Joe's the one showed me how to do this." And he handed me the knife and said, "Let's see if'n I've been as good a teacher as he was." And so I cut the rabbit up the rest of the way, Daddy occasionally saying a word or two to help.

We washed up and started cooking. If Granny couldn't do it sitting down, she didn't do it. So she sat there in the kitchen, watching what she called her two good boys when her eyes stood open, humming church hymns when her eyes closed, and taking in the smells of a kitchen that she knew she didn't rightly run any more. And though she smiled at me once when I looked back from cooking, the lard all melted and hot and crackling when we put those floured-up pieces of rabbit in, her eyes looked tired and a little sad. I reckon her poor heart couldn't push the good feeling up much further than her upturned lips. And even though she bragged on my rabbit and how good it tasted, she didn't eat very much. I think even meals had gotten tiresome for her.

After Daddy and I cleaned up, she worked on her quilt. She napped between stitches, and sometimes, I think, dreamed good dreams. I guess I thought, inasmuch as a thirteen-year-old boy can pick up on this kind of thing, that the quilt was being made for Uncle Joe, but that its real purpose was to help Granny remember "Joey" and think back on days long past.

XVIII

You can look at something all your life, but if you haven't ever done it, it seems all brand new and spooky, especially if it's supposed to be something special. It was that way for me the last Sunday of October, because that was the first time I got to partake of the Lord's Supper.

We always had the Lord's Supper four times a year in our church, or once a quarter as Preacher would say. Once asked Granny, then Daddy, why we did it once a quarter, and the only reason they knew of is that we had always done it that way, which seemed to them to be a good reason to keep doing it once a quarter. I reckon that made for as good a reason as any. I decided I wouldn't get too far asking why it was always held on the last

Sunday of the month, or reckoned I'd get the same answer, so I figured the question was as good as asked.

I'd always been fascinated by the Lord's Supper. Every time we had it Preacher would stand behind this big oak table with the words "In Remembrance of Me" carved in the front. And he'd read about how Jesus had a last supper with his disciples; then he'd read a section about how Jesus said to do this in remembrance of him and so that was what we were doing.

Remembering Jesus seemed to be about mostly remembering how Jesus died. Preacher did good at helping us remember what Jesus felt. He'd get us to thinking about how we had a nail in our hand or foot once, or if that hadn't ever happened to us then maybe we had got us a big old briar stuck in our hand or foot or leastways we'd been scratched by briars. Then Preacher'd make as how Jesus had the biggest nails and the biggest briars for the longest times in the tenderest parts of his hands and feet and wasn't the pain awful. He would have me hurting by the time he'd finished describing it all. And then he'd say as how it should have been all us hurting like that for real, not Jesus, but that God sent Jesus to hurt for us. That constituted remembering right, Preacher would say.

Then, after Preacher had repeated the words from the Bible about "This is my body, this is my blood, do this in remembrance of me," the deacons would fetch trays full of broken-up crackers, and they'd pass the trays around, everybody who was baptized taking a piece then handing off the tray to the next person until the tray made it to the end of the pew. Then another deacon would take it and hand it back to the next pew full of folks.

Everybody would hold onto their piece of cracker until everybody had a piece because Preacher said the Apostle Paul hollered at some folks for eating before others had a chance, so we ought to all eat together. Preacher would then put that piece of cracker in his mouth and chew on it like a regular big slice of bread, chewing and chewing with his eyes all closed like it was the best bread he had ever tasted, excepting he wasn't glad because sometimes after he had finished eating he'd open his eyes and they'd be all red.

Then the grape juice would get passed around. Now the Bible part Preacher always read said bread and wine, but we always had crackers and grape juice. I always thought our little cups looked like shot glasses, which I remarked on once. That brought a glare from Granny that would peel paint off a wall. So I didn't say it anymore, though I still thought it.

Juice got passed out after the crackers in the same way, and everybody would hold the cup real still until everybody had some so everybody could drink together. Then Preacher'd say, "This is my blood, which is shed fer you," and everybody would drink. The racks that held the hymnals had little cup holders attached to them, and you could always tell the Lord's Supper was over because you'd hear the clickety click of folks dropping their empty shot glasses into the little hole that held them. Then we'd always sing "Amazing Grace" and leave.

Course, like I said, it was one thing to watch this solemn-like event four times a year; another to participate. Since I'd been baptized, I got to be part of it. Granny said it would be real special, because I'd just turned thirteen, meaning I was growing up, and that I was growing up in the church, too, being all baptized and eating the Lord's Supper. She was proud, I could tell, as Daddy and me took off for church. By then, Granny didn't go anymore—the steps challenged her poor heart too much.

So there I sat, with everybody from the family who was there, including Daddy. He always came down from the choir and sat with the family during the Lord's Supper. I got all nervous. With the cracker, I held it in my hand a long time it seemed. My palm sweated, and I thought as how I might ought to put the cracker in my other hand so it wouldn't get all wet. That's what I did, and as soon as I did it, Aunt Lois leaned across Mildred and said to me in a loud whisper meant for Daddy as well as me, "That ain't to play with. Hold still."

So Aunt Lois kind of ruined my first taste of communion cracker. But the cracker was nothing compared to the grape juice. It may not look too hard, but it's harder than it looks to sit there and hold that shot glass all still and making sure nothing spills out. I about went dizzy trying to hold the thing all straight and even, and I kept worrying that it was tilted some, and my grip was too tight, and my hands got all sweaty again, and I hoped Aunt Lois would keep her whispering to herself. More with relief than a thankful heart like Preacher said to have, I took my first little swig of that grape juice.

We all started to shuffle out after singing. Course, since we sat up near the front, that meant we brought up the rear of the line to shake Preacher's hand, and so we always had us a bit of a wait. Bobby had come with his mamma and all—his daddy didn't have a place worn out in the pew, though he came sometimes. But I reckoned lots of times somebody had to stay home with Bobby's brother. They sat near the back. Bobby would wait on me, though his mamma would usually mosey on home. If it was nice weather, Bobby and I would walk home, him leaving me and heading on once we got to my place.

So Bobby walked out and I waited with the impatience of a boy inside on a cool, crisp October day. All of a sudden, I hear as how Mildred let on to her mamma that she really needed to go, and so she headed out toward the basement stairs, which would take her out a back door and round about to the outhouse. That surprised me, because at Aunt Lois's house they had an inside bathroom, and Mildred didn't much like going to the outhouse at our place, so I figured she really had to go to use the one at church.

We finally made our way up to Preacher, and we got to say our greetings and all. Surprise took hold of me when Daddy said, "I'll see you a little later on." Preacher said he'd be at our house at the appointed time, and it sounded all solemn. "Preacher coming again fer dinner?" I asked Daddy. He said no, and I let it drop there because we had stepped outside, and I wanted to find Bobby.

I looked around but didn't see him. I didn't see Mildred either, so I thought I'd head back around the church toward the out-house and see if she was headed back.

I scooted down around the corner of the church and headed for the back. I got to the back corner of the church, and I didn't see anybody heading my way from the outhouse, and so I stopped about the time I passed the back corner.

Out of the side of my eye all of a sudden I saw two people, and all of a sudden I knew it to be Bobby and Mildred. For a second neither one of them realized that I stood right there, and I saw Mildred giving Bobby a kiss on the cheek. Then I reckon I must have made some noise, because all of a sudden they looked over at me and turned all embarrassed and red. Mildred told Bobby right quick, "I'd better go find Mamma 'fore she wonders what happened to me," and then she quick stepped it past me. As she went by, though, she gave me a little shy smile and said, "See you at dinner."

So I was left with just Bobby, and we headed toward the road to go home. We didn't talk much because I think we were both a little embarrassed, but when we got to my house and him fixing to leave, I asked, "Was it nice?" and he said "Yeah."

I walked on down to my house, and I saw Mildred on the porch waiting for me. She had that shy smile again. And when she said, "You won't tell Mamma or nothing will you?" I wasn't surprised and said, "Course not." And then we walked in together and went about our normal Sunday routine, getting Sunday dinner together.

About midafternoon Preacher came by. He stood with Daddy out on the porch a while, and Aunt Lois said she'd go tell Granny that Preacher had come. Granny had gone to take a nap after the little pecking at dinner she did.

Finally, Daddy brought Preacher in, and Daddy indicated that we should all sit down real nice. Then Aunt Lois walked out with Granny shuffling along behind her, all dressed up in her Sunday dress and with her Sunday brooch that she'd gotten from her mamma sitting at the top of her dress at the neck. She went and sat down in her chair, and when Daddy went to lift her legs up on the stool so her feet would be up, she said, "No, thank ye, son. I'd like to sit proper fer this."

And with that, Preacher opened up his Bible and laid it on his lap. Then he opened a tin he had with him and reached in and pulled out a soda cracker, a little vial, and two little shot glasses, and placed them on the table next to him. Then I knew the Lord's Supper was being celebrated again for Granny. I reckoned it'd be just Preacher and Granny because only two cups sat out and the rest of us had already had communion that morning. I reckon Preacher had brought church to Granny because Granny always found the remembrance of Jesus' last supper to be real meaningful. I knew because I'd seen the way she acted at church.

Preacher opened with a prayer, and we all closed our eyes and listened to him. A right kindly prayer issued forth, a lot of it about Granny and her sickness and God taking care of her and all. He talked about Jesus' troubles and how if God stood with

Jesus during his troubles then surely he'd stand with Granny during hers. Then he read all the same Bible verses that he'd read at church that morning. Then he and Granny shared the Lord's Supper, and the rest of us watched. Granny sat straight up all during the reading. Her head tilted up a mite, like she was looking at heaven. And when Preacher said, "Remember," I know she remembered, because tears began to run down her cheeks, and in a quiet voice she said, "Bless the Lord."

Granny did same as Preacher with the cracker half—she chewed on it a right smart, like savoring a good piece of meat, eyes all closed, thinking about nothing but the chewing. She took the shot glass and drank the sip of grape juice in it, and when she gave the cup back to Preacher she whispered, "Thank ye, Buford."

With that, Preacher stood up, and he started in on singing "Amazing Grace," just like we always did at church. Granny stood up, too. Aunt Lois went over and tried to see if she didn't want to sit back down, but all Aunt Lois got for her trouble was a look that said no. Preacher knew Granny's weakness, though, and as we sang he jumped straight from the first verse to the last verse. Then, as the singing stopped, he went over, took Granny's hand, and whispered something in her ear, a prayer I reckon, and then he took his leave, Daddy walking out with him.

Granny sat back down in her chair, and Aunt Lois placed the stool under her feet, what as had a big feather pillow on it. We all waited for Granny's dismissal, and she looked around at us all and smiled, saying, "Wasn't that awful thoughtful of Buford?" And she hadn't no more than said it as her eyes closed up, and that meant time to rest.

Granny's spirit reached us all, and it made for a peaceful Sunday. We didn't all take naps, but a quietness sat on us, compared to how we could sometimes be. And so I spent the day mostly with Mildred, occasionally in the company of Daddy and Uncle Henry, and never in the company of Aunt Lois and Mildred's sisters. They stayed inside while Mildred and I stayed outside mostly enjoying what little warmth that was left to the year. And in quiet conversations about nothing in particular and everything in general, the day slipped away.

Lazy days sometimes bring lazy nights, the kind of night that's just an extension of the daytime, where you lie there all quiet and comfortable but not all that sleepy. A good time for recollecting and enjoying being in bed. That's the way it was for me that night. And so as the recollecting went on, my mind found its way around the corner of the church, and there stood Mildred and Bobby kissing.

I stood and watched for the longest time. I wondered what it felt like, to have a girl you liked kiss you and all. I watched and wondered what if it was me getting kissed, and then, the way it works in those slow-moving daydreams, the kind that verge on night dreams, there I stood back behind the church, and I could feel the lips on my cheek, and it was Joyce there instead of Mildred. And I lay there just thinking about Joyce, about her kissing me and all. I lay there thinking about that and about her presence, her just being with me, and how that made me feel. I enjoyed her presence, almost so real that it seemed she was there with me. And nothing seemed wrong about it, and I don't think there was.

XIX

Arvil Davis raised the best blue tick hound dogs in Gilmer County. About anybody who did any serious coon hunting would end up haggling with Arvil over the price of a hound. Arvil didn't haggle too much, though more than he used to.

My Daddy told me that back in the late teens and early twenties, after the war and him just home from Europe, recovering from being gassed a bit (more than a bit and he'd be dead, he said), that a good coon skin hide would bring eighteen dollars, more than you could make working all month at the mill. Said the danged Yankees were in the middle of some craze, and that they all had to have coonskin coats, especially the college crowd.

Well, Arvil provided the dogs, and the price coon brought was so good and Arvil's dogs were so good that just about all the coons got killed out around town, in the valleys, and the easy-to-get-to places. Brought in a lot of money, and Arvil, they said, got a hundred fifty dollars for a trained coon dog, and blue tick hound dogs made the best coon dog.

Course, times had changed by the early forties. If you were going to hunt coon, it was more involved, first of all because you had to head up into the mountains a spell to find much coon. Second, you didn't make as much on each skin as when that coonskin coat craze was going on. Third, you needed a dog from Arvil Davis, and he still remembered the good ol' days, and he still tried to charge the same, though he couldn't. Still, a good coon hound cost a right smart, so you had to be sure you were going to hunt enough to make up the difference. And that's what Bobby's daddy did—he hunted coon for a living, and he hunted a good deal, and he brought in a right many coons.

Bobby's daddy had three blue tick hounds, all trained by Arvil Davis. But that was alright, because Bobby's daddy knew the mountains good and he had one of the best shots around and he had the personality for a life of coon hunting. He was the kind of feller who could stay out all night, come in and see to things around the house, then sleep during the day. His nights and days didn't go getting all mixed-up like with some folks. He, along with everybody who knew him, considered himself a natural born coon hunter. Good thing, because I couldn't ever see Bobby's daddy holding down a regular job.

Early November had come, and it seemed kind of cold for the time of year. I waited outside Bobby's house because I was going with Bobby, who was going with his daddy and some other folks to go coon hunting.

I sat out on the steps, petting on the oldest of the coon dogs— Ol' Blue. Reckon everybody who had a blue tick hound dog named it some variation of Blue. Bobby's daddy called his three dogs Ol' Blue, Blue Boy, and Bluford, that last being a joke on Preacher, reckon, because Preacher's name was Buford. Sometimes Bluford would start in howling the way hounds do, just because they like to howl sometimes like a boy just likes to run sometimes even when there's no place to be running to. Bobby's daddy, if he was outside on the porch or out gathering honey or something, would just laugh and say, "Bring the word, Bluford, bring the word."

Ol' Blue sat next to me with his head leaning against my leg, with me petting and scratching his head real good. He made for a fine dog, having the black, tan, and white coloring you see on most beagles. Plus, of course, the patches of blue-tinted fur that showed up all the bluer for being laid against the white fur. He lay there a right calm dog, saving most of his energy for the hunt. He liked to be petted, and he liked having his belly scratched like all dogs do. He was good company just for sitting a spell. If you wanted to play fetch, the younger dogs were best for that. But I was satisfied just to sit and wait and pet Ol' Blue's head.

Finally I heard the door open, the screen door's metal spring screeched as it stretched, and Bobby came out dressed for the hunt. He looked a lot like me—boots, thick pants, a good shirt and jacket, and a hunting cap with pull down covers for the ears, lined with rabbit fur. He plunked down beside me, and we both waited for the men to come on out.

I was a little surprised that Bobby was going—he'd been sick earlier in the week, intestinal problems, and he still looked all flushed out. He hadn't been to school all week, but I reckon the thought of going hunting made him feel better. His daddy had stopped by and asked my daddy if I could come along, and Daddy said sure. That was on Thursday, and this was Friday. Daddy wouldn't have let me go on Saturday because of church—no use going to church to sleep, he said, and if I stayed up all night I'd be wanting to sleep. But it was Friday, the air was nippy enough to make you feel good and alive, I was going coon hunting, which was exciting because of how late you stayed up and the way it all worked, and I was going with my best friend, who I hadn't seen all week at school. I figured that made for a danged good Friday night.

Directly the men all came out. There were Bobby's daddy; his youngest brother, Matthew; Bobby's mamma's oldest brother, Andrew; and a friend of theirs from off Northcutt way, a feller named Ed Neeley. I reckon they had all grown up together, but Ed's wife had property of her daddy's out Northcutt way, so he'd always lived out there after getting married. They all stood around at the bottom of the steps. Bobby and I hopped up as soon as the door flew open so as to be out of their way.

Bobby's brother stood looking out the screen door—it was cold, and he didn't get out much in the cold, not sitting on the porch like he did in the summer and early fall. Whenever Bobby talked about it, it sounded like his brother wasn't getting any better. Bobby said Doc thought maybe a big shell exploded near his head, and he had shell madness. Doc told Bobby's daddy that they might be able to do something for him down in Atlanta at the veteran's hospital. But Bobby said his daddy told Doc that he reckoned they could sit and watch him as well as any nurses, and he figured that's all they'd be doing—watching him, because he told Doc he hadn't ever heard of anybody getting over shell madness.

Then Bobby's daddy told Doc of a feller near his age, one who'd gone off to war when Daddy did back in the teens—a feller who still marched the fields like he was at war if nobody stopped him. Wasn't let out much, but he got out every now and again. I remembered about a year before, maybe less because fall wasn't so far along, I'd seen the feller when Bobby and I had gone off walking—walked past the school, past the church, and after a couple of miles came to the place where the man lived with his daddy and mamma and a sister who never got married because she had to stay home and help with her brother. Good thing, probably, because the daddy and mamma were Granny's age now, and they needed help.

Anyway, he had gotten out that day, and I saw his sister trying to chase him down, him dodging around in the garden. He had pulled up a cornstalk, using it like a gun, shooting at his sister and screaming and hollering. Bobby and I watched until the sister caught her brother and took him in, talking with words I couldn't hear but that seemed to calm him down. Then I think he started in crying, because his shoulders started hunching up and down. Seemed real sad. I reckoned Bobby remembered it too, and that made him sad enough never to want to talk about his brother much. Just pieces, here and there.

We all took off for the hunt, Bobby throwing his hand up in a half wave at his brother as we left. Bobby marched along fast, like he was a soldier himself, putting distance between himself and the house like he was at the front. He walked fast, and soon we had made it to the end of his folks' pasture. We stopped there while waiting for the men to catch up. We'd need Bobby's daddy to know where up in those hills to go.

Soon the menfolk caught up with us, and Bobby's daddy told Bobby he'd better slow down or he'd be all tuckered out with a lot of walking still to do. So, while light lasted, Bobby and I walked behind the men. Bobby's daddy led the way, seeming to follow deer trails after a while because there wasn't much in the way of people trails.

Bobby and I took the chance to catch up on the week. I told him what had gone on at school, though wasn't ever much that went on, so there wasn't much to tell. I told him about a ten-year-old boy who had put a tack in the seat of an eight-year-old, and the eight-year-old jumped up screaming. The teacher didn't know what was going on at first, but when she got the whole story that ten-year-old got his what for. Miss Stover could be real nice if you stayed on her good side, but she had an arm on her and could blister your backside if she needed to, and she did that day.

Bobby then up and asked me if I had walked to school with Joyce all week, and I told him I had. He laughed and poked me in the ribs. But he didn't poke too hard, because directly he asked me if he could come over on Sunday for dinner. I told him I didn't see why not. Daddy and Granny were used to seeing him at our table, and it wouldn't seem odd. Then came my turn to poke back.

"Course, you could just come fer dinner tomorrow. Come back to the house with me, and we can sleep a spell and then eat. Don't got nothing to do tomorrow other'n usual chores, and I'll probably take care of 'em 'fore going to bed in the morning."

Bobby scrunched his shoulders a bit and said, "Naw. I was a-hoping fer some fried chicken, and I reckon I'm more likely to git that on a Sunday." He was right, of course. But I poked again.

"Well, shore," I said, "but I might talk Granny and Daddy into something special tomorrow."

"Naw, I don't think so. Reckon I'll be too tired."

"Well, alright, come on Sunday, but Aunt Lois ain't coming, so I don't know as how we'll have fried chicken."

That got a rise out of Bobby. "What d'ya mean she ain't coming?" he asked. "She always comes on Sunday. The whole danged family comes on Sunday. From what you said yore Aunt Doris is coming ever' other Sunday now." That was true. Aunt Doris visited more often, knowing Granny to be sick and all. With her and hers and Aunt Lois and hers, us children were left to find a place to eat as best we could, just so long as we weren't at the table, which was filled up with adults mostly, and Mildred's two oldest sisters. I once said it wasn't right, but then Aunt Lois let me know that her two oldest weren't young'uns anymore, not like me. Probably never were young'uns—always trying to act older than they were ever since I could remember.

"Still," I said to Bobby, "Aunt Lois has been visiting a lot, and I reckon she said last week that they was all a-staying at home this Sunday."

Bobby mulled that over a minute. "What 'bout church? They'll at least be coming to church."

"Nope," I said. "Aunt Lois said as how they all needed some rest, and so she reckoned they might just stay in Ellijay and run over to Ellijay Baptist."

"Oh," Bobby said, obviously disappointed.

"You can still come over and eat, though. Yep, sit there and moon over Mildred not being there."

Bobby turned his head to say something, but I burst out laughing. I knew why Bobby wanted to come eat with us—to see Mildred. Those two had been sweet on each other since the summer. With school starting and with Granny sick, Bobby and I had less and less reason to run into town as it got colder—no apple crates to make and no apples to pick. So he didn't get to see Mildred too much. Sometimes we still went into town for the movies, but not like back in the summer. Plus, with school going on, Mildred didn't come out much except on Sundays for church. Bobby was hoping to see her somewhere outside church. They talked a little before and a little after church, but that didn't make for much visiting time.

Bobby gave me a little shove and just said, "Dang you." Then we just walked, although I noticed Bobby's pace had slowed up. I reckoned him to be tired from being sick the front end of the week.

We walked along the trail until darkness crept up on us. Bobby's daddy stopped, and we settled down for our supper. Bobby's daddy said we'd gone as far as we were going along this particular deer trail, and we'd start heading deeper into the mountains after supper, so me and Bobby better stay caught up so as not to get lost.

Soon the men had a little fire going, and we sat in a little clearing near a creek. The menfolk passed around a mason jar full of whiskey before supper, and then we all sat down to eat. Bobby's daddy had a satchel that had some biscuits and ham, and he warmed them up over the fire. He sent Bobby down to the creek to get a kettle full of water to put on to boil. I thought to myself that Bobby must have been really tired from being sick because he limped down and back. His daddy then made some strong coffee, told everybody to drink up so everybody would stay awake. Even Bobby and me had some, though I didn't much like it. The hotness, though, felt good going down in the November cold.

After we finished up supper, Bobby's daddy washed out the utensils—the iron skillet, kettle, and tin cups used for coffee drinking—down at the creek; then he put it all back in the satchel and tied it to a tree limb near the creek to pick up on his way back. The menfolk passed around the mason jar once more, and we headed out.

The lanterns were lit so we'd have light to cross the creek. Bobby's daddy had been this way many times, and he had put out some big rocks so you could get across without getting your shoes wet. Creek wading felt nice in the summer without shoes, but nobody wanted wet feet on a cold November night. We still had miles to walk.

Bobby's daddy stepped across first, holding a lantern to light the rocks. Then he stood on the other side, holding the lantern out so we all could see. Bobby and I went last, and I let Bobby go ahead of me.

Bobby's first step came down solid. But on his second, it looked like his leg buckled, and he lost his balance and fell into the water. He spluttered as he pulled himself up out of the creek, and his daddy let out a loud, "Well, God Almighty, son."

There wasn't much to be said after that. No question about us going on. Bobby stood wet all over, chilled to the bone, and already shivering up a storm. His daddy didn't even come across to see if he was alright, just told him to get on home and get out of the wet clothes he was in. Then we watched as Bobby's daddy turned and went on up into the mountains, men laughing at Bobby's fall, Bobby's daddy cussing it, and hound dogs happy to be out on the hunt.

Bobby's pride was sore hurt. A half moon showed itself, and we might have made it home going real slow and careful along the deer track until we got back to nearer Bobby's home, but we didn't have to rely on just the moon. Up by the satchel hung an extra lantern, Bobby saying his daddy always left one extra there in case he needed an extra for some reason. So we lit it up and made our way back, and though it took only a little over an hour to get to where we parted off the deer track, it must have taken a couple to get back to Bobby's house. Bobby had to drag his leg, and when I asked him what was wrong, he said it felt like his leg had gone all numb.

We finally got to Bobby's house. I went in with him, but everybody was already sleeping. The coal stove they had for heat was going, but I went out with the coal bucket and got a bit more in, threw it on, and fanned it good until the flames blazed good and hot. Bobby sat nearby, trying to warm up some but shivering like crazy. He kept pounding on that leg of his. Said he'd beat the feeling back into it if he had to. I couldn't figure out why it had gone to sleep like it had.

Weariness had settled on us good, so I grabbed a couple of blankets out of his room, being careful not to wake his brother, and we slept by the stove that night, Bobby and me. I figured I'd just stay the night since nobody expected me back at my place until morning.

There we slept until the sound of men full of whiskey and heavy with coon woke us at daybreak. I reckoned that as good a time as any to make my own way home so I could milk the cow and bring in the eggs and throw out hay. Heck, I'd been helping Daddy with the cooking lately, so I figured I might even surprise Granny and Daddy if they weren't up yet and fry up some eggs for their breakfast. So off I went, waving at Bobby at the door and hoping the racket of the menfolk would wake Bobby's mamma so she could attend to him. It was clear his daddy wouldn't be seeing to him anytime soon, and I thought then that that made for a sorry state of affairs.

Things got sorrier.

By Tuesday they had closed the whole danged school. All that weekend Bobby had a bad time, and by Sunday his folks figured something really was wrong, so his daddy went to fetch Doc Miller. By Monday Doc Miller had diagnosed Bobby with polio, and by Monday evening school had been called off for a spell.

I sat thinking about Bobby, about how on the one hand they said they thought he was lucky, because it looked like just the one leg would be crippled. It could have been worse—could have been both legs, could have been where he had to go in an iron lung, though I'd never seen one and didn't rightly know what it was at the time. He could have died. So "lucky" was how people talked about it, but I don't reckon Bobby thought himself lucky, because he'd never be the fastest runner again.

I couldn't see Bobby for a while because they weren't letting anybody in but Doc Miller—under quarantine, they said. So, with no school, I spent a whole lot of time reading and sitting with Granny and making sure the house stayed warm. About the only thing to break up the time was Sunday, when everybody came over like usual. I was glad to see Mildred. Course they all came over after church, and after dinner got cleared away, Mildred and I set out to walk a spell to get out of the house. Nobody seemed to care so we went on.

Mildred wasn't her usual self—she seemed right down. After we had kicked our fair share of rocks down the road we found ourselves in front of the church. We took it upon ourselves to sit on the front steps and look over at the new part of the graveyard, looking all the more grave because the cold fall air had taken the leaves off most of the trees at the back border. They had taken on their dead look—dead for a season, anyway.

After we sat in silence a while, taking in the scenery, Mildred up and said what I figured had been gnawing at her.

"Mamma says ain't no shots or nothing fer Bobby."

"No, reckon not," I answered.

"Is he bad?" she asked. I think she wanted to know all about Bobby but didn't want to appear none too interested to her mamma. So she'd been saving up questions to ask me.

So I told her all I knew. I told her that he'd been sick in the stomach and then told her about him falling and his hard time with his leg going numb. Then I told her what I'd heard Granny and Daddy saying, how it looked like it'd be just the one leg crippled up, and how with a metal brace he should be able to get around.

"Can we go see 'im?" she asked.

"Naw," I said. "His place is quarantined. Just family and Doc Miller." She sat and thought a minute.

"I bet he's scairt," she said. And I reckoned how I thought she was right.

"Why don't we write 'im a letter, you and me, and we can go put it in his letter box," she said.

So we walked back home and wrote on some letters. It surprised me that I didn't have too much to say, mostly that I hoped he felt better. But Mildred. Danged. She must have written three pages. We found some envelopes, and I asked Daddy if Mildred and I could go as far as Bobby's letter box to put in a letter meant to cheer him up a bit. Mildred said not to mention anything about her letter. Daddy said "yes," Aunt Lois wanted to say "no," but she figured if I went to the trouble to write, then Bobby ought to get the letter and maybe it'd help the poor boy feel a mite better. She sounded right nice until we left, and I heard her tell Daddy that now she reckoned Bobby'd have to slow down and not go barreling into places like a danged wild animal. I didn't think it was right to say that. Still, she said go and we went and delivered our letters. And as we left Bobby's house, Ol' Blue came and offered his head for petting. I obliged him, him being a dog and not really knowing the sorry thing that had happened since I last petted that head.

XX

THANKSGIVING CAME UP on us and brought with it a real special time. With Granny all sick everybody pitched in so we could have our regular good meal. We ate good all the time, but Thanksgiving was different. All the family gathered in, and we had us enough food to feast on for a couple of days. Even me with my appetite ate my fill on Thanksgiving. And I reckon everybody that year gave special thanks that Granny still walked among us.

No matter how many folks came into the house, Thanksgiving taught a good lesson; there was always room enough. I didn't ever feel crowded out, and instead of feeling aggravated, the bumping elbows with everybody just made it seem more like family. The grown-ups ate at the table, and us young'uns ate where we could. If

November ran warm, we even ate out on the porch. But it was too cold that November. I heard Uncle Henry tell Daddy that it could be a right cold winter with snow. Daddy reckoned he might be right—squirrels were danged full in the tail, and he figured they knew of something headed our way.

Some folks would remember the sight of a table set nice, or the sight of all the food in the kitchen. Some might remember the noises—the clinking of dishes, smacking of lips, appreciative grunts, all mixed in with a goodly amount of talking. But me, I always remember the holiday smells. The smell of a couple of days cooking seemed to settle right into the very wood, and it made for a right homey smell, a right Thanksgiving-y smell.

The fine fat bird that we gnawed away at was Daddy's doing. He'd told Granny he knew where he could find some wild turkeys, so we'd have turkey for Thanksgiving. He'd brought it in and dressed it, then we'd taken it down to Aunt Lois to take care of. I reckon Daddy thought that with us taking care of Granny and all, Lois would have more time to do the turkey up right. And, I have to admit, she'd done a nice job. She'd smoked the thing up, and Mildred said she'd worked right hard, going between the stove in the kitchen checking on pies and running outside to check on the turkey, where she had set it up to smoke.

Turkey tasted good, but when anybody'd brag on the squirrel and dumplings I let them know how it was me as shot the squirrels. The whole feast did Daddy and me proud. Though everybody brought something, it was Daddy and I who'd put on the beans, warmed up the corn we had creamed back in August, and cut up the taters to fry, taking them from their cool place in the barn, buried beneath some straw. And Daddy had fixed up the squirrel and dumplings, Granny giving instructions as he went but him not needing them too much, because that was something that Daddy could already fix.

Now, we ate good on Thanksgiving. But I thought that we always ate good. So, after getting through all the meat and vegetables and bread, time came for what made Thanksgiving Thanksgiving to my mind—the desserts.

Thanksgiving and Christmas were the only times of year when we had more than one dessert. And even though I ate good on all that other stuff, I craved the desserts. Aunt Doris had brought a couple of pecan pies and a sweet potato pie. Aunt Lois had brought in a cherry pie and a peach pie. Daddy and I had fried up some apple pies. And being a boy of thirteen and all, I had at least a couple of bites of it all. There was plenty, and there'd be plenty left, but Thanksgiving wouldn't be Thanksgiving if I didn't have a bite of five or six desserts.

The end of Thanksgiving dinner came gradually but surely. For one thing, more talking went on, but it was real slow and lazy talking, like most of the effort had gone into eating and what was left was conserved for the kind of easy speaking that would linger on the rest of the day. And nothing seemed better than just a few more bites of a piece of pie to make the afternoon conversation right peaceful. That end-of-dinner pie nibbling worked like grease on a hinge—helped open things up with a minimum of squeaking. Everybody talked nice and quiet after a good meal followed up by pie nibbling, a big ol' glass of sweet tea to wash it all down.

Much as Granny enjoyed things, she excused herself to go and take a little nap. Daddy helped her up and to her room, her taking the little baby steps that had started to mark her walk. Daddy pulled her door to some, but not all the way—the heat from the stove in the living room needed to make its way in so Granny didn't get too chilled. Mildred and I had finished our pie nibbling, so we spread out on the living room floor, taking it easy, letting our stomachs settle. We had out the checkerboard. Aunt Doris's brood had slipped on coats and were walking around outside the house. They were younger than me, all of them, and couldn't hardly stay cooped up all the time—no patience for it. Mildred's sisters sat cozy together on the couch, looking bored and uppity and having time only for each other.

During that end-of-meal quiet time, while Mildred and I played, giving out the occasional grunt in recognition of each other's moves, I listened in on the grown-ups in the dining room. They still nibbled at pie, and I reckon that relaxed atmosphere loosened up Daddy's mouth a bit, lots of times a hinge rusted shut, it seemed, and I heard him talking about Granny. Mostly he talked about her hopes for Christmas, and what it would be like in her mind when Uncle Joe came.

"I hope he ain't playing some danged trick on her," Daddy said.

"She's pining away wanting 'im to come. She's got just a bit left on that quilt, and then she's done." He stopped and let out a big sigh. "Sometimes I think her a-working on that quilt's all that's keeping her alive. I hate to see her finish it. Seems to enjoy it so."

"Think Joey will really come?" Aunt Doris asked. She asked it in her fragile voice, and I turned back to look at them all. Uncle Olin had his hand on her shoulder, like he had to prop her up, like she would have fallen right over if he didn't have that hand on her. Nobody ever talked about Aunt Doris being sick, but danged if she wasn't one of the feeblest-looking well persons I'd ever seen.

"I dunno," Daddy said. "Normally I reckon I'd say no. But we got us a letter just recently, a real long letter, and Joey ended up saying he was a-coming fer shore. That made Mamma real happy."

Daddy said something else, but I didn't catch it. Mildred grunted out, "Ha," and I realized that she had my last piece trapped. "Two in a row," Mildred said. "Ain't you paying 'tention?" she asked.

"'Nuff to beat you," I said, and we set up again. I figured the best way to keep listening in was to keep Mildred occupied with the game, even if it meant I didn't pay attention and was getting whipped pretty badly. Mildred was good, and you had to pay attention to beat her.

By the time she had made her first move and me mine, quietness had fallen on us again, and now I heard Aunt Lois talking in a real low voice, hard to make out, sounding not much like Aunt Lois because it sounded soft.

"What was all diff'rent 'bout the letter?" she asked. "He didn't say nothin' outa the ordinary, did he?" Something stood behind that question, and I could tell that Aunt Lois wanted to see if she could find out something without having to say what she was worried about.

"A right queer letter," Daddy said. "Mostly 'tware 'bout how much he missed Mamma and all the rest of us, and he spent a couple of pages talking all 'bout some of the favorite things he did 'round here as a young'un. Joey never talks that way in his letters, you know." Daddy sat and mused a minute, letting what he'd said settle in.

"What else?" Aunt Lois asked. I could hear that she sat on the edge of her seat, if not really then in her head.

"Well, 'twarn't no talk 'bout his work or his girlfriend or his 'agenda.'" Daddy said that word with special emphasis because he thought it nothing but Yankee talk for stuff you had to do that made it seem important whether it was or wasn't. "Just recollecting 'bout old times and looking forward to being here and spending time and all with ever'body."

"That all?" Aunt Lois asked.

"That purdy much covers it," Daddy said, knowing Aunt Lois wanted to know something but being polite enough not to ask what. "Want to take a look at the letter?" he asked.

"What fer?" Aunt Lois asked. "I reckon you told it all purdy well. I just hope this ain't one of his danged fool ways of gittin' Mamma's hopes up just to break her heart. Pore thing couldn't stand it."

Don't know if Aunt Lois meant Granny couldn't stand it, or her bad heart couldn't stand it. Reckon it didn't matter—one and the same, really. With that, Aunt Lois stood up—her way of saying the talk about Uncle Joe had come to an end. She had found out what she wanted to know. By the sound of it, I knew the grown-ups had started to clean up the table and put things away. Course the pies stayed out where anybody who wanted a piece or a nibble could get at one.

The grown-ups stayed at the table for a spell longer after the clearing, sipping tea and saying nothing much. Finally, we heard Granny's voice, and Aunt Lois went in to see to her. I got up off my stomach and turned around to sit cross legged, getting serious. I had to fight my way back with Mildred, who had taken a goodly lead in number of games won while I listened in to what was said.

I saw Aunt Lois come out of Granny's room with the pot; normally, in houses like ours with only an outhouse, the pot only got used at night. But Granny didn't go out to the outhouse anymore—too much effort and trouble, so somebody always had to run the pot out a few times during the day. By the time Aunt Lois made it back in, Granny shuffled into the living room. She made for her chair, Daddy got her legs up, and she gave the word she always gave at some time after Thanksgiving dinner. "Time fer the singing, son."

Lots of folks, reckon, sing at Christmastime, but we always sang at Thanksgiving, too. Danged, we sang a lot anytime, because Daddy could play his guitar, and I liked to sing, and Granny liked to hear and hum along. But Granny especially liked to hear the whole family, so we all got ready for the singing.

I went out and told Aunt Doris's young'uns time for singing, and they knew that meant they had to get in. Course once the adults moved to the living room, it meant all us children had to sit on the floor because there wasn't enough room for everybody in the good chairs. And that settled okay with me; I already sat on the floor and was right comfortable. Mildred's two sisters made a show of not wanting to sit down with us like children, so they went and got the straight-backed chairs out of the dining room. Their rolled-back eyes also made it clear that they thought this singing made for foolishness, but one look from Aunt Lois and their eyeballs set aright pretty quick.

Ever since I could remember, we started Thanksgiving singing with "Over the River and Through the Woods." We did all go to Granny's house, and I reckon she liked having it sung. Course, no snow lay on the ground on Thanksgiving, and all in our family used cars, but it was the thought of grandmother's house that Granny liked so well, even if we didn't have horses or sleighs, open or otherwise. Matter of fact, Granny liked the song so well she even knew who'd written the song—a woman named Lydia Maria Child. I asked Granny what she knew about her, and she said not much but that she wrote a right nice song.

Other songs followed, like "We Plow the Fields and Scatter" and "We Gather Together to Ask the Lord's Blessing." Everybody sat happy and full (except maybe for Mildred's sisters who were just full), and our singing was something that makes you know what family and home and Thanksgiving all mean.

At the end, Granny asked that we all sing "Amazing Grace." Granny hummed along. When we sang the part about "through many trials, toils, and snares" she shook her head up and down like she knew all about that stuff. And when we finished up singing "when we've been there ten thousand years, bright shining as the sun, we've no less days to sing God's praise, than when we first begun," she said "Amen" and smiled at all of us, each and every one, going around the room with her lips turned upward on a wrinkly and worn-out face. It seemed almost like a spell had been put on us by it, and we all sat real still and quiet until Granny said, "Reckon I have a hankering fer an apple pie," and that let us all go. And so we ate a little more, talked a little more, then came time for everybody to go home, and Thanksgiving was done for.

XXI

A REAL BUSY time followed after Thanksgiving. We didn't raise hogs, but Daddy always bought a couple late in November. That's when we'd have us a hog killing, and then we'd have to do all that went along with it—making up bacon and ham, rendering the fat into lard, using the skin to make cracklin' corn bread, and all that stuff. It made for a load of work, and we had us a mess of folks out to help.

All of Aunt Lois's family were there; Aunt Doris came down, but nobody else. Daddy paid for the hogs, but folks got to take some things home for helping out, course, the way it should be in a family. I hung around outside with Daddy and Uncle Henry, helping as best I could. The pigs would have to be shot and then strung up by their hind legs, and then the draining and cutting would commence. The womenfolk worked inside, cooking and smoking and frying up the skins for the cracklin' corn bread, some of which everybody'd get to take home.

Since Aunt Doris didn't stand stout like Aunt Lois, Daddy figured she should sit with Granny and tend to her for the day so everybody else could do their jobs. This worked out good because Granny had about finished the quilt. Only the edges needed sewing up. Then the quilt would be done. So while I came in and out, running after anything Daddy might need, I'd see Granny and Aunt Doris working, though oftentimes Granny had her eyes closed, napping and resting as best she could with her gurgly breath. Reckon Aunt Doris mostly finished it up. But it looked a right peaceful scene coming in, seeing Granny in her chair, feet propped up on her stool, the quilting frame turned flat like a table before her. On the other side sat Aunt Doris, working quietly away, a look of determination on her face. She meant to help Granny finish that day, and it was something that she wanted everybody to know.

We worked, all of us, a long day, and we had something to show for it at the end. All of us that worked outside figured on having to wash up real good before supper. Our clothes stank and we stank, and nobody wanted to spoil the good supper we were going to have by having the smell of pig on us.

So by the time supper came around, we all brought growling stomachs to the table. We had us a feast of cracklin' corn bread smeared with butter, fresh bacon fried up good, potatoes cut up and fried with onions, and some white half-runners cooked with some of the first bacon to come off. Most of everything had been smoked and salted so as to keep, but we held back enough for a few days of fresh meat.

Aunt Doris and Granny, late in the day, had closed the front door and told everybody to keep to the back of the house. We reckoned Granny didn't want any disturbances, being tired and all. And when suppertime came, Aunt Doris helped Granny shuffle in to the table, closing the door between the living room and dining room so nobody could see in. Doris said Granny had a surprise for everybody after supper dishes got done.

So we ate up and ate good. We ate in silence, except for the appreciative grunts that popped out all of a sudden, involuntary like. It'd been a hard day, and everybody had a hard day's appetite. Hardly a word got spoken until, finishing off the last bite of corn bread, Uncle Henry said, "Now that was good." And everybody agreed. Then we all cleared the table and washed up dishes, mostly us young'uns while the grown-ups enjoyed just sipping on glasses of tea.

Then Aunt Doris said, "Time fer the surprise. Everybody git up and come to the door, but don't nobody go through 'til me and Mamma say so." Aunt Doris helped Granny up, and they slipped through the door, leaving us there to wait. Directly, the word came to come on in, and we did.

Aunt Doris had turned Granny's chair around and moved it to the other side of the room. There sat Granny with her feet propped up. The quilting frame set next to Granny, all upright instead of flat, with the quilt hanging from it. We all filed in the room and stood there, admiring Granny's work, her sitting there all proud, with Aunt Doris on the other side of the frame.

Now, everybody said that Granny made quilts like nobody else in Smoky Hollow. And this quilt proved it all over again. Most quilts were square patches made up in some design, and they looked pretty, but they always seemed to be put together in a repetitive pattern, just sewing one square to another. Not Granny's quilt, though. An artist's heart beat within her, and she could think up designs in her head and then cut things so as to make pictures, using a combination of triangles, diamonds, and squares, then sometimes on top of something putting in a rounded shape if need be. She was ahead of her time in the designing of quilts, and in 1942 Smoky Hollow or anywhere else in North Georgia, she was the only one people knew of who made these quilt pictures. And she did it with no pattern; it all came from her head, and she knew how to cut things out so as to fit together and come out right.

This quilt radiated beauty. I knew more or less, like everybody else, that Granny was working on a Christmas quilt, and we all knew that it would be about the star on Christmas night and all. We'd seen it as she worked on it. But until we saw it all sewn together and whole, the quilting frame set upright for all the world to see, there was no way to know the effect it would have. Everybody just stood speechless for a while, admiring.

Granny had sewn the quilt in whites, blues, and grays mostly. On one side hung the star of Bethlehem, with Granny using white at the center but then moving toward gray then blue as the rays of the star radiated out. A big star, it was, and it hovered right over a stable. Couldn't see baby Jesus; there was no people of any kind there in the stable area. But you knew from that special star that what lay in the stable was special. It said "Here's baby Jesus" without using words.

But the other side was plumb amazing. A hill had been sewn in, and on the hill stood a few sheep. Not too far from the sheep was the center of the quilt, and the middle of its meaning, reckon. There stood a shepherd.

Danged if I could say how Granny had made it up out of patches of quilting fabric, but I saw for the first time in person, rather than pictures in a book, something that you could really call art. Mostly because the shepherd wasn't just a picture; it was Granny's feelings there. The shepherd was obviously walking away, walking to his destiny, to see the baby Jesus, to see something bigger than anything he'd ever seen as a shepherd feller. Nobody could ignore that star, it calling out to come and see the biggest, bestest thing that'd ever been or ever would be. So nobody could blame the shepherd for going; he had to.

But the main thing about that quilted shepherd was the fact that, while he had his feet set toward the star and he had to go and he would go, his head turned back to his sheep. He knew he had to leave, but the quilt said that he wanted to stay, too. And so it was with an eye back at the life that was that he walked toward the life that called.

"Mamma," Daddy said, "that there is the purdiest quilt I've ever set eyes on. You did good, real good."

"That's something as Joey can be proud of," Aunt Lois said. That's all she said. I expected some other comment, kind as Aunt Lois always made when talking about Uncle Joe. But she didn't say anything on this night, just that he'd be right proud of it. We all stood around, saying nice things about Granny's Christmas quilt because it was the sort of thing that asked to have good spoken of it. I could tell Granny felt real proud. It was like she had poured what life she had left into it, and anybody could see what a right fine life it was.

Everybody hates to leave that kind of an evening, especially after seeing something special like Granny's quilt. Finally, though, about everybody filed on out. I walked out to wave everybody bye because Daddy stayed in with Granny. They were about all piled in—a little more crowded than usual because Aunt Doris was riding back with Aunt Lois and Uncle Henry— and I was telling Mildred how as I'd see her later on, and that I'd do what she'd asked me. She had written a note for Bobby, and she'd asked me to make sure he got it.

All of a sudden, Daddy came bounding out of the house and off the porch in a single long-legged leap. He ran up to the driver's side and told Uncle Henry, "Go git Doc Miller. Something's wrong with Mamma. Somethin's changed." Then he turned around and went back in, knowing that Aunt Lois would see to it that Uncle Henry didn't waste any time. I watched the car as it made its way up to the main road; then I walked on toward the house, though not in any hurry. Maybe I should have been running, running like Daddy had been running, but I was afraid I'd be running into something I didn't want to bump into.

I went inside and saw an empty living room. So I went to Granny's room and peered through the doorway. Daddy had gotten Granny to bed. She was all covered up, sitting up on her pillows, the way she was supposed to sleep. Her eyes lay closed. Quietly I walked in and stood next to Daddy, who was sitting in a chair next to the bed holding Granny's hand.

"What's the matter, Daddy?" I asked. I said it real quiet, not wanting to disturb Granny. She didn't seem to stir. "Don't rightly know," Daddy said. "Right after ever'body stepped outside, she said her chest hurt real bad and then she slumped over and fell unconscious." He didn't say anything else, so I didn't ask anything else.

Directly, Granny opened her eyes. "Hey, son," she said to Daddy. "Why am I in here?"

"Don't you 'member, Mamma? Yore chest was hurting. You passed out."

Granny didn't say anything. She closed her eyes and let out a tired-to-the-bone breath. Finally, she up and said, "Feels like my heart's a-gonna run outa my chest." Daddy patted her hand and said, "Doc Miller'll be here soon. Just close yore eyes and rest 'til he gits here."

So we passed the time, somehow the hour seeming to last two or three, and after I'd wondered to myself for the hundredth time what in Sam Hill kept Doc Miller, there came a knock at the door.

I ran and opened the door for Doc Miller. He'd been out enough to know to go to Granny's room, and I'd been around enough to know that I should stay out. He spent a goodly amount of time in there, and finally he and Daddy came out.

"That orta help her sleep fer a while," Doc Miller said.

"So what is it that's wrong, did you say?" Daddy asked. He wore a worried look.

"Well, I don't know if'n you 'member," Doc Miller said, "but you was tolt that with cases of dropsy a couple of things could happen. Yore mamma could just keep gittin' weaker and weaker, having more and more breathing problems, maybe some blood poisoning 'cause her body can't 'liminate all the waste, the kidneys starting to shut down, and all that. 'Tother thing 'tware said was that she could develop problems with her heart rhythm. Called cardiac arrhythmia." Doc Miller paused for a minute to let us take in the fancy word, until Daddy asked, "What does that mean?"

"Means the heart don't beat right," Doc Miller said. "Heart speeds up, kinda quivers rather than pumps," he said. "Causes chest pain, lightheadedness, blackouts. It's bad fer a heart that's already sick to beat too fast—wears it out. Or sometimes the signals that tell the heart to beat git all mixed up and the heart just stops altogether. With arrhythmia, yore mamma could go at any time; ain't no telling. But probably won't be long."

"Why do you say that?" Daddy asked.

"'Cause what I've given yore mamma to help her heart beat stronger—the digitalis—also regulates the heart rate. If'n she's developed an irregular heartbeat, that means that her heart must be a whole lot worse, 'cause the medicine ain't working like it was."

"Well, what reckon we orta do?" Daddy asked. "Maybe if'n you give her more digitalis stuff she'd do better."

"We can give her a little more," Doc Miller said, "but not much. 'Member, digitalis is a toxin, that's to say, a poison. Just a little helps the heart some. More'n a little will kill her. So we have to be careful. If'n she gits too bad, we can give her morphine a little more often, though we have to be careful with that, too. But if'n she can sleep through the worst spells, she'll be more comfortable and less likely to git all agitated, which'd just make matters worse."

Daddy let out a big ol' sigh. There was no good way to take what Doc Miller said. Daddy knew Granny was going to die, but now he knew it would be sooner rather than later. About that time I heard a car pull up. I looked out the window and saw Aunt Lois and Uncle Henry. Aunt Lois jumped out of the car before it had stopped good, and she marched her mad steps toward the house. She must have made Aunt Doris stay with her children.

And so Doc Miller had to say everything again, and it didn't come out any better sounding the second time, so I told Daddy in the middle of it that I was going off to bed, and he said go on. I told him to wake me if he needed me, and he said he would. So, exhausted from hog killing and an emergency that was punctuated in the middle with the prettiest piece of work I'd ever seen, I fell off to sleep with thoughts of life and death and hogs and stars chasing through my mind.

XXII

GRANNY HAD SAID that the best thing to do was to go on living and not start waiting on dying. So that's what we did. Granny needed a lot of help, and I learned a good deal about responsibility, both about how hard it could be and about how it could make you feel like you had done good, even if nobody was there to tell you so. School was still called off until after the first of the year because of Bobby's polio spell, so all I had to do was my chores and look after Granny while Daddy worked.

When Granny talked about living life rather than waiting for it to end, I think she meant mostly Daddy and me, because she had gotten so she couldn't do too much. She slept a lot. With no quilt to work on, she didn't reckon she had to do too much of anything, so when she wasn't sleeping she read her Bible; some-times she'd ask me to sing hymns to her a while, and when Daddy came home at night we'd usually sing several songs while he played the guitar. Granny'd always say, "That was real purdy, son," after every song, so if she didn't say it we knew that she had gone to sleep, and we'd up and sneak on out of her room, trying real hard not to make the old hardwood boards squeak too awful bad.

Part of what Granny meant about us going on living was to start getting ready for Christmas. She once gave me a weak smile and said, "Joey's gonna need more'n his quilt present; he needs a right happy house to come home to. Help yore daddy and Aunt Lois fix things up right." And so we did. Granny always loved Christmas—that's what made the quilt so special. And she always liked to have the house done up—a nice tree set up by the front window, some fresh-made pine wreaths hanging about. So we all helped make the house all Christmassy.

About a week and a half before Christmas, while Aunt Lois sat with Granny, Mildred and Daddy and I went out searching for a Christmas tree. Daddy and I both, starting about October, had kept an eye out for a good tree while we hunted or walked the woods. I had a couple of trees in mind, and Daddy said he'd look at them, even though he figured he'd seen the best Christmas tree ever a couple of ridges over from the creek.

We stomped about—since we weren't going hunting, we didn't have to be quiet. White smoke puffed out of our mouths, and the leaves that had fallen away on autumn's breath crunched under our feet good and loud. Going up and down the ridges made for hard work, but the cold kept the sweat at bay for a while—that'd wait for when we came back, lugging the tree behind us, getting it in, then realizing how hot the stove burned as we'd peel off the layers of clothes that kept us warm.

Daddy said that we'd better look at the trees I had marked, but I could find only one of them—a nice looking Virginia pine, six feet high or so. Mildred thought it looked good, and Daddy said so, too. Then he started marching around it, looking it up and down.

"Don't reckon this'll do," Daddy said. Then he told Mildred and me to come look at the bottom of the tree. "See where the trunk is all crooked near the bottom? If'n we cut that off so that it stands good and straight, then yore cutting off this whole bottom section, and 'twouldn't be as purdy or full."

I saw what Daddy meant. I hadn't thought to check the trunk. So we went on to Daddy's place. Down in the hollow between two good-sized ridges lay a little clearing where there'd once been a little house. Some younger trees grew there. "Come look over here," Daddy said.

We went to where Daddy wanted to go, and we stepped between a couple of trees, and then I saw the tree that Daddy meant. A beautiful little white pine stood there, real full with long needles. First thing I did to show myself a good learner was to go and look at the trunk—nice and straight, it was. Mildred plopped down beside me and stuck her head between branches and looked, too. We both crawled back a little, stood up, and congratulated Daddy on finding such a fine tree. We knew it'd make a fine Christmas tree. We walked around part of it, but on one side there was another smaller tree growing up close, and so we had to go around it—not enough room to go between the two trees. Daddy pulled out his little hand saw and went to sawing. Soon the tree came down, and we were ready to take it home.

Daddy took hold of the trunk, and he told Mildred and me to take hold of each side near the top, reaching through the branches to grab hold of the slender top of the trunk. Daddy said not to let go and not to hold onto the branches lest they break. And so we tromped off back home, up ridge and down, careful to keep our tree all in one piece, not even wanting to let one needle fall. We were huffing and puffing by the time we came down the last ridge, crossed over the creek, and made our way up to the house.

"Real gentle like, let's lay the tree right here on the porch," Daddy said. I saw Aunt Lois peering out the window to see what we had brought home. Daddy sat down in a rocker and said, "You two young'uns go fetch a bucket whilst I rest a spell." So off we went to the barn, looking for a feed bucket or something that'd hold our Christmas tree.

When we got back with the bucket, Mildred held the screen door open, Daddy opened the wood door, and him and me took the tree in real careful like, trying not to damage any branches as we squeezed the thing into the house. Daddy told Mildred to go and fetch some water from out back, and while she did that Daddy placed the bucket in front of the window, and the two of us placed the tree in the bucket. Daddy had cut it just right—there wouldn't be any need to cut any of the lower branches to make it fit in. Mildred came back with the water, and Daddy poured it in.

Then Daddy said, "You two go and fetch some rocks now, and I'll make shore the tree don't git up and walk away." So we did that, too, same as every Christmas I could remember since I stood big enough to gather up rocks and bring them in. Mildred and I went back to the barn, got another bucket, and went to pick some of the good-sized rocks up in our road and up near the main road, filling the bucket almost full—it didn't need to be all the way full, because the tree trunk would take up some room.

Doing something for Christmas like we were doing made the work seem more like fun. We practically ran back to the house with our rocks, feeling all good about them like it was something special to be able to pick rocks up off the road. Well, in a way, I guess it was special because the rocks would hold up the tree, which always seemed special to me. It made the house smell all good, looked real pretty, and served as a daily reminder that something special was coming that only came once a year.

Mildred and I flew into the house, but our wildness got put to flight by the look of Aunt Lois as we came in. But she didn't have any words for us right then. She stood talking to Daddy.

"Well, 'tis a purdy tree by and large, but I don't see how in the world you missed seeing that big ol' bare spot there." Aunt Lois pointed to a place on the tree where a hole looked out at you, and you could see all the way into the trunk. I was sure I hadn't seen that, and I reckoned maybe the tree hadn't grown as full over where that other tree stood so close to it. I thought Aunt Lois was mad or something, the way she talked at first. Then something funny happened. She started laughing.

"It ain't in yore blood to pick out a good tree," Aunt Lois said. "You ain't ever brought home a tree that the hole didn't have to be hid and turned away."

"Reckon not," Daddy said, a hint of disgust in his voice. He sounded like somebody who was going to say "Told you I could do it" who turns out couldn't. "They just always look diff'rent out in the woods. Ever' tree is a purdy tree, and hang it all anyway, Lois, don't reckon God made trees to sit purdy in a bucket but to grow in the woods."

"Maybe so," Aunt Lois said, "but I seen me some awful purdy trees that come outa God's woods, and they ain't all got the holes yore's always has." Then she snorted a short laugh.

"Well, if'n I brought home a perfect tree," Daddy replied, "don't reckon you'd have any fun trying to dress it up and turn it so's it looks best. So's let's just leave it as me a-doing you a favor." And with that, they both snorted. They looked at each other for a minute, like they knew something good but couldn't tell anybody.

Finally, they looked over at us. "Well, don't sit there like lumps on a log," Aunt Lois said, sounding more like her usual self, "them rocks ain't gonna jump in on their own." And that signaled Mildred and me to fill up the bucket while Daddy held the tree and moved it back here and yon as Aunt Lois told him to go this way, then that way, then perfect, then no, danged if he didn't move it. After a while, though, the tree stood straight, and Aunt Lois had made sure the bad side faced away from the room toward the outside window.

"I should be able to cover it up 'nuff that nobody can tell from outside what kinda tree yore Daddy drug home," she said, looking at me. Daddy snorted again and patted Aunt Lois on the shoulder as he moved away from the tree. It was an affectionate pat, and one I didn't see Daddy give much, and one that I don't reckon I'd ever seen Aunt Lois get. They both smiled, like fixing up that Christmas tree was the dangedest thing they'd ever done.

Daddy moved away from the tree and toward a chair because he figured his work was done. He didn't ever help with the decorating of the tree—said he was no good at that sort of thing. Granny usually put things up, but she lay asleep in bed, and so that left Aunt Lois in charge. Most years she came out and helped with the decorating, partly because, as a child, she made some of the decorations that went on the tree, and she liked putting them up. But Granny said where things got to go, and Aunt Lois mostly helped. This year Mildred and I were the helpers, and Aunt Lois stood in charge. She went to pull out the decorations from where they stayed put, Mildred and I stood by the tree ready to do what Aunt Lois would let us, and Daddy picked up the *Times-Courier* that Aunt Lois had brought out. Daddy was set to read while we decorated.

Aunt Lois brought out the box that held the decorations. All were homemade, mostly out of crepe paper. Granny had taught Aunt Lois and Aunt Doris how to make decorations, and Granny was good at that like she was good at quilting. Mildred and I started to stick our hands into the pile of stuff when Aunt Lois let out an "Uh-uh." We looked up at her, and she said, "I don't want you two messing these up or tangling 'em up or tearing 'em or nothin'. Reckon I'll decorate this here tree myself." But before we could say how that wasn't fair, she looked over at my daddy and said, "Did you pick up the popcorn?"

"Yep," Daddy replied.

"Well, let these two know where it's at so's they can pop it."

So Mildred and I ended up with a good job. We got to pop the popcorn and then string it together to go around the tree. We popped plenty so we'd have plenty to eat and string, and I reckon even Aunt Lois knew we'd do that. She seemed pleased with herself to give us something to do, something to eat, and a way to keep us out of the more delicate decorations all at the same time. So there we sat, chomping on popcorn, running string through it with a needle, and watching Aunt Lois put up the handmade ornaments. Daddy read out loud, reckon to keep Aunt Lois company, reckon to see if she'd read the paper herself, and some to let us in on the news.

"Well, looky here," Daddy said. "They finally stopped volunteer enlistment. Says here that the president has tolt folks that the Selective Service System has to be used to fetch recruits."

"Reckon folks'll fight as don't want to?" Aunt Lois asked Daddy.

"Put 'em in a place where they's people shooting at 'em, and don't matter much whether they want to or not. They will."

Daddy read about other stuff. Turned out the Gilmer County sheriff had resigned to go fight. Course, he could, him being awful young to begin with. Ed Rackley's daddy had been sheriff, and when he suddenly died everybody reckoned he had trained Ed good enough to be sheriff, though Ed had barely reached eighteen. Daddy said he'd been a good sheriff. Lois reckoned so, too, though she wouldn't mind, she said, having somebody a mite older.

Daddy read an interesting article about Pearl Harbor. It told how many ships had been sunk or damaged—all of them, it turned out, though I couldn't understand why the Navy hadn't said so to begin with. Eight battleships, ten other ships, and almost two hundred planes destroyed. "But, Lordy," Daddy said, "look at the loss of life." Then he read the numbers: 2,117 killed, 960 missing, and 876 wounded. Danged, I thought, put all of them together and that's more than all the people in Gilmer County!

But then Daddy read the danged silly stuff, or least it seemed silly to me. I wondered why in the world they printed some of the things they did. Daddy said, "Listen to this here headline." And then he read on:

Kills Canadian Wild Goose on Blue Ridge Lake. 'Celie' Pinson, of Blue Ridge, killed a Canadian wild goose on Blue Ridge Lake Monday. On the band on one of its legs it read: 'No. 36 F. C. Write Jack Miner, Kingsville, Ont., Canada. Have Faith in God. Mark 11-22.' Mr. Pinson said the goose weighed more than nine pounds and he got enough feathers to make two pillows.

"Ain't that the stupidest story you ever heard in a paper?" I asked Mildred. She shook her head yes, but then Daddy said, "Ain't nothing stupid 'bout it. I thought it to be right interesting. Probably think it more interesting, though," he said, "if'n I was the one gittin' two new goose feather pillows." And with that he laughed.

All in all, with Aunt Lois decorating, Mildred and me popcorning, and Daddy reading and conversing, it made for a real nice time. The tree looked good, and the way it sat you couldn't see the hole. Aunt Lois guaranteed that, unless somebody stuck their nose to the windowpane, nobody would notice the bad side from the outside either. "Anyway," she said, "Why would anybody be loitering 'round 'bout on the porch when it's December anyway?"

We all stood back a ways, looking and admiring and taking in what it all meant, Christmas coming and all. "It's real nice, Lois," Daddy told her. "Yep," she said, "and it's gonna be nice, too, reckon." And she left it at that, though I reckon her and Daddy were talking about something Mildred and I hadn't been told about. But it did look pretty, and the pine scent and the green tree and colored decorations made for a house getting ready for Christmas coming, and it's that feeling of getting ready for something important and happy that feels almost as good as the thing itself.

"Mamma will think you did real good," Daddy said.

"You, too," she told him, "and I won't even tell 'bout that hole in the tree that you didn't see or nothin'." And they both snorted.

As Aunt Lois and Mildred went out the door, Aunt Lois stopped and looked at me and said, "You git that fatwood?"

"Yep," I said.

"Well, go fetch it and put it in the car," she said, "then I'll give you the money Mrs. Foster sent fer it." I'd gone out and collected pine branches full of resin and chopped them up into kindling. Folks called it fatwood, and they'd pay for it, especially people who lived in Ellijay, if they didn't have woods to go off to or were getting too old. I collected fatwood for a fair number of folks, making me a little money in the wintertime.

So I went to bed that night satisfied. Tree hunting with Daddy, a nice decorated tree, Christmas just around the corner, and me with a little spending money. I'd saved up enough that, if I could get into town on Saturday while Daddy was with Granny and didn't need me, I could go to the movie and get a popcorn, and that'd take twenty cents of what I had. I'd have enough left over to buy something for folks for Christmas, probably bags of penny candy or something. It couldn't have been a better winter day, reckon, except for Granny being sick. But, even with that, and her saying as how we should go on living rather than waiting on dying, I reckoned it a good day, and I figured she would have liked me feeling that way.

XXIII

CHRISTMAS DAY FINALLY came, and I rose early like usual. I set about doing my chores real quick so as to have them done for the day; cows and chickens got hungry whether it was Christmas Day or no, so I didn't mind it. Gave me a chance to anticipate the good day that was coming.

I didn't look into the living room—I wanted to wait until after chores. I knew there'd be stuff under the tree for me—well, for all of us. I could smell some of the things that made Christmas Christmas. For one thing, mixed in with the pine scent, which wasn't as strong as when we first put the tree up, was a new smell, one that always waited for Christmas Day to come—oranges. The scent of oranges hung in the air. We always got us our first oranges of the season at

Christmas. I reckon they came in a little before Christmas, but we always waited for Christmas Day, don't know why. Back in 1942, that was the way of it—they didn't bring oranges in from all over the world all year round—what we got grew down in Florida, and that crop made its way up to North Georgia in December. Pine tree and oranges—a special and memorable smell.

The smell of the night before's cooking also wafted through the air. Daddy and I did up good like we did at Thanksgiving, and even if Aunt Lois and Aunt Doris brought a bunch, I reckon we'd done our part, too. Daddy figured the night before, when he put me in charge of cooking the fried apple pies, that I'd done up enough to feed an army. Well, danged, I told him, with us and Aunt Lois's brood and Aunt Doris's brood here all at once, we were a danged army. He laughed and reckoned it so.

Of course, nothing could have prepared me for what seemed at the time the best Christmas surprise of all, because none of us planned it or had anything to do with it. After milking the cow and taking in eggs and putting out feed, I walked out of the barn and stopped dead in my tracks. My head took in the picture as I turned it from side to side, and then I ran to the house, then around and around it, arms out, embracing the cold air and what it held. Snow. Snow on Christmas Day.

It wasn't a blowing snow, or a wet one. Big lazy flakes came floating down as if they didn't have anything to do but fall all day. They were big, but they didn't come down hard and heavy; it was like God sat up there rationing out the snow like things were beginning to be rationed because of the war, just a few fat flakes at a time. I thought that if I ran fast enough, there were few enough that I could catch them all. I'd see one coming down, take off for it, arm out, and catch it on my sleeve so as not to melt it like if it fell on my hand. Then I'd look at how pretty the flake was. Then I'd take off for another. Snow on Christmas. I reckon I couldn't remember that ever happening before. We had snow in North Georgia, but it usually came after Christmas; either that or we'd have us an early snow that'd get melted real fast because it wasn't cold enough for it to linger.

After I was good and tired from the running, I went inside. First thing I did was stoke the fire in the living room stove so we'd have us a nice warm house for everybody. Try as I could, I couldn't help but look at the tree. Danged if my stocking didn't overflow. The stocking held the usual fare, but I loved seeing it anyway: nuts and oranges and candy, especially peppermint. Danged if sitting right next to the tree didn't make you think that you could practically smell Christmas so real that your nose held the whole holiday. Presents circled the tree, and I saw that two were for me; there was one apiece for about everybody else besides what I'd put out. The biggest lay wrapped up nice with a big red bow, and I knew what it was—Uncle Joe's Christmas quilt. Granny said he'd be there and that he'd have him a wrapped present like everybody else. Aunt Lois did the wrapping for Granny, and she didn't make any remarks, just saying how much Uncle Joe would like it.

I couldn't figure out if she really thought Uncle Joe was coming or if she was just trying to pacify Granny and not upset her. Hard to read Aunt Lois on that one. For a couple of weeks she hadn't been her usual self when talk about Uncle Joe came up. She generally kept to herself any negative comments, except when somebody might mention Uncle Joe's girlfriend coming and all, and how he was marrying into the Ford family. Then she'd just look with her usual look and say, "Don't talk nonsense none. Makes you sound like you ain't got no brains." And that's where the conversation stopped.

Wrapping Uncle Joe's present a couple of days before Christmas had been real special, though. Starting about that time, Granny seemed to be a mite better. She helped a bit with the wrapping, and she did it sitting up in a chair—said she wanted out of that ol' bed. So Daddy and Aunt Lois helped her out, and she sat there a spell, maybe half an hour or so. Next day she wanted to sit again, and this time she went a little longer. She talked more, too, and without the rasping and shortness of breath that she usually had. Said she reckoned she felt better because Joey was coming home and all, and she'd live to see all her children under the roof their daddy had put over all their heads. She said it would be a right fine day, that.

On Christmas Eve, I heard Daddy and Aunt Lois talking in the kitchen in low voices. I sat at the dining room table eating a biscuit for a snack, which meant I wasn't snooping or anything, me just sitting there and being able to hear them talk. I did eat a mite slower than usual, though.

"Do you think Mamma could be gittin' better?" I heard Aunt Lois ask Daddy. "She seems a right spell better, and her breathing don't seem so bad as 'tware."

"Now, Lois, don't go gittin' yore hopes up none," Daddy said. "You know as good as I do what all's been said by the doctors. It's just a matter of time. Let Mamma enjoy it without no talk to raise up her hopes just to have 'em broken."

"Well," Aunt Lois replied, "Doctors don't know ever'thing. I know people who doctors said was gonna die and they plumb near did, but in the end made a liar outa 'em. Could happen."

"I don't think so this time, Lois," Daddy said, saying his sister's name gentle like. "It ain't just Mamma, you know, it's you I'm worrit 'bout, too," Daddy went on. "You git yore hopes up and they come a-crashing down 'round you, and they might just take you with 'em. Don't want to see it."

"I know the diff'rence 'tween real hope and not real hope," Aunt Lois said. "Just seems she's better, that's all, and I reckon it don't do no harm to ask the good Lord fer a mite more of good time. Ain't all hopes in vain, you know, or at least I hope not." And with that they walked out of the kitchen and saw me sitting there and clammed up. I didn't see any reason to linger any longer over my biscuit, so I finished up.

After Aunt Lois had left, I told Daddy that I'd heard them, and maybe Granny was better, I said, because she seemed that way to me, too.

"Son, let me tell you somethin'," Daddy said, patting my shoulder in a way he didn't much do. "I've seen my share of people die. Some in battle, some in other ways. I sat by yore mamma whilst she died, and I know purdy much what it looks like." He paused and let out a big ol' sigh, blowing out bad memories. Then he went on.

"Reckon by the grace of God some folks git a chance to say good-bye," Daddy said. "They seem better. I seen it before. They seem alert, stronger, talkative. Yore mamma was like that. But you can't let it fool you, son," he said. "It's just God's way of letting 'em have the strength and the courage to say that they's ready to go and that they love you."

I thought about what Daddy said, and I asked, "How do you know?"

"By the look in their eyes, son," he said. "Yore granny has the look. She's sitting up a bit and she ain't needing quite so much medicine 'cause her breathing ain't causing her quite so much trouble. That's so she can talk and keep a clear head whilst she talks. But her eyes, son," he said, "they kinda look through you, and you can kinda look through them. All glassy-eyed, that's yore granny. She sees us, I reckon, but it's like she sees through us, too, like she's looking off already to 'nother world. And reckon she is." Daddy's eyes turned red. Then he said, "I heard her last night, as I was a-gittin' ready fer bed, talking to yore mamma just like she was in the room with her. And, who knows, maybe she was."

Daddy gave out another of his great big ol' sighs. "Tell yore granny you love her, son, and let her tell you that she loves you.

That's what this is all 'bout. Her eyes tell me she ain't long fer this world." And I reckoned Daddy knew.

I sat there, next to the nice warm fire I had coaxed into blazing, just taking it all in and thinking about everything that'd been going on and what everybody'd said the night before and about Granny most of all. It could be Granny's last Christmas, and that made the day a bit doleful, even with snow in the air. As I sat there figuring, a knock rapped on the door. I looked around the tree out the window, and I saw Uncle Henry sitting in the car, two neat little tracks behind his car where the tires had run over the snow.

He seemed about ready to leave, and I couldn't figure what in the world was going on because Aunt Lois hadn't said she'd be coming over especially early before anybody else or sending anybody else over. They usually had their Christmas morning time and then had breakfast. After a spell they would come over, and we'd have us a fine feast midafternoon. But here dawn had barely broken good, and a knock had come at the door, and me wondering what in the world was going on rather than getting the door like I should have.

So the knock had to come again, a little more forceful. It was a knock that didn't want to wake anybody up who wasn't already up, but it was a knock too that said, "Let me in if you can hear me." At that second knocking I went to let in Aunt Lois or whoever she'd sent. Maybe she figured a little extra help on Christmas morning would make the afternoon dinner go a mite smoother,

though smooth wasn't exactly the way it went while all of
Granny's children and grandchildren sat under one roof.

I opened up the door, but with a funny feeling. If Aunt Lois
knocked at all, she always had the screen door already pulled
open ready to blow in, and so did Mildred and her sisters. But I
opened the door, and the screen door was still shut. I looked up a
bit because I had to; even though I'd grown to be a fairly tall feller
for my age, this person at the door stood taller than me. For that
matter, he stood taller than Daddy.

He had on a pair of pants pressed right nicely. He looked
almost like pictures I'd seen of soldiers dressed fancy with creases
in their pants so sharp you reckoned you might cut yourself on a
crease like that. A good-looking pair of pants, they were, though
not new, just well taken care of. He wore his jacket buttoned up
to the top because it was cold and snowy, but that's when I had
me my first surprise. On the left side of the jacket, the cuff lay
pinned up near the shoulder so that the jacket sleeve folded
neatly in half. I had a feller standing there that didn't have but
one arm. Then I looked up at the face, and then I did have me a
surprise. Except for being too tall and a little balding and turning
gray there where he did have hair, I'd have told you, if he had
stood twenty or thirty feet away, that it was my daddy. Course,
there was the arm, too; my daddy had two arms. Other than that,
though, they looked an awful lot alike.

My eyes wandered off toward the missing arm. It's hard to ignore
something like that, especially when it's a surprise and you don't

have time to prepare yourself not to look. When I reckoned I'd been staring, my head snapped back to the feller's face to say something, but once he caught my eyes he spoke first.

"Hey, son, I know who you are, but I reckon you don't quite know who I am. I'm yore Uncle Joe."

Because of the shock I guess my eyes wandered off some more. I saw that Uncle Henry had turned the car around, heading off up the road, so I reckoned he wasn't coming in and that the feller standing in front of me wasn't leaving. I looked for a great big new fancy Ford, the kind I thought Uncle Joe would be driving, but nothing like that sat outside. There was no girlfriend, either. Just this feller who looked an awful lot like Daddy with no arm. And he looked tired, awful tired, big bags under his eyes like he hadn't slept for a goodly while. Finally, I pushed open the screen door for him and said, "Come on in, Uncle Joe." And he did.

Once inside Uncle Joe took in the room, real slow like, taking in the living room, the decorated tree, then his eyes stopped at Granny's chair. He looked real hard, like looking would make Granny appear out of nowhere. Finally, his eyes moved back to me. "Right warm in here," he said. "You tending the fire this morning?"

"Yep," I said, thinking I might say something else but finding that I didn't have anything else to say right then.

"Well, it's good and warm in here, right warm. Reckon I'd better take off my coat."

Then he pulled off his coat, and I said I'd take it, which I did, and laid it on the back of a dining room chair. His shirt looked like his pants, pressed all crisp. He'd done up his long sleeve like his jacket, it folded neatly in half and pinned at the shoulder. He still stood there, like he was company, not making to sit down. I started to say something about taking a seat when I heard my daddy's voice behind me.

"Joey? Lord have mercy, it's you, ain't it?"

I turned, and there stood Daddy at the door of the hallway to the bedrooms. He stared hard, and his head tilted to one side, as if looking at something strange and wonderful and like he didn't know how to make heads nor tails of the thing.

"Hey, Bobby. It's good to see you, real good." Confusion struck me for a minute because Bobby was my friend. Everybody called Daddy "Robert." Daddy laughed.

"Ain't nobody called me that fer years, not even Mamma," Daddy said. "But it shore sounds good right now." And with that he walked over to Uncle Joe. He started to reach out his hand to give Uncle Joe a handshake, but then he changed his mind and just gave Uncle Joe a great big bear hug, and Uncle Joe did his best to bear hug back with his one arm.

"When'd you git here, and how?" Daddy asked.

"Henry brought me here this morning," Uncle Joe said. "I caught a ride from Marietta to Ellijay with a lumber truck yesterday. I started out a few days ago from Detroit on a bus, got to Atlanta, and took a bus to Marietta. 'Twarn't no service out to Ellijay 'fore Christmas, though, so I hitched in from there. Stayed with Loey and Henry last night."

"You don't say," Daddy said, surprise not hid too well in his voice.

"Yeah," Uncle Joe said. "'Tware Loey who wrote 'bout Mamma back a few months ago. Knew 'tware serious if she had taken the trouble to write. Reckoned I'd better git on down here when I could, and it worked out I got here 'bout when I had tolt Mamma in my letter that I'd be here. Took a while to git up the money to come," Joe said, "'cause I had to sell what I had up in Detroit, and I had other arrangements to make, too. I'm back fer good, Bobby, so I had to take a little longer gittin' down here than I wanted, 'cause I had to git my affairs in order and all that."

"Well," Daddy said, "there's a bunch of questions I got fer you, but I reckon it'd be best if'n you came in to see Mamma. If'n yore the first thing she sees this Christmas morning, it'll be a Christmas gift fer the soul." And so we all went back to Granny's room.

There Granny lay, all propped up on her pillows, seeming to sleep better and easier than in a long while. Daddy walked over to her, Uncle Joe close behind. Daddy reached down and gently touched Granny's shoulder. "Mamma," Daddy said, "Mamma. It's Christmas morning, Mamma. Time fer yore present."

Granny slowly opened her eyes. It took her eyes a few seconds to focus. She set her sight on Daddy, and she said with a smile, "Morning, son." Then she saw that Uncle Joe stood next to Daddy. Her head relaxed back into her pillow, and she closed her eyes. I thought maybe the shock was too much for her, but it wasn't the shock. "Thank ye, Lord, fer listening to an old woman." After her prayer, she opened her eyes back up, and they shone wet. "Joey," she said, and it sounded like she was saying the sweetest word that ever human tongue could speak. But then Uncle Joe said, "Mamma," and the air grew sweeter still because the two words went together so good. If Christmas is about love, then those two words filled the room with Christmas spirit in a way I haven't ever known since.

Finally, Uncle Joe said, "Mamma, they's certain things I need to tell you 'bout, certain things that need explaining." But then Granny said, "Son, they ain't nothing needs 'splaining. All that's needed right now is fer you to spend a little time with yore mamma."

Daddy pulled over the chair that we used to sit with Granny when we were in there for a spell, and he placed it beside the bed for Uncle Joe. "Let's leave 'em alone fer a while," Daddy said to me, so we left the room. And as Daddy closed the door, he said, "Well, if'n this don't beat all." And he reached over and rustled my hair like I was a little kid again and said, "Merry Christmas, son," and I knew he meant it. Then I told Daddy, "It's snowing a bit," and then he said, "Reckon that makes things 'bout as perfect as they's gonna git." And we walked over to the living room window and looked out as the snow gently fell, blanketing the whole world around us.

XXIV

THE SNOW FELL, but none too deep, only an inch or two in all. Aunt Lois and Aunt Doris made it out with their families, and it made for the merriest Christmas we'd ever had. Every time somebody'd start to ask Uncle Joe about Detroit and his work, Granny would say, "Don't bother the boy with questions right now. Let's just enjoy our time and be glad we's all here together. Questioning and celebrating don't make fer a fit match, so's we can hold off the questions 'til later." And everybody did as Granny said. She looked real special, sitting at the head of the grown-up table, looking over her own, and being awful proud. She stayed up so long and ate a little bit and talked and listened, I'd be danged that, if except for what Daddy'd said, I'd have thought that she wasn't even sick. Everybody kept saying what a special day it was.

It made for one of those days that, when you look back on it, you have a hard time describing. It was like a real nice dream you have, and it feels so real, and the colors and sounds and smells make you think you're in the real world, and then you wake up. It's a good kind of waking up, happiness swelling up inside you, and you think that you'll never forget a dream so sweet and special and happy. Then, within a few hours, the details are all hazy, then the dream itself is gone, and all you're left with is that feeling of happiness that went with it, knowing it was good but not being able to say exactly how anymore. That's the way I remember that Christmas Day, like a wonderful dream that's hard to recollect now except for the good feeling and knowing the day made everybody happy.

After dinner had been cleaned up (though Christmas was like Thanksgiving—it wasn't completely cleaned up because folks would be nibbling the rest of the afternoon and on into the night), we went and opened the presents. It wasn't much, in a way. Yet, it was plenty, because it was never about the presents but about family and eating together and laughing and thanking God for Jesus and everybody else ever born as a baby.

I do remember Uncle Joe opening up his present. Granny's face shone like a summer sun after a hard rain—made everything light and glistening that it touched. Granny was right proud of the present she'd made Uncle Joe, and Uncle Joe was even prouder to get it, though mixed in with some shame, too. He seemed to keep looking at Daddy and Aunt Lois and Aunt Doris to see if they didn't want to have it because he figured that they deserved it better than him. But they just shone and glistened in Granny's pride and good feeling. All together I reckon it made for sunshine in the showery places in Uncle Joe's soul because of the smile that finally lit up his face. He hugged Granny with a hug that held all the words that regular language couldn't say. That was Christmas 1942, and the best part of it. But more came.

When things went bad, sometimes, Granny would quote out of the Bible, especially the book of Job, where God tells Job you have to take the bad with the good. God gives good things, so when things that don't seem so good come along, don't complain. What seemed like evil from the hand of God to me was that such a Christmas Day should end the way it did. Granny died that night.

Everybody had gone on except Uncle Joe. He planned to stay with us until things got settled. Granny'd gone into the bedroom to get ready for bed. She felt plumb tuckered out, reckon. She'd been up for a longer spell than she had been for months. Every time Lois would say, "Mamma, you better go lay down and rest some now," Granny'd say, "Time fer resting will be soon 'nuff." And so she stayed up, sitting in her chair in the living room with her legs propped up. And she looked right happy.

"I'll go check on Mamma," Daddy told Uncle Joe after Granny'd been in her room a spell. "Sometimes she nods off purdy quick, and I like to catch her 'fore she does so's I can see if'n she needs something."

"I'll step in with you," Uncle Joe said. So they went on into Granny's room.

I guess I figured they stood speaking a long good night to Granny, because they stayed back there a long time. But when they came back to the living room, I could tell something had gone wrong. They both were red in the eye and carried hang-dog looks. Uncle Joe slumped into the nearest chair, and Daddy came and sat with me on the couch. He patted my leg just up over the knee, then said, "Yore Granny's gone, son." That little short sentence cast a long shadow, and we all sat there for a while, waiting for the darkness we felt inside to snuff out the light in the room.

But, of course, that didn't happen. The world didn't go dark, and it didn't stop for us, even though we figured it ought to. So finally Daddy said to Uncle Joe that folks needed telling and affairs needed ordering, and so the slow-motion action of funeral preparations got started.

From that night to the funeral, things seemed blurry to me. Daddy had to go and tell Aunt Lois, and he reckoned I ought to come with him. Uncle Joe said he would sit with Granny until folks came back, and Daddy said okay. At first I didn't know what Uncle Joe meant about sitting with Granny. Always before, sitting with Granny meant that we sat in there to keep her company or to sing to her or to get what she needed, and mostly to see to it that everything was alright. But then I figured he just wanted to sit a spell with her since it'd been so long since he'd spent time with her.

We went and told Aunt Lois and hers, and then Daddy said she should run over and get the mortician because he ought to go tell Aunt Doris over in Canton. Aunt Lois in her practical way said Daddy could wait about Aunt Doris until morning. But Daddy reckoned he'd want to know as soon as possible if he wasn't there, and so he reckoned Aunt Doris ought to get the same treatment. Lois got ready to fetch ol' Ben Baker from his bed so he could go get Granny ready for the laying out, and we went on.

I slept mostly, though I meant to keep Daddy company. But he didn't seem too talkative, and it's hard to stay awake if the only sound you hear is the bumpity bump of the road and the steady hum of the motor engine. Daddy woke me up to go in with him at Aunt Doris's, but I don't recollect much, and I sat dead to the world on the way home as well. We pulled up, Daddy woke me, and we saw Uncle Joe sitting up on the front porch, no coat or anything. Snow still lay good on the ground, so it had to be below freezing outside.

"They took Mamma on," he told us as we walked up to the porch. "I made shore they was real careful and all," he added, though I reckon Mr. Baker always took care with carrying bodies out. "Loey rode out with 'im to make shore he knew how to git here in the dark and all," he said. Then he blew out a big ol' puff of white breath and stopped talking.

"Purdy danged cold out here," Daddy said. "Why don't you come on in, and I'll get us up something warm to drink."

Uncle Joe's eyes fixed on the tracks running out to the main road, like he was still following the car leaving with his mamma inside. "I'll be in d'rectly," he said. "I just want a little quiet." Then, just as Daddy and I headed in, he said real low, "Ain't no place quiet like here." And I stood inside for a spell, watching Uncle Joe watching whatever it was he saw in his mind. Then I went off to bed just as I smelled the smell of coffee about done. I heard Daddy go out and get Uncle Joe, and I heard them talking low over their coffees, and then I fell asleep.

The next day everybody came out to our house that could be of use. All the family and a few friends came by. They helped a little, but we didn't need much. They offered to cook us up something during the day, but Daddy said with having just had Christmas dinner we'd just eat on leftovers. I picked up around the outside good, Mildred lending me a hand, and the grown-ups set the house up right nice. Aunt Doris worked on the kitchen, did some dusting and stuff like that. Aunt Lois did the hard work, scrubbing the wood floors down good with sand until they showed nice and clean. Daddy and Uncle Joe moved some furniture, and they went to get a few extra chairs from here and there for folks to sit in, since we'd be having a crowd later on. They carried the couch back to mine and Daddy's bedroom, and they said that could be for family who got tuckered out. Daddy said the coffin would be set up where the couch normally sat, and he arranged chairs in the living room so folks could sit. Then we all had to get cleaned up good. Aunt Lois and Aunt Doris, along with theirs, went to Aunt Lois's house, while Daddy and Uncle Joe and I got ready at our house.

Not long after a good scrubbing but before I got into my Sunday clothes, Mr. Baker came with Granny. I peeped around the hallway door as Mr. Baker and his helper, Mitchell Hall, who wasn't much older than me and had big ol' ears so folks called him "elephant ears" and who appeared a mite strange to everybody's reckoning, brought in the coffin with Granny inside. Daddy and Uncle Joe helped direct them where they should set things up, and once everything was put in its place to everybody's satisfaction, Mr. Baker said come look see and opened up the coffin for Daddy and Uncle Joe.

Mr. Baker stood back while Daddy and Uncle Joe took a couple of short steps up and looked in at Granny. I couldn't see Granny from where I stood, but I could see the other folks. Mr. Baker stood off beaming, real proud of the job he'd done. "Nellie Picklesimon fixed up her hair good," Mr. Baker said, hoping, I think, that somebody would say, "Why, Mr. Baker, you done worked wonders fer Granny." Reckon the biggest compliment the morticians got was when somebody said, "Why, don't she look natural." But the truth of the matter was that, what showings I'd been to, nobody ever looked too natural lying in their deathbed.

Daddy and Uncle Joe stood before Granny. Daddy looked on with lingering sad eyes, like they'd seen too many sad things and this was just another to add to the pain.

Uncle Joe looked like he'd been hit head-on, like the pain was so near and sudden he had to close his eyes to keep them from popping from his head and running away. His eyes looked like they'd seen something beautiful for the first time, then it was gone, so he had to close his eyes trying to hold on to how beautiful the thing must have looked. But I could tell neither Daddy nor Uncle Joe thought that Granny looked all natural lying there.

Mitchell had crept over toward me. He kept looking down, then looking up, down then up. He looked like he knew something and was keeping it secret. He gave me a dopey smile that said something like, "Ain't this purdy swell what I git to do?" It made me think everybody was right to think him a bit fetched in the head.

Finally, Daddy said, "You done a real nice job, Mr. Baker. You know that the funeral's at the church tomorrow at eleven o'clock?"

"Yep, I'll be here 'bout ten to gather 'er up," Mr. Baker replied, and with that he went on toward the door, and him and Mitchell went on.

Finally, the hour came for the showing. Lots of folks came out to pay their respects to Granny and the family. You could tell that everybody wanted to get at Uncle Joe and talk about what he'd been up to for so many years, but all but two or three of the thickest knew it wasn't time for that sort of thing. Uncle Joe politely told those few that there'd be plenty of time to talk about that later.

Nobody said Granny looked natural, because she didn't. Now that life had run off, her body looked like it'd been drained. Granny's spirit must have been awful strong, because it kept her from looking all drawn up in the face; now that it was gone, her face sort of swallowed into itself despite the best work of Mr. Baker.

People did comment some on her covering—I'd heard Uncle Joe and Daddy talking it over before the showing. Uncle Joe wanted to be able to give Granny something special, something to show his respect for her. And the most special thing he had was the quilt she'd made for him. Daddy said Uncle Joe talked nonsense, that Granny meant him to have that quilt. Uncle Joe said that that was right, that Granny'd given him the quilt, and he could do what he pleased with it. And what he wanted to do was to make sure she had a special cover. People were normally laid out in their good clothes, but lots of times they had a covering from just up above the waist down, I reckon to make it seem more like they were just sleeping good rather than being dead. Hands were usually placed up at the top edge of the covering, one folded over the other. And Uncle Joe wanted Granny's covering to be that quilt. And he had his way, and lots of folks commented on what a fine and pretty thing it was. Uncle Joe made sure that everybody knew that Granny had made it and wasn't she awful special to be able to make something like that.

Course there's only so much a feller my age could take of a bunch of grown-ups milling around and talking, so I finally went outside for a spell to gather my thoughts and get some fresh air. The air felt nice and crisp. It had warmed up some that day, melting most of the snow, but it had gotten cold again as soon as the sun had set. But that was good. Too many extra bodies taking up too little space had made it hot inside. I had to get away. I slipped out the front door, but people kept coming in and out, so I walked around a bit until I found myself sitting on the back steps. I reckoned nobody would begrudge me a few minutes of time to myself.

I'd been back there a while when I heard steps coming around the house, real slow like; the person either wasn't sure in the dark if they were going to run into something or they were looking for something. Danged if I couldn't even have a little while alone. But I reckoned if somebody came out looking for me, I'd best let them know where I sat.

"Hello," I said. I waited a second; then a familiar though unexpected voice said back, "Hello?"

"Hey," I said, "I'm just sitting here on the back steps." Joyce came around the corner of the house and took a seat by me.

"I'm real sorry 'bout yore Granny," Joyce said.

"Thanks," I said. "I don't guess it's really sunk in none yet. I feel kinda strange inside, you know?"

"Yeah," she said; then she didn't say anything else. We just sat there a few minutes, her and me. Directly she looked over and said, "Reckon I'd better go on back in 'fore Mamma and Daddy start to miss me."

"Alright," I said, not sure whether or not I was going to go in with her.

She looked away for a second, and I looked down at my feet some, reckon to see if they were still there. And while I looked downward, I felt Joyce scoot a little closer to me, and then I felt her lips on my cheek. After she kissed me, she said, "I really am sorry," and she got up to go.

I reckon then my mind was made up real quick. I walked Joyce in, and before we had moved two feet away from the back steps she reached over and took my hand, so we held hands as we walked around to the front porch, though as soon as we were where anybody might see, Joyce slipped her hand out of mine. So we walked back in, her and me. And even though it still wasn't any fun to be there, it was less unbearable than before, and somehow it didn't seem quite so crowded.

After everybody had left, Daddy and Uncle Joe and Aunt Doris and Aunt Lois made plans about what time everybody should be at the house to accompany the hearse to the church. I made my way to bed. Daddy had a cup of coffee, and Uncle Joe had a chair pulled up next to Granny. He sat there with a piece of the quilt pulled a little ways out of the coffin fingering it real slow and thoughtful. I had me a headful of feelings that hit the pillow with me, but I reckon I felt so tired it didn't matter. Sleep came in no time.

Like all funeral days, the next day was a blur. There were actions to walk through, but nobody much paid attention to what they did. Everybody attended to the details of getting dressed and getting going and sitting in the right places and making sure everything had been set up just right at the church, like a list of one thing after another to do, forgotten as soon as done. Reckon walking through it like you weren't hardly there made it bearable for everybody.

I don't much remember any of the words, but I do remember

the way Preacher preached that day at Granny's funeral. He preached quiet and respectful and all about love—the love of God and the love of family. Preacher left out the usual fire and brimstone and threats and warnings. And I know that when Preacher preached about some lost soul, sometimes tears would come to his eyes, and he'd weep over the lost sheep, like Jesus weeping over Jerusalem he said. He let a few teardrops fall at Granny's funeral, too, but it was different. They weren't tears for some lost soul—he cried tears for a very specific soul, one that he cared a great deal about apparently. I don't know why I should have been able to see it, but I'm pretty sure that Preacher loved my granny. Genuine tears trickled down his cheeks that day, and he seemed a little ashamed of them, like they weren't something for others to see.

We buried Granny next to my granddaddy, who lay next to my mamma. I could look in one place and see my daddy's mamma, daddy, and wife all in one place. It was a sight that looked all wrong, and from the way Daddy's face looked, I knew that he felt that way, too.

After the burial, the church put on a fine dinner for the whole family. They must have served up all kinds of good things to eat, I reckon, because funerals I've been to since have always had real good things to eat. Folks tried their best, in the way they could, to show the family respect for their loss. So people in Smoky Hollow cooked up a storm, and I know it must have been good. I don't really remember eating a thing, though. All I remember about the whole meal was thinking about going home and Granny not being there. And when the time to go came, we all pushed away from the tables, made our way out to the cars, and drove off to the same place where I had always lived. Yet, as I stepped into that house, I knew it wouldn't ever be the same place again.

XXV

UNCLE JOE LEANED against the old shaggy-bark hickory tree, his forehead touching the wood and his hand wrapped around loose pieces of bark like he was greeting an old friend. And maybe he was. Seemed he was saying hello to something special.

"Know where yore at?" he asked me. I didn't rightly know. I'd been that way a few times, but not too awful many. It lay in a direction away from where I normally went hunting, so I didn't have much reason to be there. I couldn't recollect Daddy bringing me there none either.

"This is part of the old homestead, where my granddaddy—yore great-granddaddy—first settled here in Gilmer County. They came in from Western Carolina." Then he stopped talking for a minute, though I don't know if it was to let things sink in with me or to let it sink in with him.

"This is Hickory Station," Uncle Joe said. "Back in 1832, when the gover'ment surveyed Gilmer County, they marked it off in 160-acre tracts. If'n they was a tree near a corner of the 160 acres, they'd mark the tree, carving in the lot number and what corner of the lot the tree stood on. They was called station trees. This here shaggy-bark hickory stands almost right on the northwest corner of this lot, which is what Granddaddy bought."

I looked up at the tree. It stood high, maybe seventy feet high, so I knew it had to be old, though a really old shaggy-bark hickory could go up maybe ninety feet. I looked here and yon, and I could see that Uncle Joe was looking around, too. We'd set out early in the morning, and you could see the fog lifting up out of the valley. "Fog's lifting and going heavenward like a slow-spoken prayer," Uncle Joe said. "That's what Daddy always used to say whenever he'd see fog lifting in Smoky Hollow." Saying something about his daddy put Uncle Joe in a mind to talk, reckon.

"Now, my daddy," he said, "he ended up buying the place where me and yore daddy was raised. Didn't want to be back in the hills quite so far, he didn't. Daddy knowed it'd be best to be near where they was a-starting to put in roads and all. Course, back when yore daddy and me was little, they wasn't putting in roads fer automobiles but fer horse-drawn carts and all. Still, 'tware a good thing, reckon, 'cause when folks did start having them horseless carriages it wasn't too awful much work to make the road fit fer 'em. Horse or horseless, wheels still gotta be able to turn."

Uncle Joe seemed to be thinking a right long spell about long ago, reckon, back to his growing-up years. Finally, he said, "I used to love to come up here and walk 'round, visit with Granddaddy and all. Let's go find the old place." So we went off until we came to a place where an old house stood, or barely stood, the sturdiest thing about it being the rock chimney. The rest of the house had fallen in around it. Looked to have been abandoned a long time.

After looking about, Uncle Joe said, "Why don't we walk the property lines?" So we spent that day making our way around the perimeter of his granddaddy's property, him telling me things he had done here and there when he was my age. It turned into an all-day affair. Walking the perimeter of 160-square acres is about a couple of miles, and walking in the woods can be a slow affair, especially when you stop ever so often to hear about something special that happened here or there.

Dang, seems that for a year or so all Uncle Joe and I did was tramp in the woods up in Smoky Hollow. Daddy was right—Uncle Joe knew all about the woods—where to look for sign for deer, bear, wild pig, and all. He knew what to call all the trees and plants. He'd see a small lump on the ground, like a little tiny hill, with grass and everything growing on it, and he'd ask me how it got that way. I said I didn't know, and he explained to me how trees would get blown over and the roots would pull up a big ol' pile of dirt with them. After the tree rotted all away and years passed and ground cover crept up over the dirt left behind, it made a little mound. Then I noticed for the first time how it was that when you saw mounds they were shallow to one side, where the dirt was pulled from when the tree fell over—that's the direction the wind blew from, Uncle Joe said. Uncle Joe taught me good, and he hadn't seemed to have forgotten anything about the woods and where everything was even after being gone for so long.

I say we tramped the woods for only a year or so, because Uncle Joe died. He'd come home because Aunt Lois had written him a letter telling about Granny, asking him real nice to come. He said that probably would have done the trick. But, as it turns out, Uncle Joe was thinking about coming anyway. Doctors had told him there was something wrong with him that would only get worse, so Uncle Joe decided to come home.

I reckon it made for a hard decision, to come home after all the years of trying to pretend that he'd made something of himself that he wasn't. Uncle Joe was talking to Daddy and Aunt Lois and Uncle Henry, but I figured it didn't matter if I heard, so I sat me right still and listened one night at the end of the hallway. Uncle Joe had had an accident early on while in Detroit. He did work for Ford, and he was doing okay until the accident. But when he lost the arm that ended his work on the assembly line. Since it was something that happened at work, the Ford folks made a big deal about taking care of Uncle Joe.

What that ended up meaning was that they kept Uncle Joe

on—as a janitor. He cleaned offices every night after the big shots left. That's where he got the fancy stationery to write on. While he cleaned offices, he would take a few pieces of paper and an envelope every now and then. Reckon it made the secretaries wonder—they didn't miss the few pages he took, but Uncle Joe said he always left a little money at the desk where he took the paper. He told a funny story about how glad he was that one time when Granny wrote telling him not to send any more typed letters. Apparently it had taken a pretty danged long time to type with just one arm, him not even being a typist really.

It was hard for Uncle Joe to talk about, I could tell, but he wanted the story told. Aunt Lois asked why he didn't come on home after the accident, but Uncle Joe said how ashamed he was—ashamed about making a big deal of leaving, about how he was going to make it big. Then, once he painted a bigger life for himself than he had, he figured he couldn't come. Turns out Uncle Joe had spent most of his adult life homesick. So, for the time he had left, we spent it where he wanted—around where he grew up and played and hunted and fished and lived life as a boy.

But after that year, things changed for me quite a bit. Daddy and I moved in with Aunt Lois and her family shortly after Uncle Joe died. Daddy said he would have done it sooner if Uncle Joe hadn't wanted to live out his days there in Smoky Hollow. So we sold the house and land where I'd been born and raised, Daddy paid off some bills, especially some doctoring bills he owed still on Granny and some on Uncle Joe, and he spent the rest paying for materials to build onto Aunt Lois's house so we'd have our own room.

At one time I would have thought that'd be the worst possible thing to have happen to me, but it wasn't. Uncle Joe being home, then him dying, seemed to soften Aunt Lois up. She could still be stern and all, but she didn't seem out after me like before. Reckon the resemblance in attitude between Uncle Joe and me didn't bother her so much anymore. Seemed nice to have a little bigger family nearby, what first with Granny gone then Uncle Joe, and for the most part it was a good thing. Mildred and I had our occasional fights, like anybody living under the same roof with mostly equal status, but we were always real close, and I reckon she was mostly like a sister to me after that.

It certainly made going to school a whole lot easier. The Ellijay Academy was right there, and I got to go through high school without too much trouble. I did good and was always right smart about book stuff.

Bobby and I stayed good friends, but maybe not best friends, him living still in Smoky Hollow. He didn't have a mind to go to the academy, the way he felt about school. But I'd visit sometimes, and we'd go to the movies on Saturdays. He wore a metal brace on his leg, and he limped, but that running boy stayed in his heart somehow or another. He became one of the most decent fellers I've known.

Funny how things turn out when I think back on it. I went into the army after graduation, and then came the war in Korea. They called it a conflict, but only the people who weren't there could say that with a straight face. I did my job best I could while trying to keep from getting dead. So I came back whole and for that I was grateful. Bobby's brother came to mind now and again, and I reckoned, after I got back home, that it was only by a miracle that more folks didn't come back like Bobby's brother.

I didn't stay home for long. The GI Bill made it possible for me to go to college, and I took off for Athens to go to the University of Georgia. Reckon the Ellijay Academy wasn't a fluke, because I did good there, too. Then I moved further south a spell—four years down in Augusta attending the Medical College of Georgia. I don't rightly know how it come about that I ended up a doctor. It wasn't that I liked science better than some other things—I loved reading books, and in some ways that sort of thing suited the kind of imagination I had a bit better than science, I sometimes thought.

Reckon it was mostly my past life, though, that spoke for my future one. I saw a lot of people die; I saw a lot of people sick. At times I felt sorry for myself, which I reckoned only natural— before I turned fifteen I'd had my granddaddy, my mamma, my granny, and my Uncle Joe all die. I got where I respected Doc Miller a good deal—he took care of people best he could, and it was never about money but doing right by somebody who needed what you could do for them. I wanted to help the way Doc Miller had helped. Course, I couldn't feel too sorry for myself. I knew a boy in school whose mamma had buried two husbands and five of her seven children by the time this boy came to the academy. Still, knowing other's misery don't exactly wipe the slate of your own clean.

At first I settled down in Marietta. I had a nice little practice, and I made a decent amount of money. But an incident in Europe, of all places, sent me back to where I'd come from.

I always wanted to go everywhere, anywhere, but Smoky Hollow. Thing is, the older I got, the more I thought about it, and I missed it. It wasn't like I didn't go visiting, but I have to admit that when I visited back in Gilmer County it seemed like home; my house in Marietta always felt like a danged hotel room or something. Never felt like home.

After I'd been in my practice a while, I took a trip over to Europe. I had developed an interest in World War I based on some of the things Daddy told me once I had grown up. I figured it would be a way to see the world and retrace some of Daddy's steps while he served. Thing is, there were a lot of interesting places, and a lot of things I hadn't ever seen except in books. But while there, it was the quiet places, the out-of-the-way places, that called to me. And I'd sit and I'd listen, mostly away from the cities, preferring the countryside. Then one day I heard, clear as clear, Uncle Joe's voice in my head. He said two words, but that's all he had to say because I reckon the quiet put me in a mood to listen. "Go home" is what I heard.

Once we got back in the States, I told Joyce about my desire to head back to Gilmer County. I don't know why, but I thought she'd be upset. She seemed to adapt lots better to city life than I did. I wasn't sure she'd want to give it up to head back up into the mountains where there'd be less money and more work. Joyce surprised me. "Only reason I'm here is 'cause of yore talk 'bout leaving Smoky Hollow. I figured leaving home would be the price to pay for being yore wife. I ain't got no reason to be anywhere but home." And with a smile and a kiss we started the process of moving back.

It's been a fine life. Course we didn't live in Smoky Hollow most of the time. We bought us a house in town where we'd be close to the clinic and near the hospital. Also, Ellijay was centrally located. I tried to keep up Doc Miller's habit of going where the sickness was instead of waiting for it to come to town. I found out, probably like he had, that if you wait for the sick people to come in you have a right more doctoring to do, and sometimes to no account.

But life's been good. I did another thing, too. As soon as I was able and the owner willing, I bought back the old house in Smoky Hollow. It had been updated by then, having electricity and running water. And being a doctor, I couldn't do without the phone. Also, I did appreciate having an inside bathroom, which had been added on. But for the other stuff, most of the time I just run the kerosene lamps for light while we're here and go out back to draw water for drinking and cooking. I use the old stove in the living room for heat unless it's fearful cold. Dinner up here once a week has become a tradition, and sometimes I show off to Joyce all the things I learned to cook while Granny was sick. Being a doctor, I finally realized that we were eating way too many fried apple pies for our own good, but we keep eating.

Weekends we spend up here, if nothing much is going on at the hospital. And holidays. We keep Thanksgiving and Christmas right well in this house where I learned what they were all about. While the children were little, they liked coming up to the old homeplace. When they were teenagers, they didn't much like it. But now with their own young'uns they like it again, maybe because the little ones like it so much.

Maybe the biggest surprise for me came in the form of a garden—we started keeping one. Joyce has always loved to garden, and because I love her I've always tried to help. So even after many years, on into my older years, I've never graduated from being garden help. But somehow or other, time spent on my knees in red dirt isn't so bad with Joyce there, and she loves it so much that I can't help but put aside the bad feelings gardening always seemed to stir in me while I was young. Still, I've never learned to really like it.

It's a wonder this old house still can hold so many folk, what with everybody accustomed now to bigger houses and bigger things and more conveniences. Still, while family's visiting, the place never seems as small as it would to the casual passerby. I reckon that's because of what Granny had once said. I asked her once as she worked away on her quilt, "What you reckon made the star so big that ever'body could see it on Christmas?" I asked because she had made the star on her quilt so big. She didn't hesitate a second. "Love, son. Love makes ever'thing bigger. And folks who don't know that miss out on what Christmas was meant to bespeak us." And she was right. There's a history of love in this old homestead that makes it big enough for anybody who wants to fit inside. It's only too small if you don't want to be with the people who're there.

Danged if sitting here doesn't make it easy to remember all these things. I sit in a rocking chair near the stove, warming my feet, looking at Granny's Christmas quilt hung up on the wall. It hangs there prettier to me than anything I saw on the walls of museums in Europe. Daddy told me after Uncle Joe died that he'd gotten with old man Baker and told him to pull that quilt out before Granny got buried. He said on the one hand he understood that Uncle Joe wanted to give Granny something special like that. On the other hand he thought it foolishness to let something Granny had poured her heart into follow her to the grave. He said Granny wouldn't have wanted that—that her gift was for people to see and get joy from. He had kept it, intending to give it back to Uncle Joe if he ever indicated that he was sorry he'd put the quilt in. But Uncle Joe never did, so it wasn't until he died that Daddy pulled it out. And from that day on we took care of it because it was, we all reckoned, the most precious family heirloom we had.

About every Christmas Eve now I come out here early to meditate a bit, to think over life and think about those that are gone, and I always end up thinking about that year back in 1942. I can't help it with the quilt hanging up big in the living room. I tell folks I'm coming out to warm the place up good so it'll be nice and comfortable for everybody. I also have to cut down the tree we've picked out so everybody can decorate it the way we used to with popcorn and crepe paper ornaments. But I reckon Joyce knows why I come, because she makes sure nobody comes out until she comes. And she always gives me plenty of time for my work and to reflect a mite. She always gives me this smile that says, "I hope you've had a nice visit with your memories," and I give her one back that says, "Yes, I have, and they're even nicer because you're part and parcel of them."

I hear cars coming down off the main road, right about dusk it is, so I get up from my comfortable spot, put on my shoes and coat, and go out to greet the family as they come in. I want to greet them with a greeting that's big like the Christmas quilt star is big, one that says, "Love lives here." So I go out the front door, and I stand on the front porch. I see them all coming down the road, the tires of the cars making little tracks. Danged if it hasn't been snowing while I sat reminiscing. And I look around, and I figure it's not such a bad thing after all, one small flake following another, settling on the ground soft like a kiss from heaven, covering Smoky Hollow like a blanket of grace that shines white with goodness.